WAYWARD HEARTS

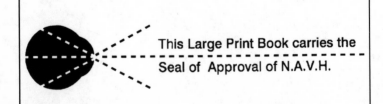

This Large Print Book carries the
Seal of Approval of N.A.V.H.

WAYWARD HEARTS

SUSAN ANNE MASON

THORNDIKE PRESS
A part of Gale, Cengage Learning

GALE
CENGAGE Learning·

Farmington Hills, Mich • San Francisco • New York • Waterville, Maine
Meriden, Conn • Mason, Ohio • Chicago

GALE
CENGAGE Learning®

LIBRARY OF CONGRESS CATALOGING-IN-PUBLICATION DATA

Names: Mason, Susan Anne, author.
Title: Wayward hearts / by Susan Anne Mason.
Description: Large print edition. | Waterville, Maine : Thorndike Press, 2017. |
  Series: Rainbow falls ; #2 | Series: Thorndike Press large print Christian romance
Identifiers: LCCN 2016046411| ISBN 9781410497222 (hardcover) | ISBN 1410497224 (hardcover)
Subjects: LCSH: Large type books. | GSAFD: Love stories. | Christian fiction.
Classification: LCC PR9199.4.M3725 W39 2017 | DDC 813/.6—dc23
LC record available at https://lccn.loc.gov/2016046411

Published in 2017 by arrangement with Pelican Ventures Book Group, LLC

Printed in Mexico
1 2 3 4 5 6 7 21 20 19 18 17

To my wonderful critique partners, Julie, CJ, Eileen, and now Sally, who have shared their time and talents to help improve my writing! I appreciate and cherish our friendship!

1

"Ninth floor penthouse." The musical voice oozed from the speakers as the elevator slid to a smooth stop.

The doors whispered open, and Maxi North stepped out into the magnificent lobby of *Baronne's Salon*. She paused, latte in hand, and smiled at the sheer luxury on display. The ornate crystal chandelier glittered above the mahogany reception desk that housed a striking array of orchids. Sometimes Maxi had to pinch herself to make sure she wasn't dreaming — that this former farm girl from Rainbow Falls, North Dakota, now worked as a junior stylist in one of the top salons in New York City.

She hiked her purse farther onto the shoulder of her satin jacket as she strode into the heart and soul of the salon — the chrome and glass stylist stations, where the employees worked their magic for a pampered clientele. The familiar scents of floral shampoos, coconut conditioner, and hair spray swirled around her.

Coming in for the afternoon shift meant that most of the stations already bustled with activity. On the way to her own station, second chair from the back, she waved to her friend Cherise. With a contented sigh, Maxi set down her latte, threw her purse in the bottom drawer, and plugged in her curling irons.

"You're early today." Cherise stood on tiptoes, stretching to reach one of the sliding cupboards at Maxi's right. She grabbed some towels and blew her pink-tinted corkscrews off her forehead before flashing a dazzling smile.

"Nothing to do at home. My Internet connection died, so I figured I might as well come in and get a head start on my shift." Maxi fished her cell phone out of her jacket pocket and deposited it on the counter in front of the huge beveled mirror. "Mrs. Rothman's my first customer. You know how picky she is."

Cherise snickered. "Uh-huh. Better you than me." She swung back toward her customer, then pivoted, her ebony eyes twinkling. "Rumors are flying today. Philippe and the other partners have been in a meeting all morning."

The numerous cups of coffee Maxi had already consumed churned in her stomach. "Good news or bad, do you think?" She hadn't dared heed the latest gossip that the Baronnes might be considering taking on another partner.

"Hard to tell." Cherise nodded toward the hall leading to Philippe Baronne's private office. "Guess we'll know soon enough."

Lillian Rothman's formidable figure crossed the room, a frown already creasing her forehead under the silver-gray swoop of hair, leaving Maxi no time to dwell on what may or may not be happening in that meeting.

Maxi put on her brightest smile. "Good afternoon, Mrs. Rothman. How are you today?"

"Terrible, if you must know. Let's get on with it, shall we?"

Maxi gritted her teeth and managed to keep her expression pleasant. "Of course. Please have a seat."

After washing and setting Mrs. Rothman's hair in large rollers, something the eccentric woman insisted on instead of curling irons, Maxi positioned her under one of the dryers and provided her with an espresso and some biscotti before ushering the next client to her chair. Once Maxi finished the quick trim, she finally found a spare minute for a sip of her now-cold latte. She grimaced and swallowed, her eye catching a movement in the mirror. The two other senior partners spilled out of Philippe's office. Philippe's wife, Suzanne, laughed before flitting off in the direction of the spa, high heels tapping across the marble floor.

The timer dinged, signaling Maxi to check Mrs. Rothman. She escorted the woman back to her station, and as Maxi started to remove the rollers, heavy footsteps sounded behind her.

"Miss North, my office, ten minutes." Philippe barked the order and disappeared down the back corridor.

Maxi froze, hand poised over her client's head. Why would her boss want to see her now? Could it have anything to do with the morning pow-wow?

She bit her lip at the giddy thought. Then she quickly dismissed the idea. They'd never consider someone so young for the position of partner. In all likelihood, Philippe wanted to review her list of clientele. Or discuss the new ad campaign. Still, as Maxi continued styling Lillian Rothman's hair, she couldn't help but fantasize about the possibility.

"Quit daydreaming, girl. I haven't got all day." Mrs. Rothman's raspy voice brought

Maxi crashing back to reality.

Keep the customer happy. Maxi repeated the salon's mantra to herself and pasted on a smile. "Yes, ma'am. I'll be done in a jiffy."

Ten minutes later, with Mrs. Rothman primped, sprayed, and satisfied, and a sizeable tip tucked in Maxi's pocket, Maxi crossed the busy salon, neatly avoiding Cherise with a tray of color. Outside Philippe's office, she smoothed down her green jacket and knocked on the door.

"Entrez." Philippe's lilting French accent made Maxi's lips twitch.

She opened the door and stepped inside, inhaling the scent of opulence. Each time she'd had the occasion to come into this office, the magnificence of the space took her breath away. A huge picture window overlooked the spring greenery of Manhattan's Central Park. To the right, Philippe's oversized chrome and glass desk sat on a rakish angle. An impressive space for an impressive man. She still couldn't believe her luck in landing a job here.

Maxi shifted her gaze and frowned at the sight of Sierra Scott, one of the other junior stylists, already seated in a guest chair. As usual, Sierra had her honey hair pulled back in a perfect coif, complementing her champagne blouse and black skirt. Maxi resisted

11

the urge to fiddle with her own hair or adjust her clothing. In comparison to Sierra's sleek style, Maxi always felt garish and overdone. Today, with the help of some styling gel, Maxi's red hair spiked out in all directions. The total opposite of Sierra's chic elegance.

Maxi ignored the smug expression on the other woman's flawlessly made-up face and smiled at Philippe. "Here I am. What's up?"

"Have a seat." Philippe waved to a second guest chair. For a man in his early fifties, Philippe's vitality gave him the air of a much younger man. Faint threads of silver at the temples, as well as a few lines around his eyes, were the only concession to his age. His steely gaze could still wither anyone with one glance. Now his guarded expression gave nothing away as he watched Maxi sit down.

"I'll get right to the point," he said, looking from one girl to the other. "You may have heard rumors that we are considering taking on another partner for the salon."

"There's been talk." Sierra crossed her long legs, accentuated by her skimpy miniskirt.

Philippe raised a well-groomed brow. "Well, for once the rumors are correct. We are looking for a new junior partner."

A surge of adrenaline spurted through Maxi's system. She didn't dare breathe in case she missed her mentor's next words.

Philippe leaned back in his leather chair and waved a hand in the air. "We would like our new partner to be someone young and vibrant. Someone with fresh, innovative ideas, full of creative energy, who will attract a younger clientele."

Maxi forced her brain to slow down and take in every word Philippe said.

"After much consideration, we have narrowed our choice down to you two." He looked at his watch. "I have a conference call soon, so I'll make this brief." He slid two large brown envelopes across the desk. "Over the next few weeks, we will make our final decision. Here are the details of what a partnership would entail. You will find we require a substantial investment fee, should you be chosen. Please read the documents carefully, and if you're interested, give me your answer by tomorrow. I'll need an updated portfolio as soon as possible as well." He rose, indicating the meeting was at an end. "I wish you both *bonne chance.*"

Maxi picked up the envelope with a smile. "Thank you, Philippe. I'm honored to be in the running, and I am very much interested."

Sierra stood and took Philippe's hand. "Oh, I'm definitely interested, Philippe."

A slight frown creased his brow. "You must read the paperwork before you give me your answer."

Undaunted, Sierra winked. "Believe me, I will."

As she left the office, Maxi pushed back her annoyance at the other woman's blatant flirtation with their *married* boss and focused instead on the amazing opportunity just handed to her — the very real possibility that her lifelong dream could now be within her grasp. Excitement buzzed though her veins while her mind reeled.

The diversity of her skills gave her a distinct advantage. She could do almost any job in the spa. Pedicure, manicure, any style of hair — even colors, weaves, and extensions. And she was learning more every day. She breathed a sigh of thanks to Peg Hanley for taking her under her experienced wing while Maxi was still in high school. Who would have imagined that working at the *Cut 'N Curl* in Rainbow Falls would lead to a position in the top salon in Manhattan?

Memories of Peg brought about a sudden, sharp pang of homesickness. Maxi absorbed the wave. Then with great effort, she shook it off. She could not afford to be distracted from her goal. Instead, she strode over to her station, deposited the envelope in the drawer, and tidied her area in readiness for her next client.

Still, Maxi couldn't seem to shake her lingering thoughts of Peg. She longed to call her and share her incredible news about the partnership. But Maxi couldn't be sure *he* wouldn't answer the phone.

Before she could stop herself, Maxi rifled through the contents of her drawer in search of the treasured dog-eared photo within. The familiar shaft of joy and sorrow seared through her at the sight of Jason Hanley's engaging grin. It seemed a lifetime since she'd seen Jason or heard his voice. Peg had snapped this picture of them at their high school graduation several years ago. He stood with his arm draped around her shoulders. Both their faces were filled with youthful exuberance — one of those perfect moments in time, captured forever.

If only they could've stayed in that moment.

"You know you don't stand a chance against me." The hiss of Sierra's voice behind her startled Maxi out of her daydreams.

She turned to glare at the tall blonde.

"Don't go ordering your new nameplate yet."

Sierra snorted. "I'm not intimidated by a farm girl from Hicksville. As far as I'm concerned, the partnership is already mine." With a dismissive wave of her hand, Sierra sashayed back to her own area.

Maxi let her irritation roll over her and slide away. Sierra would not ruin the deliciousness of this moment. Maxi's days in "Hicksville" were long over, and her future as a partner at *Baronne's* shimmered as brightly as the mirrored lights. Nothing or no one would get in her way.

She allowed herself one last glance at the tattered photo in her hand before slipping it into the pocket of her purse inside the drawer. With one sharp click, she shut away the past and focused her energy on the future.

A little after nine o'clock, Maxi jogged up the stairs to her second floor walkup on West Fifty-Sixth Street, excitement pumping through her system. Fumbling with the key in the door, she pushed her way inside, dropped her takeout Chinese food on the scarred coffee table and kicked off her heels. She already itched to take out her portfolio and see where she could improve it. Ideas buzzed in her head for innovative, new hair-styles.

Her cell phone jangled as soon as she opened the takeout container. She jumped to grab it out of the jacket she'd draped over the arm of the lumpy brown couch. Must be Lance. He said he would call her tonight to make a date for the weekend. She smiled, ready to share her good news with the man who was becoming an important part of her life.

But it wasn't Lance.

She stared at the display and blinked, not believing her eyes.

Jason Hanley?

Her heart took off at a gallop in her chest. Why, after two years of silence, would he call now? On the very day she'd dug his picture out of her drawer. Maxi's hands shook so hard she had to set the phone on the couch beside her. What would she say to him? Unbidden memories of their last encounter crowded her thoughts. The ugly accusations, the words hurled in anger. She wasn't prepared to deal with all that right now. So, coward that she was, she let the call go to voice mail.

Her relief was short-lived when the phone chimed again seconds later.

She groaned. Knowing Jason, he'd keep

calling until she picked up. She paused for one deep breath. "Hello?"

"Maxi?"

Her heart stuttered at the gruffness of his voice. "Yes."

"It's Jason. Sorry to call out of the blue like this."

The serious tone had her rising off the sofa to pace the small living area. Something was wrong. She could sense it. Panic clutched her throat. "What is it? Is Mama all right?" Her mother's multiple sclerosis had been under control, but you never knew when a setback could occur.

"Bernice is fine."

Thank You, God. If anything had happened to her —

"It's your dad."

A flash of hot anger shot through her chest. She tightened the grip on the phone until the metal bit into her flesh. Hadn't her father caused the family enough misery? "Let me guess. Another drinking binge?"

"Not this time." He paused long enough for Maxi's palms to grow damp. "There's been an accident at the farm. Your mom asked me to call you."

Maxi eased herself down onto the arm of the sofa, dread pasting her mouth closed.

Jason gave a long sigh. "There's no easy

18

way to tell you this, Max. Charlie's dead.
You need to come home right away."

2

Jason Hanley ran his fingers around the tight collar of his dress shirt and wished he could loosen his tie. If he lived to be a hundred, he'd never get used to wearing a suit. Felt like a straitjacket, all stiff and confining. The last time he'd worn this brown monstrosity had been at Lily and Nick Logan's wedding. Now, seated in the fifth row of the Good Shepherd Church, he waited for Charlie North's funeral to begin.

Jason's stomach did a slow roll in anticipation of seeing Maxi again. He hadn't heard from her since she'd left for New York over two years ago. Any minute now, she'd walk through that door, and Jason wasn't sure how he felt about that.

His mother sat beside him, dressed in black, a tissue pressed to her nose. Jason draped an arm around her shoulder and squeezed, eliciting a watery smile in return. Ever since Maxi had worked at his mother's beauty shop during high school, Ma had looked on Maxi as the daughter she never had. Today, she likely grieved more for Maxi's pain than for the loss of Charlie North.

The organ began its sad refrain. From his position at the end of the aisle, Jason turned his head to watch the procession enter the church. Pallbearers carried the coffin up the main aisle, followed by the somber figures of the family. Jason's pulse sprinted as he strained to see around them. Right behind the coffin, Calvin North pushed his mother in her wheelchair. Multiple sclerosis had ravaged the proud woman and turned her into an invalid. His gaze moved past them and a burst of red made Jason's lips twitch. Maxi hadn't changed her hair, at least not the color. But today her usual spiky cut was tamed into submission. She looked different somehow. All sleek and sophisticated, like a real city girl.

Why did that thought irk him so much?

Maxi's big hazel eyes stared straight ahead, dulled by sorrow. The smattering of freckles she so hated stood out in stark relief against the pallor of her skin. Knowing firsthand the volatile nature of her relationship with Charlie, Jason guessed she would be suffering from a wide range of emotions

— the main one being guilt.

As the procession moved past, Maxi's ravaged gaze flicked over to Jason. Their eyes met and held for a brief moment before she jerked her head back and stumbled forward. Her brother, Aidan, caught her arm to steady her, and they moved past.

Jason hardly heard a word of the service. His attention remained riveted on Maxi several rows ahead. Her shoulders shook as she wept in Aidan's arms, and Jason wished he could be the one to comfort her. Like he had all through high school.

His heart ached for her pain. Despite Maxi's difficult relationship with Charlie, Jason knew his death would devastate her. He shifted on the hard pew, the scent of candles and funeral flowers drifting by him. He must be a real jerk, because in spite of everything, he envied Maxi. At least she knew her dad, even if they never got along. And now she'd have closure — something he would likely never get with his own father.

When the service finished and the family filed out of the church in solemn procession, Jason hurried after them, hoping to catch a moment alone with Maxi. But as he sifted through the crowds in front of the church, he couldn't see her anywhere. At the curb, Aidan North helped his mother into the car. Jason tried to peer into the backseat, sure Maxi must be inside.

"Hello, Jason." Even after the trauma of losing her husband, Bernice North still had a smile of welcome for him. She looked much older than a woman in her mid-fifties. He imagined her illness had something to do with that.

She held out her hand to him. "Thank you so much for coming. I hope you have time to come back to the house for refreshments. Everyone's welcome."

There would be no trip to the cemetery since Charlie was being cremated. Jason didn't hesitate for a minute. No matter how mad Maxi might be at him, he couldn't pass up the chance to see her again.

"Thanks, Mrs. North. I'll be there."

Maxi moved like a robot through the living room of her parents' sprawling farmhouse, offering drinks and trays of sandwiches to the people who'd come by to pay their respects. Keeping busy allowed her to avoid thinking, or feeling, anything. On automatic pilot, she smiled at neighbors, gave the appropriate responses to their words of condolence, and scurried on to the next guest as soon as it was polite to do so.

She still couldn't believe Charlie was dead. Crushed by his own tractor. Her family had worried his drinking would end in something like this one day. Now their worst fears had come true.

A waving hand from the other side of the room caught her attention. Her mother motioned her over and a pang of guilt swamped Maxi. She should be paying more attention to Mama, instead of running from her emotions. Mama was the one who'd be most affected by Charlie's death. After all, she depended on him for everything.

Too bad Charlie wasn't dependable.

She set the tray of sandwiches on a side table and weaved her way over to the wheelchair in the corner, crouching down so her face was level with her mother's. "What is it, Mama? Do you need something?" A breeze at the open window lifted the curtain and ruffled Maxi's bangs.

"I'm fine, dear." Despite her assertion, the strain of the past few days showed in the lines on her face. Her light brown hair, streaked with a good deal of gray, needed trimming. Her mother reminded Maxi of a wilted rose — once beautiful but now withered by time and disease. Much like the faded furniture in this living room.

Her mother smiled. "Look who's here. It's Jason."

Maxi's hand froze on the arm of the wheelchair. How had she missed Jason standing off to the side? She grappled to keep her expression neutral as she slowly straightened. Faced with the reality of seeing him again, she found herself unprepared for the onslaught of conflicting emotions. After two years without contact, she had no idea what to say to him. So she said nothing — and simply stared.

He looked so different, she almost didn't recognize him. He'd filled out through the chest and shoulders, giving him a more rugged look. His hair, which skimmed his collar, had deepened into a beautiful chestnut color. His stunning blue eyes, however, remained as intense as ever. Right now they shone with sympathy.

"Hello, Maxi." He stepped forward to kiss her cheek. "I'm so sorry about your dad."

His breath tickled her ear before he moved back. With that one tiny action, and the familiar scent of his cologne swirling around her, her long-standing crush roared back to life.

"Thanks. You sure look . . . different." The words were out of her mouth before she could think. In order to steady her hands, she crossed her arms over her chest.

He smiled at her. "I suppose I do."

"Jason was one of the first responders here when I called for help. He's a volunteer firefighter now," Mama told her.

Maxi looked down at her mother and blinked. She'd almost forgotten Mama was there.

"Remember, I wrote about it in my last letter?"

Maxi couldn't admit she didn't remember — that she tried her best not to think about Jason Hanley at all. Instead, she shrugged. "I guess." She turned back to the intensity of Jason's gaze.

"I'm training to be a fireman over in Kingsville."

Maybe that explained the fire in his eyes.

"I never thought you'd leave the auto body shop."

Jason tugged at his tie as if he wanted to pull it off. "Guess you didn't hear that Tony's garage burnt down. Ironic that I'd choose firefighting because of a fire where I worked, huh? Anyway, that type of work never did anything for me. I want to do something that will make a difference for people."

Maxi couldn't conceal her surprise. When had Jason Hanley grown up? Before she left, he'd been adolescent in his ways, riding motorcycles and running with resident bad boy, Marco Messini. A multitude of questions raced through her brain, tangling her tongue, but now was not the time or place to rehash old issues.

"How about you? What are you up to these days?" Jason asked.

"Didn't Peg tell you?" Maxi always worded her letters to his mother in a careful manner, conscious that every bit of news would be relayed to Jason.

"She said something about a swanky shop in New York."

Maxi smirked. Sounded just like Peg. "Yeah. I'm at *Baronne's* on Fifth Avenue. You've probably never heard of it, but it's pretty prestigious."

"I'm glad. I know how much you wanted this."

An unidentifiable emotion flashed across his features. Features she had to admit were very attractive. For several seconds, she couldn't tear her eyes from his.

"I have to go . . . serve more food." She waved her arms in the direction of the kitchen.

"Sure." He paused. "Listen, can we get together before you go back?"

She hesitated. *Bad idea,* her brain

screamed. She scrambled for an excuse to say no, but when nothing came to her, she shrugged. "I guess so."

"Great. I'll call you."

He kissed her cheek again. Maxi closed her eyes, drinking in the familiar scent of him. Then she forced herself to step away into the safety of the crowd.

After the majority of the guests had departed, Maxi sought a moment of solitude outside on the porch steps. With only the family's faithful farm dog for company, she stared out over the expanse of their property. Acres and acres of green pasture interspersed with newly growing wheat fields, spread out as far as the eye could see. Good thing they'd have time to hire workers before the crop would need harvesting. If they didn't sell first. Off to one side, Maxi could see the outline of the barn and the offending tractor parked outside. It sat askew, like no one had bothered to park it properly after finding Charlie underneath it. She wondered who had found him and how they got the tractor righted again.

She swore silently at her father's stupidity to drive such a dangerous machine after drinking. How could he be so reckless with his life and end up leaving Mama all alone when he knew how she depended on him?

Waves of anger rippled through her. How she hated this farm — loathed it with every fiber of her being. She hated it as much as Charlie had loved it. Every bad thing that had ever happened in her life, she blamed directly on this farm.

Including Drew's death —

"There you are. I've been looking everywhere for you."

Maxi jolted on the wooden stair and twisted around to see her best friend, Lily Draper — no, Lily Logan now — step out onto the porch. She stood with one hand on her very pregnant belly and pushed her long, dark hair off her face with the other.

Maxi tried to smile. "Sorry. Just needed a few minutes alone."

Lily took a seat beside her, her stomach protruding in front. "I thought you might be hiding from Jason." The teasing quality to her voice brought a snort to Maxi's lips.

"That, too."

Lily wrapped an arm around Maxi's shoulders. "I'm so sorry about Charlie. How are you holding up?"

A storm of tears lodged in Maxi's throat. She'd managed fine all day and would not break down now. "I'm fine." *Liar.*

"I know you didn't get along well with

him. Still, this must be difficult for you."

Maxi shrugged. "It's no real surprise he's gone. I think we all knew his drinking would lead to this one day." She bit her lip to keep her emotions contained. "It's my mom I'm worried about. She can't live here by herself. Her condition's become much worse since I left."

A soft breeze blew the scent of Lily's subtle perfume across Maxi's nose.

"Is there any way to slow the progress of MS?"

"Not really. Sometimes she's stable for a while. Then she gets worse again."

"So what are you going to do?"

Maxi leaned her head against the railing for a moment and sighed. That one simple question summed up her whole dilemma. "I wish I knew." Maxi pushed to her feet. "I'd better get back inside. Aidan will worry. And the dishes won't wash themselves."

"If I can help in any way with your mom, you know I'm here for you." The sympathy in Lily's eyes was genuine.

"Thanks, but I'm sure we'll figure something out." She opened the screen door and waited for Lily to enter the kitchen.

"How long are you staying in town?" Lily walked to the long counter that lined the wall of the country kitchen.

"I'm not sure. I need to get back to the city as soon possible. But first I have to figure out what to do about Mama." Maxi took a block of cheese from the refrigerator and set it on the wooden cutting board. She would keep the finger foods going until the remaining handful of friends had left.

Following Maxi's example, Lily began to chop cucumbers to refill the vegetable tray. "I can ask Nick to look into some facilities for you, in case you decide to go that route. Being a minister has some advantages. He'll know which places are good and which aren't."

Gratitude for the compassion of her friends lifted Maxi's spirits for the moment. As much as she hated to think of her mother in some sort of facility, she had to face the cold reality that there may not be another option. "That would be helpful. Thanks."

"I saw you talking to Jason earlier."

Bands of tension returned to Maxi's shoulders. Without looking at Lily, she turned to the fridge to get another pitcher of iced tea. "Yeah, he was here."

"Was it difficult seeing him again?"

The truth of Lily's observation hit hard. Maxi took a deep breath and closed the fridge door. "Why would you ask that?"

"Gee, maybe because you've had a crush

on him for as long as I've known you."

A dozen different emotions sifted through Maxi, but the only one she let surface was anger. "That crush ended a long time ago. Just being back here makes me realize how much I hate the small town way of life. I can't wait to get back to New York."

Lily laid down the knife. "Good thing I know you better than that, or I might take offense. Seeing that I'm part of this small town."

Maxi heaved a sigh as anger morphed into weariness. She swiped her arm across her forehead. "I'm sorry. Don't listen to me right now. I don't know what I'm saying."

Lily crossed the distance between them and put her arms around her. "It's OK. Just breathe and put one foot in front of the other. The rest will work itself out in God's time. It always does."

Maxi allowed the comfort of Lily's embrace to seep into her weary soul. She envied the conviction of her friend's new-found faith. If only Maxi could find comfort in a God who cared about her.

But Drew's senseless death had destroyed the threads of her trust in God. Her father's demise only reinforced the fact that despite Mama's constant litany of prayers, God paid very little attention to the plight of the

North family.

And Maxi had no reason to believe that would change anytime soon.

3

Jason let all Sunday go by without calling Maxi. He figured she'd need time to recuperate from the funeral. Now, late Monday afternoon, he packed up his toolbox and hauled it out to his truck. He'd been working for the past few months renovating Lily and Nick Logan's main floor living area — a job that was taking longer than expected. Jason wiped the sweat off his forehead with his sleeve and slammed his tailgate shut just as Lily pulled into the driveway beside him.

He watched her struggle to wedge her pregnant belly past the steering wheel to get out. Jason tried not to smile and went to help her lift two bags of groceries out of the trunk.

"Thanks, Jason." Her large brown eyes lit up. "Everything's so difficult with this watermelon in the way." She rubbed her abdomen with loving fingers.

He chuckled as he carried the sacks up

the stairs and inside the front door. "Where would you like these? Kitchen counter?"

"Perfect." She followed him at a slower pace into the homey kitchen. "So, have you seen Maxi since the funeral?"

He put down the bags and glanced over at her, certain her question carried more weight than her casual tone implied. Especially since Lily was Maxi's best friend. "Nope. Figured she needed some time to recuperate."

Lily's warm gaze slid to his. "And now?"

Jason tensed at her scrutiny. No way was he going to discuss Maxi with her. He shrugged, attempting a casual air. "I'll probably see her sometime before she goes back."

"Good. I know she's missed you." Lily took some cans out of the first bag.

He snorted. "Could've fooled me."

Lily turned to face him, one hand on her hip, head cocked. "Did you two argue before she left?"

Her voice was soft, but the question jarred him. "Yeah, we did," he admitted. "Seemed like she was spoiling for a fight that day." He frowned. "It was stupid."

Lily came closer and laid a hand on his arm. "Don't let her avoid you this time. She needs all the support she can get with her dad gone and her mom's health so bad."

"I'll do what I can." He stepped back, hoping to escape Lily's probing.

"You still here, Hanley?" Nick Logan's voice boomed down the hall. "My wife must have you doing extra chores."

So much for his escape.

"He's helping me with the groceries," Lily called back.

Nick entered the kitchen, loosening his clerical collar. He stopped to give Lily a kiss. "You should wait for me to do the shopping," he scolded. "Doc said you shouldn't be on your feet too much."

She rolled her eyes in mock exasperation but continued to unpack the bag.

Jason bit back a laugh and turned to Nick. "How are things at the shelter?"

He'd helped Nick turn the abandoned Strickland house into a shelter for abused women and children, and though the facility had opened six months ago, it had taken awhile for word of mouth to spread of its existence.

Nick ran a hand through his dark blond hair. "Busy, but good. Another family moved in today."

Lily's eyebrows shot up, interest lighting her face. "If you need me tomorrow, I could come by for a few hours."

Nick frowned as he stored perishables in the fridge. "I thought we agreed you wouldn't work anymore until after the baby's born."

Lily planted her hands on her hips, her famous temper beginning to show. "I did *not* agree. You and Doc ganged up on me."

Jason couldn't help but smile. After working with the Logans for almost a year, first at the shelter and now renovating their home, he'd come to love their good-natured bickering. They'd overcome many obstacles to be together, thanks in large part to Maxi, who had helped them realize their true feelings for each other.

"Well, you two, I've got things to do, so I'll leave you to work out your . . . issues." Jason smiled and bent to kiss Lily's cheek, ignoring her scowl. He clapped Nick on the back and then headed out to his truck, his mind on Maxi.

Very soon, he planned to have a serious talk with his former best friend and figure out just where things stood between them.

Monday after dinner, Maxi wheeled her mother into the living room and turned on the TV for her to watch her favorite game show. She helped her onto the sofa, got her settled with a pillow behind her, and went back to the kitchen to clear the table and do the dishes.

Maxi scraped the food from her mother's plate into the trash. She'd barely picked at her meal. Maxi blew out a tired breath. As soon as the chores were done, she would find some treat to tempt Mama's appetite.

Bones aching with weariness, she filled the sink with soapy water, lamenting the fact that her father had never allowed them to install a dishwasher. One more example of his selfishness. She clanked the dishes in the sink, sloshing the water with extra force.

An arm reached from behind to still her hand. "Take it easy. Those are Mom's good dishes."

Water splashed onto the counter. "Aidan. You scared me."

She looked over her shoulder at her sibling and flicked suds at him. He grinned, reminding her of the little boy he'd once been. His gray-blue eyes, so sincere, always contained a glimpse of humor or mischief. His sandy hair had darkened somewhat over the years, but he'd only grown more handsome. Maxi thought Drew might look very similar if he'd lived this long. Immediately, she wrenched her thoughts away from that painful subject.

Aidan picked up a towel and began to dry

the dishes. They worked in companionable silence until the need to talk overcame Maxi.

"I can't believe how much worse Mama is since the last time I was home. I don't think she can live here by herself, Aidan. What are we going to do?" Her shoulders slumped. None of the possible solutions to this problem sat well with her. "I can't move back here to look after her. My career is at a crucial point right now."

Aidan stopped drying. "No one expects you to give up your dream, Max."

"Well, you've just started teaching. You can't move back either."

They'd all been so proud when Aidan got his degree and landed a teaching job right away. The only drawback was they missed Aidan, who was way out in Arizona.

"No. I can't abandon my students right now." His face was a study in seriousness. "I've made a commitment to them."

"I know." She let the water out of the sink, watching the suds do a slow swirl down the drain. "Of course, Cal is out of the question. I can't believe he even came home for the funeral." But not surprised he left town again right after the ceremony. Just as well. Trouble followed Calvin wherever he went.

Aidan dried the last dish and reached to

put it in the cupboard, avoiding her gaze. A prickle of intuition hit Maxi. "Has Cal been in touch with you?"

Aidan had the grace to look sheepish. "He called a few months ago."

Maxi planted her hands on her hips. "Looking for money, I'll bet."

Aidan nodded. "Same old story. Lost his job. Needed something to tide him over . . ."

"Tell me you didn't give him anything." Maxi crossed her arms over her chest and leaned back against the counter, trying to contain her anger at her oldest brother. "You can't keep bailing him out of every mess he gets into."

Aidan sighed. "I gave him a little, not much."

She frowned her displeasure.

"He's our brother. What am I supposed to do? Let him starve?"

"How about letting him stand on his own two feet? And take responsibility for the problems he creates." She grabbed the dishcloth off the counter and began to scour the large wooden table that dominated the room. "He's one of the main reasons Charlie was so unhappy. Why couldn't Cal just remain here and work the farm?"

"Same reason you and I couldn't," Aidan replied in a low voice. "He hates farm life.

And the pressure Dad put on him to stay only aggravated the situation."

Maxi tensed, remembering the fights she'd had with her father over doing the farm chores, the guilt he'd laid on all of them for shirking their duty. The guilt he'd smothered her in over Drew . . . She heaved in a great gulp of air and forced her mind away from those tortuous thoughts.

No wonder she'd dreaded coming home for this funeral. All the bad family blood bubbled up, threatening to swallow her whole.

"I hope he said good-bye to Mama before he left," she snapped. "She has enough grief to deal with right now."

Aidan stepped toward her, took the rag from her hands and pulled her into a hug. "I'm pretty sure he did. You look exhausted. Why don't you head off to bed, and let me look after Mama?"

"I will soon." She rested her cheek against Aidan's soft cotton shirt. The comfort of her brother's arms made a wealth of emotions loom too close to the surface. She swallowed hard to push them back.

"We'll talk about the farm tomorrow," he said. "I guess you're right. We'll have to put it up for sale and find Mama somewhere to live."

The weight of all that they still had to do settled like two bricks on her shoulders. "I can't take too much time away from the salon. Not if I want to get that partnership."

He pulled her back to look in her eyes. "If anyone can do it, it's you. Look at all you've accomplished since you've been gone."

She gave a weak smile. "You haven't seen the barracuda I'm up against."

"Since when do you let anyone intimidate you? That's one of the things I admire most about you. You don't let anyone stand in the way of what you want." Aidan squeezed her shoulder. "Let's not worry about all that tonight. Things are bound to look better after a good night's sleep."

"You're right, as usual."

"I'm going to take a quick shower and then sit with Mama for a while. You go and relax."

"Yes, sir." She gave a mock salute, and once he left the kitchen, she turned to rinse out the sink one last time.

The phone rang as she hung the towel on the stove to dry. Maxi looked at the clock and frowned. The only call she expected was from the real estate agent. It seemed a bit late for Myra to return her call, but then agents kept weird hours.

"North residence."

"Maxi? It's Jason."

She fumbled, nearly dropping the receiver. "Jason. Hi." Her heart thumped at an uncomfortable rate.

"How are things?"

"OK, I guess." *How lame could she sound?*

"I was wondering if you could get away for a cup of coffee."

Maxi froze. Part of her wanted to jump in the family car and drive right over. The other part shied away, remembering the heartbreak that had been somewhat responsible for her leaving town in the first place.

"I don't know. Aidan's in the shower, and I don't want to leave Mama alone." *Pretty sad, using her mother as an excuse.*

"I understand. How's she doing anyway?"

She kept her voice low. "I think she's still in shock. It hasn't sunk in for any of us yet. And she's worried about what's going to happen to her now." *Like we all are.*

"I'd like to talk to you about all this. How about tomorrow?"

He wasn't giving up. "I'm meeting Lily tomorrow. She's going to show me around the shelter. I haven't seen it since they made all the renovations."

"You'll be amazed at the transformation. It looks great, if I do say so myself."

"Lily told me you worked with Nick fixing it up." Another fact that surprised her. Since when had Jason bothered with charities?

"Nick was nice enough to give me a job when Tony's garage burned down. Now I'm working on their living room."

A small stab of jealousy rocked her. How had Jason become so involved with her best friends? "Looks like I've missed a lot since I've been away."

"See, we really do need to catch up. As a matter of fact, I'll be doing some landscaping around the grounds of the shelter tomorrow. Maybe we could meet afterward."

Maxi drew in a deep breath. There appeared to be no polite way to get out of seeing him. For the sake of their former relationship, she could at least give him this. "Sure. That'd be fine."

"Great. See you tomorrow then."

She could hear the relief in his voice. For whatever reason, Jason seemed eager to see her. She'd just have to steel herself against the attraction she'd always felt in his presence.

Nothing but more heartache could come from allowing Jason back into her life.

4

The next day, Maxi followed Lily down the main staircase of Logan House to the impressive entranceway, finishing her tour of the new shelter. The mahogany railings shone as though just polished, as did the gleaming hardwood floors. She was amazed at the stillness in the big house. With two families living there, she thought there'd be more noise.

"You guys have done a fantastic job. I wouldn't have recognized the place."

Lily smiled. "Nick and Jason worked hard to get it ready."

"How did Jason end up working for Nick?" Maxi didn't mind letting Lily see her interest in Jason. After all, she'd cried all over Lily's shoulder years ago when Jason had fallen so hard for Susie Marshall.

Lily paused with her hand on the newel post. "He started as a volunteer at first, until the fire at Tony's garage put him out of work. Nick felt bad for him and liked his work well enough to hire him."

Maxi frowned trying to remember if Peg had told her about Tony's place being destroyed. She was more blown away by Jason volunteering for something. The Jason she remembered wouldn't do anything unless there was something in it for him.

"He's changed a lot since you've been gone," Lily said in a quiet voice, as though reading her mind. "You should talk to him."

"I will — later today." Maxi ignored the nerves rolling in her stomach as she followed Lily to the kitchen. "Apparently he's working on the property. I'm going to meet him after we're done."

"Good, 'cause you guys need to resolve things between you."

Suspicion hummed through Maxi's veins. "What do you mean by that?" she demanded, marching into the spacious room. A distinct citrus odor floated in the air.

Lily went to the fridge and pulled out a large pitcher of lemonade. "I know you and Jason had some big blowup before you moved to New York. And you haven't really talked since, have you?"

Maxi sputtered as her temper took hold. "Who told you that?" She hadn't discussed the fight with anyone. Not even Lily.

Her friend shrugged. "No one. I guessed what happened from the way you guys were acting. Jason confirmed it yesterday." She stretched to pull two glasses from the cupboard.

Irritation rose in waves through Maxi's body. "I'd appreciate it if you wouldn't talk to my *former* friend about me behind my back." In some small corner of her brain, she knew she was overreacting, but she was powerless to stop the tide. She paced to the far side of the room, the words of her last encounter with Jason echoing in her head.

"If you can't be happy I've found someone I care about, you might as well . . ."

"I might as well what, Hanley?"

She remembered the uncontrollable anger, flashing like fire, fueled by his words.

"You might as well leave and never come back."

The hurt had seared through her, cutting off her breath. Her whole body had shaken with the thought that Jason had chosen Susie over her. Did their friendship mean so little to him?

"Don't worry. That's exactly what I intend to do," she'd yelled back.

Those had been their last words to each other before she'd slammed out the door. The next day, she'd left without even saying good-bye.

The touch of Lily's hand on her arm made her jump.

"Hey, I didn't mean to upset you. It's just that I miss you, and I'm worried about you."

Maxi released a deep breath and let Lily's apology soften the anger inside. "It's not your fault. I don't have the energy to deal with past baggage right now. I've got enough problems with the farm and my mother."

Lily pulled her into a tight embrace, the warmth of her large belly as comforting as her compassion. Maxi stepped away before tears could blossom, and Lily moved to the counter, poured lemonade into two tall glasses, and handed one to Maxi. "So tell me about this partnership."

Maxi took a sip of the tart liquid, grateful for the change in topic. "It's exactly the type of thing I've dreamed about. Which is why I have to get back. I need to work on my portfolio and let Philippe know I'm serious about this promotion."

"What about your mom? Has she made a decision yet?"

Maxi swirled the contents of her glass and frowned. "Mama says she'll go into a home, but I don't know if I can let her do that."

Lily patted her arm. "What a terrible position to be in. I guess Bernice wouldn't move to New York with you." It was more of a statement than a question.

"No. She's lived her whole life in this town. It wouldn't be fair to make her leave her friends, her church, and everything she's familiar with."

Lily nodded her agreement. "I'll pray for you and your mom. I know God will help you find the right solution."

An uncomfortable sensation stiffened Maxi's spine. As much as her own faith had lagged in recent years, she didn't like to dampen anyone else's. "Thanks."

Maxi's cell phone rang. She read the name on the display and answered. "Hi, Jason."

"Hey. How's your visit with Lily going?"

She glanced over at her friend, who motioned for her to go on. "Just finishing up."

"Good. You still want to get together?"

"I guess, if you have the time." *Could she sound any more unenthusiastic?*

"I'm almost finished here. Why don't you meet me out back?"

Lily waved madly, pointing to the pitcher of lemonade.

Maxi rolled her eyes. "Lily wants to know if you'd like some lemonade."

His chuckle echoed through the phone. "I'd love some."

"Be out in a minute."

Lily was already pouring the drink into a tall plastic glass when Maxi disconnected. Dread pooled in her stomach, combining with the acid of the lemonade to make her somewhat queasy.

Lily held out the glass. "Go talk to him. You'll feel better. I promise."

Maxi sighed and headed out the back door, feeling like a prisoner about to face the firing squad.

Jason wielded the clippers with extra force, trying to steady his nerves. He hoped it'd be easier to talk out in the open while he worked, instead of being stuck behind a table in some noisy coffee shop.

His hands dampened at the sight of Maxi's petite figure marching across the large expanse of lawn. From this distance, she looked the same as she had in high school. He smirked, remembering the feisty, rebellious teen she used to be. The way her hazel eyes glowed with a challenge the day she dared him to skip school and drive into Kingsville to the movies.

They made quite a pair back then. She always knew how to get him to do anything she wanted.

Almost anything.

"You missed a spot, Hanley."

Jason's mouth curved into a smile at the sound of her voice. He picked up another set of clippers and held them out. "Think you can do better?"

She stared at him for a minute before she grinned in return, accepting the challenge, as he knew she would. "Sure can." Despite the fact that he held two pairs of clippers, she traded him the tool for the glass.

He looked at her blouse and dressy pants. A high contrast to his sweat-stained T-shirt and faded jeans. "Not worried about getting those fancy clothes dirty?"

"Nope."

His heart lightened as they fell back into their familiar pattern of playful competition. "Thanks for the drink." He drained his glass and set it down on top of his toolbox, ready to tackle the greenery again.

For a while, they worked in companionable silence, while Jason tried to figure out how to start the conversation. He sneaked a sideways glance at her. She seemed oblivious to everything but the wayward branches. Why did talking to Maxi suddenly seem harder than battling a raging fire? Despite the lemonade, his tongue stuck to the roof of his dry mouth. He cleared his throat and took the plunge. "Must be tough being back on the farm."

Maxi looked at him. "It is. Having Aidan here helps though." She clipped with more intensity.

"I take it Cal didn't stick around."

"Nope. Took off as soon as he could. I'm surprised he even came at all, knowing how he felt about Charlie."

Her expression became thunderous, and Jason feared for the hedge's existence. He guessed her older brother hadn't changed for the better in recent years. Best to change topics. "So how do you like the shelter?"

She flashed a wide smile at him. "It's beautiful. You and Nick did a great job."

"Thanks. Good training for my next big project."

"What big project?"

He hesitated, reluctant to say it out loud, to make it real. "I want to work toward getting a fire station built in Rainbow Falls." He glanced over to see her reaction.

She stopped mid-clip. "You're really serious about this firefighting stuff. What started all this?"

He paused, taking time to wipe the sweat off his forehead. "It's something I've been thinking about for a long time actually. Since Drew died."

The blood drained from Maxi's face at the mere mention of her brother's death.

Even now, eight years later, she still couldn't talk about it.

"I don't know if having a station in town would've saved Drew," he went on, "but it would sure help in a lot of other cases. Like when Tony's place burned down."

She raised the clippers with shaking hands. "What happened to your bike? You still ride?"

The complete change of subject threw him for a moment. "Not so much anymore." He smiled then, remembering the two of them screaming through town on his second-hand Harley, much to the annoyance of the adult population — his mother included.

"You still hang out with Marco?"

His insides clenched. The thought of his ex-best friend's betrayal still rankled. "Not anymore." He shot her a furtive glance, praying she'd let the subject go.

But Maxi's eyebrows perked up like a set of antennae. "Why not? What happened?"

Jason lowered his clippers. The fact she knew him so well irritated the crap out of him. He blew out a breath. "Marco swindled Tony out of some cash."

"That's it?"

"He also tried to steal my girlfriend." The brief hope that Maxi would let it go evaporated at her horrified expression.

"What a snake! I can't believe Susie would fall for his charm. Not when she was so crazy about you."

He began trimming again at a faster pace, avoiding her probing gaze. As much as he didn't want to continue this topic, he couldn't let Maxi think the worst of Susie. "She didn't. Turned him down flat. But that didn't stop him from trying again with my next girlfriend."

Maxi stalked over. "Your *next* girlfriend?"

Jason pressed his lips into a thin line. How had this conversation veered off track so fast? He scrubbed a hand through his hair. "Yeah, Gloria Johnson — but I ended the relationship a couple of months ago."

Her mouth fell open. "The high school tramp?"

Too late, he remembered how much Maxi had loathed Gloria in high school and clipped harder. The muscles in his upper arms burned.

"How could you go out with her? She slept with practically the whole senior class."

He sighed and stopped to wipe his face. "Call it a significant lapse of judgment. I was ready to break it off anyway, but Marco's stunt sent me off the deep end."

Maxi snorted. "Did you hit him?"

He grimaced, remembering the beating

he'd laid on Marco. "Let's just say I'm not proud of how I handled the situation. But that was before I turned my life around."

They had come to the end of the row of hedges. Maxi ran her arm across her face and plopped onto the ground in the shade of an oak tree. "You mean the firefighting thing?"

With careful precision, he set the tools down and then came to sit beside her. This was it. Time for honesty. He plucked a piece of grass and shredded it before answering. "That's one change. But the biggest one is that I've dedicated my life to God's service."

Her jaw dropped open and her eyes went wide. "You did what?"

If he'd said he was a serial killer, she couldn't have looked more shocked. He kept his gaze serious. "I needed to stop my self-destructive behavior and do something meaningful with my life. So I came up with doing service through firefighting." He waited for her to say something, hoping she would understand how big this was for him.

"Wow." She looked poleaxed. "Didn't see that coming. I thought you went to the youth meetings at the church just to hit on girls."

He laughed. "That's how it started. But Nick's words and attitude rubbed off on me. More than I realized."

She frowned as she looked at him. "You really have changed."

"Guess I have." He paused, allowing his gaze to roam over her tousled hair, settling on the familiar silver hoop earrings. Earrings he'd given her for a graduation present. Sorrow twisted in his chest. "I've missed you, Max."

She turned away but not before he noticed moisture brimming in her eyes. He took it as a good sign, that she was as invested in their friendship as he. "What happened to us anyway? What caused that big fight before you left?"

Maxi stared out across the lawn, a nerve jumping in her jaw. "Geez, Hanley. I don't know."

She was lying. He'd bet his Harley on it. "I think you do."

She leapt to her feet, brushing grass off her pant legs, not looking at him. "It was a bad day, that's all."

She took off at a brisk pace toward the house. He jumped up, annoyance shooting through his system. He was not about to let her off the hook. Not this time.

He covered the distance between them in two seconds and grabbed her arm. "Wait a minute. We need to deal with this. The way you left town has bothered me for a long time. I called, I sent e-mails, but you never answered."

She tried to squirm away, but he held her firm. Her gaze remained focused on his chest where she surely must be able to see his heart beating at a ridiculous rate. This close he could see the sweep of her lashes on her cheek, the faint dusting of freckles near her nose. When she raised her eyes to lock with his, fire blazed in their hazel depths.

"I thought a clean break would be better. My life's in New York. I figured yours would be here with Susie."

He scowled. That didn't answer his question.

"Why'd you two break up anyway?" she demanded.

"None of your business." Trust Maxi to avoid his question with an attack of her own. "What was it about Susie that made you so crazy? You never cared who I dated before."

Her nostrils flared for a moment before she struggled again to get free. He only tightened his grip, suddenly aware of how fragile she seemed compared to his own muscled arms.

The look in her eyes changed from anger

to one of almost pain, making his breath catch. When her bottom lip began to quiver, the irrational side of his brain could only manage one powerful thought. What would it be like to kiss those lips?

His breathing became labored, his chest tight. Slowly he lowered his head toward her. He heard the sharp intake of her breath, smelled the traces of lemonade on her mouth. The tension shimmered between them until the sound of her cell phone pierced the silence. Maxi jerked away from him, pulling the phone out of her pant pocket.

Jason raked a hand through his hair, his pulse rioting. What had he almost done?

"Lance. Hi. Yes, everything's fine." She turned away from Jason, one hand over her free ear. "No, I can't leave yet. I told you. We have to put the farm up for sale and find a place for my mother . . ."

Who was Lance? And since when was she selling the farm?

"Philippe understands my situation."

Jason saw Maxi's back stiffen and frowned at the sudden desire to ease her tension.

"There's no reason for you to come here." She sounded panicky. "If I need you, I'll call. Yes, I promise. I miss you, too. Talk to you soon."

Maxi clicked the phone off and stayed with her back turned for a moment, taking in a long breath.

Jason waited for her to turn around. When she did, her mask was in place, emotions contained.

"Who's Lance?"

"Just a friend."

He snorted his disbelief. "Yeah, right."

"Fine. A friend I'm dating."

"Sounds like a hair stylist."

"Actually he works on Wall Street."

Awkward tension hovered in the air between them. She fiddled with a necklace sitting at her throat. He tried not to think about almost kissing her moments before.

"So your boyfriend didn't even come with you to your father's funeral?" He couldn't help the snide tone.

Her mask slipped. "Don't you dare lecture me about relationships."

A swarm of indescribable emotions churned the lemonade in his stomach. Maxi had a boyfriend. A rich, New York boyfriend. Why did that bother him so much?

"You're right. It's none of my business." Mentally he counted to ten and backpedaled to focus on what he'd been trying to achieve. To recapture their former friendship.

If that were even possible.

The stiffness in her slim shoulders relaxed a touch, though she appeared wary.

He blew out a breath. "Look, I don't want to fight with you, Max. Can't we please go back to the way we used to be? You were my best friend, and I miss you."

She didn't move, except to blink twice. Finally she nodded. "I've missed you, too." Her chin trembled for a moment before she stuck it out, an act of defiance, like the old Maxi.

"Friends again?" Jason held out his hand to her and waited.

An untold emotion flickered over her face before she took his hand. "Friends."

Her slim fingers gripped his hand, sending a flood of warmth through his arm. For some reason, even though he'd accomplished his goal, Jason wasn't nearly as happy as he'd expected.

5

The familiar jingle of the bell brought waves of nostalgia crashing over Maxi the next day as she pushed through the door to Peg's *Cut 'N Curl.* The scent of green apple shampoo blended with hairspray fumes to assault her senses. It felt like coming home.

So much so, that she had to swallow a rush of emotion.

Nothing had changed in the time she'd been away. Tangerine walls still provided a backdrop to the hair styling stations. The same large hair dryers lined the far wall. Peg Hanley, her barrel shape and familiar topknot of wispy reddish hair, stood snipping Millie Simmons's gray curls that didn't need trimming at all.

The only real difference Maxi could see was the new girl at the reception desk. Maxi smiled, recalling the good times she'd had when Lily worked at that desk. Those simple things seemed even more memorable today for some reason.

"May I help you?" the girl asked.

"I'm here to see Peg."

The girl eyed Maxi's spiked hair and large hoop earrings and then moved down to her mosaic halter top and tight designer jeans. Her disapproving look made Maxi raise her chin. "No need to get up. I know the way."

Before the girl could sputter a protest, Maxi breezed by the reception desk toward Peg, who turned and let out a whoop. Dropping the comb, she rushed forward to envelop Maxi in a crushing hug. The simple affection had tears smarting.

"If you aren't a treat for these tired eyes," Peg said. "Haven't changed a bit, except your clothes are fancier and you're still too thin."

Maxi laughed. "Thank goodness you haven't changed either."

"Let me finish with Millie here while we chat." Peg went back to her hair cut. "So how are things at that swanky establishment of yours?"

Maxi hesitated, wondering why immediate words of enthusiasm didn't spring to her lips. She forced gaiety into her tone. "Great. I'm in the running for a junior partnership. If I can get back in time to beat out the ice queen."

"Ah, one of those types."

"You have no idea. And she's out for blood."

"Don't wrinkle that freckled nose worrying about the likes of her. If your boss has any sense, he'll recognize true talent when he sees it."

Maxi grinned. "Thanks. Actually that's one of the reasons I dropped by. Would it be OK to use the shop to practice some New York style hairdos, if I can line up a few guinea pigs? I need to update my portfolio."

Peg raised one eyebrow above her wire-rimmed glasses. "I wouldn't mind seeing some of those fancy dos myself. As long as I'm not booked up, the place is yours."

Maxi kissed her cheek. "Thanks. I knew I could count on your support."

"I'd rather you come back here to work," she grumbled.

Maxi laughed out loud. "I miss you, too."

Peg brushed off Millie's neck and sent her to pay the bill. She shook out the black cape and laid it over the chair. "So have you seen that boy of mine since the funeral?"

Tension hummed through Maxi's shoulders. "Saw him yesterday." She forced herself not to think about the near kiss.

"He still mad at you?"

Maxi frowned. She hadn't realized the extent of their estrangement was common knowledge. "I think we're back to a good place again," she replied.

Peg gave her a penetrating stare. "You still in love with him?"

An infusion of heat spread up Maxi's neck to her cheeks. She felt as exposed as a streaker in a football stadium. "In love? No. I got over that high school crush a long time ago." She tried to give a convincing smile. "Actually I'm dating a very nice guy now — a businessman on Wall Street."

Peg didn't move a muscle or even blink. "A businessman? Guess the city's changed you after all."

Peg's unsettling remark stayed with Maxi the rest of the day, irritating her mood like an uncomfortable rash. All through dinner, which her mother barely touched, Maxi couldn't help reliving Peg's unspoken criticism. Though Maxi didn't give a fig what most people thought of her, she valued Peg Hanley's opinion as much, if not more, than that of her family.

The phone rang, startling Maxi out of her brooding thoughts.

"Hey, sis. It's Aidan. Just wanted you to know I made it home safe and sound."

Aidan had left that morning, needing to

get back to his job in Arizona. The sound of his voice increased the pangs of loneliness. "Glad to hear it." She tried not to envy him being able to leave all the problems here behind him.

"How's Mama?" he asked.

"About the same. I'm not sure if it's her illness or depression over Charlie, but all she wants to do is sleep. I can barely get her to eat."

At Maxi's feet, Shep whined. She pushed open the screen door as she talked and let him out.

Aidan sighed on the other end. "Let's pray the house sells fast, and we can find a good place for her. I hate leaving you with the brunt of all this." He paused. "You sure you're OK?"

Maxi swallowed her sadness. "I'm fine. Just tired."

"Well, call me anytime if you need to talk."

"I will. Thanks."

Maxi hung up feeling more desolate than before. She tidied the kitchen, let Shep back in, and went to check on her mother, who'd dozed off on the couch. Maxi roused her and got her into her room and settled in bed with the German shepherd lying guard on the mat.

Weariness settled into Maxi's bones as she

locked up for the night. In the darkened kitchen, the lonely glow of her cell phone beckoned to her. She picked it up, her mind turning to Jason. The longing for his soothing presence became a physical ache.

They'd agreed to be friends, hadn't they? She could ask him to come over. They could talk about old times, play some cards, watch a movie. Her heart beat faster as she punched in the first few digits of his number. Then the memory of their encounter at the shelter made heat flare in her cheeks. She snapped the phone off and tossed it on the counter. Probably a very bad idea. In her vulnerable state tonight, who knew what could happen?

She walked into the living room, straightened the pillows on the couch and turned off the lamp. With no desire to watch mindless television, she decided to turn in early, hoping things would appear brighter in the morning after a decent night's sleep.

With any luck at all, she wouldn't even dream — especially not about Jason.

Jason checked his pager and his cell phone to make sure both were still on. He'd been on call for the Kingsville Fire Department for the past eight hours and now looked forward to a hot shower and the comfort of his bed.

He ran a hand over his gritty eyes and checked the time on the clock of his truck. Twelve thirty. He should make it back to Rainbow Falls by 1:00 AM. With any luck, his mother would be asleep.

He blew out a weary breath. Maybe the time had come to get a place of his own. He hated the thought of leaving, but once he became a fireman full time, he'd be working crazy shifts, and his mom didn't sleep well, waiting to hear his truck in the driveway.

His thoughts turned to Maxi as he swung the vehicle onto the country road leading into town. Soon he would pass by the Norths' farm. Would he see any lights on, or would Maxi be long asleep?

Darkness spread out before him, broken only by the long beam of his headlights. Above him the stars winked a silent greeting. He felt like the lone person alive on the planet.

A sudden flicker up ahead caught his attention. For a moment, he thought it a trick of his imagination until the flicker became a red glow. He craned his neck to see better, his instincts kicking into high alert.

Fire!

He hit the accelerator hard to get closer as fast as he could. Fear gripped his insides the minute he realized where the light was coming from.

The North farm was on fire.

Jason slammed down his foot on the accelerator and pulled out his cell phone. He punched in the speed dial number for the Kingsville Fire Department.

"It's Hanley. Fire on rural road eight. Charlie North's place. Looks like the primary burn is the barn. I'm going to check the house. Meet me there."

Gravel flew as the truck roared onto the side road leading to the property. His pulse pounded in his temples.

Please God, let Maxi and her mother be all right.

Jason watched the flames shoot from the barn as he jumped from the barely parked vehicle. Thank goodness the chicken coop was far enough away not to be affected. Not so, the main house. Smoke wisped up from the roof of the house. His blood ran cold. The fire had spread, probably from embers blown over in the wind.

He bolted up the porch stairs to pommel the front door, calling out for Bernice and Maxi. He tried the handle, knowing it would be locked now that Maxi was home.

With no response to his banging, he took a run at the door and hit it hard with his shoulder. Pain radiated through his arm, but the door didn't budge. Fear closed his throat.

You're a firefighter, Hanley. Slow down. Think logically.

Jason turned, picked up a wooden chair from the porch, and ran to the front window. He heaved the chair with as much strength as he could muster into the pane of glass. Shards flew everywhere. He leapt through the jagged opening, mindless of the sharp pieces that tore at him. He seemed to be moving in slow motion as he ran into the hallway. Shooting a glance toward Bernice's main floor bedroom, Jason hesitated for a split second. Then, at the sight of smoke in the stairway, he bounded up toward Maxi's room.

Perspiration beaded on his forehead and dripped down his spine. The smoke got thicker as he ascended, burning his nostrils and throat. Black mist, like evil tendrils, swirled around him. He coughed, trying to cover his nose and mouth with the crook of his elbow. Somewhere in the house, Shep barked. He tried to call Maxi's name but choked instead. Acrid fumes stung his eyes and blurred his vision, further hampering his ability to see. He crawled his way along the wall to her door.

Relieved the handle wasn't hot to the touch, Jason pushed into the room. Through the haze, he could only make out vague shapes. He felt his way to the bed, groping until he hit a lump.

"Maxi."

She didn't move.

Running his hands over her, he found what felt like a shoulder and shook. When there was still no response, he gathered her body, blankets and all, into his arms and staggered to the door.

Dear God, don't let me be too late.

The smoke was much thicker on the second floor than below. As he made his way down the stairs, his vision improved. He found the front door, unlatched the lock and pushed outside. Coughs racked his body while his lungs fought for fresh air. Dropping to his knees, he laid Maxi gently on the grass. He swiped at the tears blinding him, desperate to see if she were breathing. The fact that she wasn't coughing sent off alarm bells inside him. He found a weak pulse, further adding to his anxiety.

Life and death decisions had to be made. Raising his head, he looked back at the house. Shep stood on the porch, barking in frantic staccatos. Bernice was still inside, but he had to get Maxi breathing first.

He couldn't lose her. He *wouldn't* lose her.

Determination strengthened his resolve. Hopefully, Bernice had more time, since the smoke wasn't as bad on the main level. Right now Maxi needed oxygen. He checked her airway and began mouth to mouth. His hands shook as he held her face and blew.

Please God, let her breathe.

On his third attempt, Maxi began to cough. Then she gulped in large quantities of air.

"Thank you, Lord." Relief made his muscles weak.

Her arms flailed as she regained consciousness. Gently, he held her by the shoulders.

"You're going to be OK. Stay here. I have to get your mother."

He raced into the house, dimly aware of sirens approaching.

Minutes later, he returned carrying the frail older woman. The fire truck and ambulance had just pulled up. Men spilled from the vehicles. Jason brought Bernice right to the paramedics.

"She needs oxygen. So does Maxi over on the grass."

One of the men tried to put a mask on Jason, but he pushed it away.

"The women first."

Suddenly the smoke took its toll. Jason bent over, hands on his knees, gasping air into his straining lungs. When the ground stopped spinning, he raised his head and went to find Maxi.

True to her stubborn nature, she was on her feet, refusing the paramedic's offer of an oxygen mask. Her desperate eyes sought Jason. "Where's Mama? Is she OK?"

She took a few unsteady steps toward him before her legs gave out, and he caught her.

"I think so. They're looking at her now." Maxi's colorless lips matched her pale skin. "You need oxygen."

"I have to see her first."

There was no use arguing with her. She was as stubborn as a spreading fire. He half carried her to the ambulance, motioning for the paramedic to follow. Once Maxi spied Bernice lying on a gurney, she pushed out of his arms.

"Mama." Her croak turned into a cough. "I'm here, Mama."

Bernice's lids flickered open for a moment. She gave a brief smile before they fluttered closed again.

"Is she all right?" Maxi asked the attendant.

The man, in his forties with a brush cut and a no-nonsense attitude, avoided her question. "We need to get you all to the hospital." He nodded at Jason. "You too, sir."

As much as he hated it, Jason knew the guy was right. Plus he wanted to make sure Maxi received treatment. She'd been unconscious for who knew how long.

Before she could protest, he grabbed her by the waist, hoisted her into the ambulance, and then climbed in after her. With the adrenaline waning, exhaustion crept into his body like water trickling through a dry creek bed. After Maxi was settled, he let the attendant place the mask over his face, then leaned back, waiting for the ambulance to take them away.

6

Maxi fought her way through dense fog, battling for breath. She had to find Drew. He was in this maze somewhere. She coughed, unable to find air. Heat singed her eyelids.

Fire!

She shot up as a scream ripped from her throat. Strong arms pulled her close where a steady heart thumped under her cheek.

"It's OK. You're safe."

Jason. Relief spilled through her. Everything would be all right now.

"Where's Drew?"

She felt him go still and pulled back to look at his face. Under his tousled mop of hair, sympathetic eyes watched her.

"You were dreaming, Max. Drew died a long time ago, remember?"

The confusion in her brain refused to clear. "Where are we? What happened?"

Jason held her shoulders. "You're in the

hospital." His voice was low and calm. "A fire started in the barn and spread to the house."

Oh God, no. Not another fire.

Adrenaline surged through her veins. Where was her mother? She tried to push Jason away and get out of bed, but he kept a hand on her shoulder.

"Your mom's going to be fine," he said, as though reading her mind. "She suffered some smoke inhalation. Not as much as you, but because of her illness, they want to keep her for a day or two."

Tears blurred her eyes, partly from gratitude, partly from the force of what they had escaped. They both could've died. "How — how did we get out?"

She fought to recall any detail, any tiny scrap about it. All she remembered was waking up on the grass with someone pushing an oxygen mask over her nose.

"I got you out."

She wiped the moisture from her cheeks and stared at him. His face was grim; his jaw clenched tight.

Jason had saved them?

"You? How?" Her throat burned with every word.

"I was on my way home and saw the flames in the distance. I didn't realize it was your place until I got closer." He shrugged but the look on his face told her just how bad it had been.

"So you came and got us out?"

Jason looked uncomfortable. He shifted on the bed beside her. "It's what I'm trained for."

Maxi tried to comprehend the magnitude of what he had done, scrambled to find the words to express her gratitude, but all she could do was cough. It was an effort to get the air into her lungs.

"You saved our lives," she murmured. Her body began to shake, as though she was cold, which she wasn't. It was most likely from the shock of almost losing her life. Of almost losing her mother so soon after her father.

Jason pressed her back against the pillows and rang for the nurse. A heavy-set, middle-aged woman appeared at the door seconds later.

"Our patient's awake, I see." She bustled over to check Maxi's vital signs. "Back on the oxygen you go, miss," she ordered, and attempted to replace Maxi's nose tube, which had come out during her struggles.

Maxi put up a hand to stop her. "I want to see my mother first." She couldn't rest until she saw Mama's condition for herself.

The woman darted a look at Jason who nodded.

"I'll take her."

"Only five minutes. Then I want her back here."

In the room down the hall, Bernice lay still beneath the sheets of her hospital bed. A little too still for Maxi's liking. Jason wheeled her chair to the side of the bed, and Maxi reached to take her mother's hand. The skin was paper thin and cool to the touch. Bernice's lips had a bluish tinge, her cheeks looked almost gray. Maxi swallowed hard to quell the tears that threatened again.

"I want to talk to her doctor." It hurt her raw throat to speak.

"I'll see if I can find someone."

It registered in the dim recesses of her brain that Jason was being far too accommodating. He usually argued with her about everything. Did that mean her mother's condition was worse than everyone was letting on?

When Jason left, she laid her head on her mother's arm, longing for her to wake up and tell her everything would be all right. "Please be OK, Mama. I can't lose you, too," she whispered.

A few minutes later, Jason returned with a

different nurse. This woman was tall and slim with short dark hair and a kind air about her.

"Your mother will be fine," she assured Maxi. "We've sedated her, so she'll rest. Because of her illness, though, we're going to keep her for a couple of days of observation."

Maxi sensed no deception, just honesty. The tension in her shoulders eased a fraction. "Thank you."

"If there's any change, I'll come and let you know." The woman flashed a warm smile. "Now I think you should get back to bed yourself."

The last bit of energy drained from Maxi's body. All she could do was nod. She felt the wheelchair moving, was vaguely aware of being lifted into bed and the oxygen tubes attached before she succumbed to oblivion.

7

Jason ran his hands through his hair in disbelief as he surveyed the ruins of the Norths' barn. Nothing left but a pile of ashes and part of one wall. This would delay the sale of the farm for sure.

The first light of dawn peeked over the rolling hills of the property as Jason turned toward the house to see what state it was in. Kingsville fire chief, Steve Hamilton, descended the porch stairs as Jason approached. Fatigue etched the lines of Steve's face. He was probably finishing the tail end of the midnight shift.

Jason strode over to him, noting a dejected Shep lying on the porch.

"Hey, Steve. How bad is the damage in there?"

Steve looked up from his clipboard, his face grim. "Main floor's not bad, but the second story will need extensive repairs. The roof over the far bedroom is gone."

Maxi's room.

"Lots of water damage, too," Steve continued. "Looks like Charlie let the batteries wear out on the smoke detectors."

Jason shook his head, not wanting to think ill of the dead, but it was typical of Charlie. "So the family won't be able to come back yet?"

"Not for a while, I'm afraid."

Jason tried not to think about telling Bernice and Maxi they were homeless for the time being. "Any idea how this started?"

Steve threw him a dark look. "There'll have to be an investigation to know for sure, but it looks like . . ." He paused as if unsure to continue.

"Like what?"

"Possible arson."

Jason's mouth fell open. "Arson?"

Steve nodded. "I've already called the inspector from Bismarck. He should be out here in the next couple of hours."

Jason's mind raced, trying to make sense of the whole situation. Why would anyone want to burn down the North farm?

"Heard you were the first one on the scene." Steve pushed his pen through the graying hair over his ear.

"That's right. I'm the one who put the call in."

"According to the paramedics, you got the women out in good shape."

Jason straightened his shoulders, not sure where Steve was heading with the conversation. "I did my best. They're both stable for now."

Steve narrowed his eyes. "Good job, rookie. Tough thing to handle on your own. Even tougher when you know the people involved."

"You have no idea." Jason still grappled with his decision, whether he should've gotten Bernice out first because of her delicate health. But he'd gone with his gut, which usually ended up being the right call.

"I wouldn't go in the house right now unless absolutely necessary," Steve called over his shoulder as he headed to his vehicle.

"I need to get Mrs. North's wheelchair and her medication. On the main level."

"Make it quick."

"Will do."

Jason bounded up to the porch, through the door and into the hallway, where he careened to a halt. The smell of rancid smoke curled around him like phantom arms. The fear that had gripped him as he'd raced up those stairs, not knowing if Maxi was alive or dead, now roared back with the force of a bulldozer.

He could've lost her for good last night. He took a deep breath, steadied himself on the post at the foot of the stairs and determinedly squashed the uncomfortable sensation in his chest. Dwelling on what might have been was a colossal waste of time and energy.

Instead he focused on the task. In Bernice's room, he folded the wheelchair into a manageable position, grabbed the bottles of medication on the dresser, and headed back out. There was no point in trying to retrieve anything from Maxi's room. Everything would either reek of smoke or be water logged.

Jason stepped onto the porch and took a deep, cleansing breath. Shep raised his head off his paws and fixed Jason with a forlorn look. Poor dog had probably been outside all night.

"Come on, boy. You'd better come home with me."

Shep stood up, gave a slight wag of his tail, and followed Jason to his truck.

Lack of sleep caught up with Jason as he steered his vehicle home, fighting to keep his lids from drooping. He hoped his mother would be awake. He needed to run his idea past her before he approached Maxi. Shep followed him up the walkway to the front door of the bungalow.

His mother stood in her blue bathrobe at the kitchen counter, pouring boiling water into the teapot. She eyed him and the dog and put the kettle down with a deliberate snap. "Why is there a dog in my kitchen?"

Jason smiled and bent to kiss her cheek without answering.

She frowned. "You look terrible. What happened?"

"Sit, have your tea, and I'll tell you."

Ma took two mugs from the cupboard, poured the tea, and brought them to the table where Jason sat with his head in his hands. He took the cup, grateful for its warmth.

"There was a fire at the Norths' farm last night."

"My goodness, no." Alarm shot into his mother's eyes. "Are Maxi and her family all right?"

He nodded. "I got them out in time."

"You got them out? You were on duty?"

"Actually, I was on my way home." He explained what had happened and how Bernice and Maxi needed somewhere to stay for a while. "I was hoping you'd let them come here until the repairs on the house are done."

"Of course. They're more than welcome."

"The dog, too?"

She gave a mock scowl. "As long as he's house broken. And as long as you don't tell me there's a herd of cows needing shelter as well."

Jason chuckled. "No livestock. The chicken coop wasn't touched, thank goodness."

She smiled and laid a hand on his shoulder. "You're a good man, Jason Hanley. Now go get some sleep."

"Thanks, Ma. Sleep sounds like heaven right about now."

He'd worry about the rest when he woke up.

Maxi groaned as she attempted to get up to use the bathroom. Every muscle ached, and her chest wheezed like she'd been smoking for fifty years. She hadn't gotten much sleep with the constant whirring of machines, nurses coming and going, and checking her oxygen levels. But the doctor had been in to see her earlier and given her good news. She would be released later in the day — a fact that should be cause for celebration, but Maxi couldn't shake her unease. She'd feel better once she knew for certain her mother was out of danger. Now to figure out how bad the house had been damaged and whether they could go back there or not. She'd give her right arm for a cell phone right about now.

She'd returned to her bed and got settled under the covers when Jason poked his head around the doorframe. "You decent?"

"Aren't I always?"

He grinned and then stepped into the room, a huge bouquet of flowers in his arms. Maxi blinked, suspicion blooming as he handed them to her. Jason wasn't the flower-giving type of guy. He must have bad news to resort to this.

"OK. Give it to me straight."

"What? Aren't you supposed to bring flowers when someone's in the hospital?"

"Save it for one of your girlfriends. What aren't you telling me?" She tried not to notice how good he looked, his chestnut hair waving over his forehead. And he smelled like he'd just stepped out of the shower. All fresh and spicy.

He grew serious as he pulled a chair over to her bed side and sat down. "The barn's completely gone."

Maxi sucked in a breath. She hadn't really allowed herself to imagine what toll the fire might have taken. Then the irony of the situation struck her full force. How many times had she wished for this very thing to happen? That the farm would disappear. Now when she needed it in tip-top shape, a fire destroyed it. Was God trying to sabotage her life again?

"Hey, you OK?"

She pulled her attention back to Jason. "Yeah. What about the house?"

"There's some damage to the roof and the second floor." He got up to take the flowers from her and set them on the windowsill.

"So we'll have to live on the first floor for now?"

"Not exactly."

Her patience evaporated. "Spit it out, Hanley. Bottom line."

He reclaimed his chair, his expression grim. "The house won't be livable for a while. So my mom wants you and Bernice to stay with us until the repairs are done."

Instant panic rose in her chest. She could not stay in the same house as Jason. Sleep down the hall from him. Shower in the same bathroom as him. Not without her old feelings flaring up stronger than ever. "I'm sure Lily can put us up," she said, not meeting his eyes.

"They're renovating the main floor, remember? Besides your mom can't do the stairs there. And I don't think Lily needs all the extra work in her condition. Nick's on her like a hawk about taking it easy."

Jason watched her a little too closely. Could he sense her discomfort? When no other solution would come to her frazzled mind, she finally shrugged. "OK. Guess we'll be roomies for a while."

His lip twitched. "Please, curb your enthusiasm. My ego can't take it."

She hit his arm. "Cut it out. My life is in ruins, and you're making jokes."

"Sorry." With that glint in his eye, he didn't seem the least bit remorseful. "Look, we'll get the house fixed. I promise. I've already called a few guys about getting a team together to rebuild the barn. The only hold up will be the investigation . . ." He clamped his lips shut and looked like he wanted to bite off his tongue.

She stiffened against the pillows. "What investigation?"

Jason muttered an oath and dragged his hand over his jaw. "I didn't want you to know about that right now."

"Too late. What investigation?"

He looked down at his hands and then raised his head and sighed. "There's a suspicion of arson."

Maxi gasped. Her fingers plucked at the ragged neckline of the hospital gown, suddenly too tight on her throat. "Arson? Who would want to burn down our barn?"

"That's what I've been trying to figure out."

Her head swam as she tried to comprehend the significance of this new turn of events. Then her blood ran cold as a sudden thought occurred to her. "What happens to our insurance if they find out the fire was deliberate?"

Her stomach sank when he didn't reply. The sympathy in Jason's blue eyes told her the answer. "They won't pay us, will they?"

"Probably not. Unless you can prove it wasn't anyone connected with the property who might have a stake in it." His gaze seemed to ask a question. "There wouldn't be anyone like that, would there?"

Irritation rose up in waves. "You don't think *I'd* do something like that?"

"No, not you. Or Aidan." He paused. "I was thinking of Cal."

Anger lit a slow fuse inside her. Though she had issues with her oldest brother, it hurt that Jason would think him capable of such treachery. "I know my brother's no saint, but Cal would never do this to us. What reason would he have?"

Jason rose to pace the small space. "He's always hated that farm. Maybe he was afraid you'd expect him to move back and take over."

She shook her head. "But Cal wasn't even here. He took off right after the funeral."

"Who says he wasn't hanging around waiting for the right opportunity?"

Maxi pushed herself up in the bed and swung her legs over the side. "No. Cal would not set the place on fire knowing Mama and I were inside the house. I know my brother better than that."

"OK. OK. It was just a thought." With firm hands, he guided her back into bed, arranging the pillows behind her into a more comfortable position.

She scowled at him, pushing her lips together into a tight line to stop them from quivering. Tears brimmed, blurring her vision. She blinked hard to push them back. She would not break down in front of Jason. She needed time to think, to decide what to do next. Once she had a plan of action figured out, she'd start to feel steadier.

"I have to go into town for a bit," Jason said, straightening to his full height. "But I'll be back later to pick you up."

She nodded, her arms crossed tightly around her torso as if to protect herself from any further emotional blows.

Jason hesitated at the foot of her bed. "You

want me to call your friend, Lance? Let him know about this."

"No." The thought of Lance smothering her with concern made her claustrophobic. "No sense in worrying him. I'm fine."

"All right. It's your call." He stopped at the door. "Try not to worry, Max. Everything will work out. You'll see."

At the Kingsville Fire Hall, Jason found Steve Hamilton in his office finishing a hamburger for his lunch. The smell of barbecue and bacon made Jason's mouth water. His stomach growled, reminding him he hadn't eaten all day.

"Jason. You're not on the roster today, are you?" Steve waved him inside and motioned to a spare chair.

Jason perched on the edge of the seat. "No. I was visiting Maxi in the hospital and decided to drop by and see if the investigator turned up anything."

Steve's weathered face seemed to close up. "You know I can't discuss the details of the case with you. Especially since you're a friend of the family."

Jason hadn't really expected anything else. "Worth a try."

Steve chuckled. "Guess I can't fault you there." He threw a wrapper in the wastebasket. "I can tell you the investigator might be by later today with his findings. But I won't be able to tell you anything more then, either."

"I understand. Sorry to bother you." Jason stood to go.

"Hang on a minute." Steve sobered. "Rumor has it you want to lobby to open a fire station in Rainbow Falls."

Jason went still. He'd only told a handful of people about his dream, and he wasn't sure he was ready for Steve to know about it just yet. "Where'd you hear that?"

"Some of the boys talking around the station. Is it true?"

"It's an idea I've been kicking around. Once I become certified."

Steve took a sip of his coffee. "What about funding?"

"I'm hoping there'll be support for my idea from the city council. Maybe if the town holds a fundraiser, it would feel more like a community project."

"I like it. Why don't you put the proposal in writing, and we'll see what kind of backing we can get?"

Jason's eyebrows shot up. "Seriously?" He hadn't dared hope the fire chief would support his idea.

"Why not? I've always felt we could use a

few more stations in the outlying towns. Might've been able to save that barn last night if we hadn't been twenty minutes away."

Jason nodded, thinking grimly of another fire eight years ago with a much different outcome. One that still haunted him and Maxi to this day.

8

Maxi closed the door behind her as she left her mother's hospital room. Mama's coloring seemed better today, but the mild sedatives meant she slept a lot. Maxi didn't have the heart to tell her about having to move in with the Hanleys. Time enough for her to find out later.

Jason was waiting in her room when she got back. "You ready to get out of here?"

"Yeah. I'm good to go. The release papers are at the front desk." She'd already changed out of the hospital gown into the sweats and T-shirt she'd been wearing to bed the night before. They reeked of smoke, but it was the only thing she had.

"You're wearing that?"

His disapproving tone inflamed her irritation. "Sorry if it offends you." The thought of all her expensive clothes going up in smoke made her cringe. "If it's OK, I want to stop at the farm before we go to your house. I have a few things in the dryer downstairs which should be salvageable. And I need my purse and cell phone."

His brows shot together. "I don't think that's a good idea. Why don't I drop you off first? Then I'll get your things."

He was probably trying to protect her, but she didn't want to be coddled. She needed to see for herself what shape the place was in. "I have to do this, Jason. Please."

A battle of emotions crossed his face before his shoulders slumped. "Fine. Let's go."

She stopped at the nurses' station to leave phone numbers where she could be reached in case her mother's condition changed. A nurse arrived with a wheelchair. "Here you go, miss. Your friend can take you out in this."

Maxi stared at the chair and then back at the woman. They had to be joking. "I don't need that. I'm perfectly capable of walking."

"Hospital policy, miss."

Jason stepped forward before she could say another word. "Just get in, Maxi. Do you have to argue about everything?"

"I was thinking the same thing about you a few seconds ago," she muttered, glaring at him.

"I can always carry you out like a sack of potatoes." He loomed over her, hands on his hips.

The nurse smothered a grin, which irritated Maxi even more. She frowned, remembering another argument years ago in Peg's shop when Jason did exactly that. To avoid a repeat of that particular humiliation, she plopped into the chair and let Jason wheel her out.

Halfway into Rainbow Falls, Maxi's disposition had not improved. What was the matter with her? She shouldn't be squabbling with Jason. She should be figuring on a way to straighten out this mess her life had become.

Tension cemented her shoulders as they neared the farm. It hit her then that her bad mood had more to do with the anxiety of seeing her home rather than anything Jason had said or done. Facing the results of the fire would surely trigger horrible memories that she'd repressed all these years. She straightened in her seat, straining to catch a glimpse of the house. Her heart wanted to jump out of her chest as she waited.

Jason reached over to take her left hand. "Brace yourself. It's pretty bad."

Worry didn't stop her from appreciating the warmth of his hand covering hers. She swallowed, promising herself she could handle it.

Jason slowed the truck as he turned onto the gravel side road and her home came into view.

Maxi gripped the door handle as though anchoring herself to something real. Each bump in the road seemed to hammer home the horror of the situation. The dreaded barn, a symbol of all she'd hated growing up, had been destroyed. Half of one charred wall stood out from the pile of ashes. Her father's thresher, or what was left of it, sat within the burnt area, a scarred skeleton of metal. Tightness seized her throat, making it hard for her already belabored lungs to take in air. She pulled her reluctant gaze over to the house and gasped at the gaping hole in the roof.

Right over her bedroom. A shudder slid down her spine.

When Jason let go of her hand to park the truck, Maxi pushed out the door before the engine even died. A compulsion to see the inside of the house forced her up the front steps. She took note of the boarded living room window before rushing inside where the overpowering stench of stale smoke hit her like a punch to the stomach. Despite her wheezing lungs, she half stumbled up the stairs to the second floor. Her eyes stung as the smell grew more acrid. The sound of Jason calling her barely registered. She plunged into her bedroom and skidded to a halt.

"No." Her hand flew to her mouth.

Half the ceiling had collapsed onto her bed. Charred black walls gave a tomb-like quality to the formerly cheerful space. The window had melted into a large hole in the wall. Her gaze fell to the water-stained carpet under her sneakers. Amid the soot and ash, one corner of a photo stuck out. With a muffled cry, she pulled it free. Despite the film of black soot, she recognized her precious graduation photo. That picture had traveled everywhere with her since high school. It was nothing short of a miracle to find it amid the debris. As coughs racked her body, she pushed the treasure into the pocket of her sweat pants.

With a hand over her nose and mouth, she backed out of the room, her chest heaving with the effort of breathing. She jerked as strong arms grabbed her from behind and half-carried her down the hall to the staircase.

"I told you not to go in there." Anger laced Jason's words.

He helped her down the stairs to the main

floor where she staggered and would have fallen if Jason hadn't been supporting her. She tried to take a deep breath, but the lingering smoke caused her to cough in rasping spasms. Jason pulled her into the kitchen, sat her in one of the chairs, and poured a glass of water. Gratefully she drained the cup. Too many emotions swirled inside for her to make sense of anything.

Jason stood by the counter, his stiff posture evidence of his annoyance with her. "Where's the stuff you wanted?"

"The basement. In the dryer."

"You stay here. I'll be back in a minute."

Maxi nodded and leaned her elbows on the table. A fine coating of black ash covered most surfaces. Once again the knowledge of how close she'd come to dying struck her. She clasped her trembling hands together in an effort to get control.

Jason returned carrying a laundry basket full of rumpled clothing. "I brought everything I could find. Let's go."

She stood on shaky legs. Her purse and cell phone sat on the end of the counter, and she grabbed them on her way out.

The fresh air brought welcome relief to her labored lungs. She breathed in, willing them to feel normal again.

Jason headed straight to the truck but

instead of following him, Maxi found herself drawn to the burned-out barn. She walked across the field, mesmerized by the site of destruction. Had someone really caused this or had it been an accident? She hugged her arms to her torso. Even though the day was mild, a chill crept over her.

As she turned, her gaze landed on the stump of the old elm tree. The only remaining evidence of the disaster that had occurred eight years ago. Maxi lurched forward and placed her hand on the trunk.

Drew, I miss you so much.

She fell to her knees, her forehead resting against the rough bark. Against her will, unbearable memories of that horrible night rose again to plague her. Memories of how she'd hurled up the driveway in her father's old truck, so furious at Jason, and at herself for stooping so low as to spy on him, that at first she hadn't noticed the red glow coming from Drew's tree house. When it finally penetrated, she'd hit the brakes and screeched to a halt, gravel spewing from the tires. She barely remembered leaving the truck, running to the base of the elm tree, and shrieking Drew's name. Though aware on some level the fire was too far gone, she whirled to get the hose from the barn. In a panic, she pulled and tugged as far as she could possibly stretch it, but it was no use.

A movement above her had riveted her attention upward in time to see the body of her brother, engulfed in flames, stagger to the edge of the tree house. The sheer horror of the vision paralyzed Maxi, rooting her feet to the ground like the tree before her. A primal scream escaped as Drew teetered on the edge for what seemed like minutes and then dropped. The hideous thud of his body hitting the ground had jolted her into action. She raced toward him, ripping off her denim jacket as she ran. As soon as she reached him, she beat the flames from his body, but to no avail.

Drew was already dead.

She wasn't sure how long she'd sat clutching his lifeless form to her chest, oblivious to the heat and smoke, and the lifelessness of her brother before Jason found her. He pried Drew away, and with infinite gentleness, covered his blistered face with a blanket. Her precious brother with the sandy blond hair and goofy grin was gone. Forever.

"Oh, God. I can't relive this again."

The sound of her own voice startled her, bringing her back to the present, to the feel of the cool grass beneath her face. She'd curled into a fetal position, rocking back and forth as she had on that horrifying night. Sobs tore through her, along with a tornado of emotions, the toxic mixture combining to choke the breath out of her.

Her body suddenly seemed weightless, floating off the ground. Had God come to exact his punishment at long last? Maybe retribution wouldn't be so bad after all, if it meant she'd be free of the torturing guilt.

"You're all right. I'm here with you."

Jason.

Soft fabric brushed Maxi's cheek. A steady heartbeat thumped under her ear. Warm breath moved in her hair. She clutched onto Jason as though he was the only thing keeping her from floating up to the heavens with Drew.

"It wasn't your fault. You hear me. It was an accident." Jason's fierce whisper penetrated her stupor as he released her to stand on her own two feet.

Still, she couldn't seem to stem the torrent of tears that besieged her. Eventually the cocooning warmth of Jason's body seeped into her, and the shaking subsided.

She lifted her head, the breeze chilling her wet face. "We both know it was my fault. I'd give anything to bring him back. To take his place."

"So would I." His voice was gruff with

emotion.

She clung to him, allowing his hands to soothe the tension from her back muscles. Jason was the one person who understood what that night had done to her, the havoc it had wreaked on her relationship with her family and on the rest of her life. Through it all, Jason had never condemned her for her foolhardy actions — never once told her how stupid she'd been. He'd remained her staunchest defender.

He pulled her closer as if their bones could melt together, offering her his solace and strength. On an inhale, she became acutely conscious of that strength, the band of steel his muscled arms formed around her. His lips in her hair, whispering words of comfort.

In that moment of awareness, something changed between them. Jason's lips moved to her cheek, then slowly downward, inch by silky inch, until they neared her mouth.

Her breath tangled in her lungs. He hesitated for a fraction of a second before he touched his lips gently to hers, as if experimenting to see how she'd react. Her body began to hum, like a thread of electricity moved through her. She strained to press her mouth more firmly to his.

Somewhere through the haze of grief, passion sparked. Reaching up, she entwined her arms around his neck, plunging her fingers into the thick mass of his hair. She kissed him back with a fervor long held in check — years of repressed longing bubbling forth. His hands moved up her back. She thought she heard him groan, and then, as quickly as it had started, he pulled his mouth away.

She stared at him, dazed. His eyes appeared black, the pupils almost fully dilated.

He shook his head. "I'm sorry. I shouldn't have done that."

"I'm glad you did," she whispered. She wanted to tell him how long she'd dreamed of his kiss, imagined the feel of his arms around her. The words hovered on her lips, but she hesitated.

His eyes burned with untold emotion. He raised one finger and brushed the remaining moisture from her cheek. "Come on. Let's get out of here."

When he pulled his body away from hers, the cool air whooshed in to form a barrier between them. She trembled for a moment, wishing they could stay locked together forever.

What a crazy, impossible thought.

When she didn't move, he took her by the hand and led her back to the truck.

With the warmth of Jason's kiss still on her lips, Maxi knew with absolute certainty her world would never be the same again.

9

Shep danced circles around her as soon as Maxi stepped into the Hanleys' living room. His tail waved madly back and forth as he jumped, trying to lick her face. Instead, she bent to hug his neck.

"Hey, buddy. I'm glad you're OK."

Silly tears formed once again, and she pushed them back. What was wrong with her? She hardly ever cried.

Peg came out from the kitchen to wrap her in a tight hug. "I'm so sorry about your house, honey."

In the comfort of Peg's ample arms, Maxi breathed a great sigh. Here with this woman's unconditional love and support, Maxi could believe everything would be OK.

Peg pulled back to smooth a hand over her cheek. "I thank God you weren't hurt. You must have some amazing guardian angels watching out for you, girl."

Maxi frowned. She didn't see it that way

at all. Instead, it seemed like she was cursed.

"How else do you think my boy arrived right in the nick of time to save you?" Peg raised one ginger eyebrow above her bifocals. "You believe what you want. I know the angels were looking out for you."

Peg put her arm around Maxi's shoulders and steered her into the kitchen where a big pot of some great smelling food simmered. Maxi hadn't really eaten since the previous day. She was ravenous.

"Sit down. I'll get you some stew. Jason can join us when he gets back."

Peg had sent him to get milk and bread at the corner store. Maxi was glad for a few moments without him to allow her system to settle. Jason obviously regretted their kiss. He hadn't been able to look her in the eye since. She gave an inward sigh. It would be better if they both forgot it had ever happened. Especially since they'd be living under the same roof for an indefinite period of time. The last thing she needed in her life was another complication.

Peg set a plate of steaming beef stew and a basket of hot biscuits in front of her, and Maxi gave herself over to the pleasure of a home-cooked meal. Peg poured her a large glass of juice and then sat down across the small table with her own plate.

"Thank you so much for taking us in," Maxi said between bites.

"Pishposh. I wouldn't have it any other way. Bernice can have the spare room, and I've fixed Jason's up for you."

Maxi swallowed a groan. Sleep in Jason's bed? What had she done to deserve this kind of torture? "I don't want to put Jason out. I can sleep on the couch."

Peg paused, her fork in mid-air. "Jason wouldn't hear of it. He's very much a gentleman, if I do say so myself." She grinned the smile of a proud mother. "Besides, we have a perfectly good spare bed in the basement. He's already moved his things down there."

Sometimes Maxi envied Peg and Jason their close relationship. Since Jason's father left, it had been the two of them against the world. Jason was devoted to his mother, enduring endless ridicule from his friends for still living at home. Only Maxi knew he couldn't bear to think of his mother all alone — that the scars of his father's abandonment ran far deeper than he would ever admit.

Jason returned just as Maxi finished her cherry pie and tea. His presence in the small kitchen seemed to suck the very air out of the room. A hum of tension returned to her veins as she struggled to let on that everything was normal.

Peg stood at the sink washing the dishes. Jason grabbed a plate from the cupboard and ladled the stew out for himself. He sat down, still not looking at her, and attacked his plate. She grappled for something ordinary to say, but there was nothing ordinary about this situation.

She finished her drink and rose to take her cup to the sink. "That was wonderful, Peg. Best food I've had since . . ."

"Since New York?"

"Since my mom's cooking. She hasn't felt up to it . . . lately." Maxi picked up a towel to dry the dishes.

"Give her some time. She'll come around." Peg nodded toward the living room. "You go and relax. You're still recovering from your ordeal."

Maxi shook her head. "If I'm going to impose on you, I'm at least going to do my share of the work."

A chair scraped the floor. Jason thrust his plate, already empty, into the sink and took the towel from her hands. "Go and sit down."

Strained emotions vibrated between them, and for once she obeyed without arguing.

"I'll go call the hospital and check on

Mama."

Back in the living room, Maxi retrieved her purse and took out her phone. She spoke briefly with her mother, reassured that she seemed to be faring well. She was about to put the phone away when it rang in her hands.

Lily's concerned voice came through. "Hey, I just heard about the fire. Are you all right?"

"I'm fine.

"Where are you now?"

"At Peg's. She's offered to put Mama and me up until the house is fixed."

There was a chuckle on the other end. "This is an interesting twist."

"Let it go, Lily," she hissed in a low voice. "It's very temporary." She pushed all thoughts of the kiss out of her mind just in case Lily had some latent psychic ability.

Lily only laughed louder. "I can't wait to see how this pans out." She turned serious again. "You sure you're OK? I can come over if you want."

"No. I'll see you soon."

"OK. Call if you need anything."

"I will."

Maxi clicked her phone off. Sudden exhaustion hit her like a two-ton truck. The onslaught of emotion earlier in the day must've taken a lot more out of her than she realized. She looked at her watch to see if it was too early to retire for the night. She didn't want Peg and Jason to think she was avoiding them.

"You look beat." She jumped at Jason's voice behind the sofa. "If you want to turn in, go ahead."

He sat down, not beside her on the couch, but across the room in an armchair.

Her shoulders sagged. She didn't have the energy for this tonight. "I think I will. Thanks — for everything."

His eyes met hers for the first time since he'd kissed her. He nodded once, picked up the remote for the television, and clicked on the screen.

Jason left the house before 7:00 AM the next day. He wanted to go by the North house before he headed over to work at the Logans'. He was leaving early to avoid seeing Maxi, but he didn't care. He needed the space to get over what had happened between them.

The mess he'd created, more like.

What on earth had possessed him to kiss her? He'd gone and done what he always swore he'd never do — he'd crossed the fragile line of friendship by violating the unwritten code. You didn't kiss your female friends. His one moment of insanity could have cost him everything. Cost him Maxi's friendship — a friendship they'd just started working their way back to.

He smacked his hand on the steering wheel. A spurt of pain shot up his arm. A romantic relationship with Maxi was not an option. He'd vowed long ago that he would never marry or have children. He wouldn't risk turning out like his father, causing some other poor woman and child the type of anguish he and his mother had endured. That's why he kept his romantic dalliances to short intervals with women who were not interested in a serious relationship.

The one exception had been Susie Marshall, but once she started hinting at an engagement ring, he'd broken all ties with her. He'd made a big mistake with Susie, allowing his emotions to override his resolve. In the process, he'd hurt a girl he cared a great deal about.

No wonder he'd turned to Gloria Johnson — a girl no one ever got serious about. But after his disastrous interlude with Gloria, when his life and his morals had seemed to be careening out of control, Jason had sought counseling from Nick Logan. With Nick's help, Jason had come to a new level of commitment in his faith and had taken a personal oath not to ever play with the affections of a woman again.

Jason scrubbed a hand over the stubble on his chin. He doubted he'd ever change his mind about marriage and children, yet deep down where it mattered, he feared Maxi could be the one woman to make him disregard his resolution, and he wasn't about to let that happen. Maxi deserved a husband and children, something he wasn't prepared to offer, even if it meant living his life alone.

No. Getting romantically involved with Maxi was a terrible idea on many levels.

After taking a few measurements upstairs at the North house, Jason headed over to Nick and Lily's. They were usually up by seven, so he wasn't worried about arriving too early.

Nick smiled as he let him in. "Here's our hero." He clapped Jason on the back.

Jason scowled. "I'm no hero. I did what anyone else would do in the situation."

Nick only grinned. "OK, Mr. Modesty. There's coffee in the kitchen if you're interested."

Lily, clad in a bulky bathrobe, turned toward him as he entered. She walked straight over, wrapped her arms around him, and squeezed. Stunned, Jason stood as rigid as a statue.

"Thank you for saving my best friend's life."

Sheesh, if he'd known people would make this kind of fuss, he'd have disappeared before the paramedics arrived. "You're welcome. Can I get a cup of coffee now?"

She unwound herself and wiped her eyes. "Sorry. Pregnancy's making me weepy."

She went to the cupboard and got him a mug, which he took to the coffeemaker.

"Are you going to be home today?" he asked. "Because the work I'm doing will be noisy."

Lily lowered herself gingerly to a chair that sat at an awkward distance from the table to allow for her belly. "Nick won't let me help at the shelter. Maybe I'll go visit Maxi, make sure she's all right."

"I think she'd like that. It'd take her mind off things."

Like me kissing her socks off.

"How long do you think the repairs at her place will take?"

He took a swig of coffee before answering, knowing whatever he said would be repeated verbatim to Maxi. "Probably a few weeks."

Lily sighed. "This is going to mess up

Maxi's plans for the partnership." She looked at him. "If you need to take time off here to concentrate on the farmhouse, I'm sure Nick won't mind. Anything to help Maxi get back to New York as soon as she can."

Nick came in, fighting with the top button of his shirt under his clerical collar, saving Jason from having to respond. He didn't want to think about Maxi leaving yet.

Nick walked up behind Lily and put his hands on her shoulders. "You sure you're feeling OK?"

She smiled at him. "I'm fine. Just huge."

He frowned as if he didn't believe her. "I can cancel this conference today and stay home."

"I've got three more weeks to go. You can't stay home every day 'til then." Lily reached over to pat his hand. "I'll be fine."

Nick looked at Jason. "I've got to go into Bismarck today. You'll be around, won't you?"

"Most of the day. Don't worry. We'll make sure she's covered." Jason smirked at Lily's glare and drained his cup.

"I don't need a babysitter," she announced to the room in general.

Nick bent to kiss her. "I know you don't, but can you humor a nervous father-to-be?"

Her face softened and the mutinous glare disappeared. "I guess so."

"If you need me, I'll have my cell on."

Jason discreetly left the room so the two could say a more private good-bye.

Maxi waited in Peg's salon for Lily to arrive. It felt like old times, setting up her former workstation in preparation for her next client. She remembered one of the first days Lily had worked there as a receptionist. Maxi had persuaded Lily to let her work on her gorgeous long tresses. Today, she hoped to try something a bit edgier on Lily. She was so beautiful, anything would look good on her, and Maxi would have another masterpiece for her portfolio.

It felt good to be doing something constructive instead of dwelling on her problems. Later, she would head into Kingsville to visit her mom in the hospital, maybe take her some of her favorite chocolates.

The door jangled announcing Lily's arrival. Maxi walked over to greet her and startled when Lily grabbed her for a hard hug.

"I can't believe I could've lost my best friend." Her large brown eyes brimmed with tears.

Maxi waved off Lily's display of emotion.

"It'll take more than a little smoke to kill me off. I may be small, but I'm tough."

Lily laughed through her tears. "You don't need to remind me." She looked around the shop. "Where's Peg?"

"She had a break for an hour, so she went home. We have the place to ourselves for now."

"Just like old times." Lily smiled as Maxi led her to the chair. "Remember the first time you did my hair?"

Maxi laughed. "I was thinking about that before you got here. This time I'm much more experienced. I'm going to do a modern city do on you."

"As long as there's no cutting involved."

"I promise." Maxi began to brush out Lily's long, dark locks. She had the type of hair most women would kill for. Thick and wavy with natural highlights.

"I see you haven't got your spikes today," Lily said as Maxi worked.

Instead of her usual porcupine style, Maxi'd worn it tucked behind her ears. The bangs remained a little spiky, just for effect. Of course, the standard large hoop earrings were still the highlight of her look. "I thought I'd try something different for a change. Besides, I couldn't find any hair gel at the Hanleys' this morning."

Lily laughed as Maxi twisted long strips of her hair into interesting loops on top of her head. "I'm glad you called. Jason's working at the house, making a lot of noise. I needed an escape."

"Glad I could help." Maxi didn't want to think about Jason at the moment.

She worked with feverish intensity until she captured the look she wanted. Then with Lily's permission, she added an interesting flare of makeup and got out her digital camera for the photos.

"Make sure you don't get my belly in there," Lily demanded as she posed.

Maxi laughed. "We could start a whole new line of *haute couture* for pregnant women."

They were still laughing when the bell jangled at the front of the store.

"I'll see who it is. You take a break," Maxi ordered.

She headed toward the front of the shop, camera in hand, only to stop cold when she saw who had entered. Gloria Johnson, of all people, stood at the reception desk, her bleached blonde hair pulled into a high ponytail. She wore a low-cut, black top. The hem of the shirt didn't quite meet her belly button or the top of her low-rise jeans. A dragonfly tattoo peeked out from beneath her right sleeve. A strong tide of long-dormant dislike rose in waves through Maxi's frame. As far as she could tell, nothing much had changed about Gloria. Maxi tried to keep a neutral expression on her face as she approached her.

"Can I help you?"

Through her obviously fake lashes, Gloria looked Maxi up and down. "I didn't know you were still in town. Slumming, are we?"

Maxi struggled to put a leash on her temper. "Hello, Gloria. Do you have an appointment?"

"No, but I'd like a manicure. And there doesn't seem to be a line."

"Sorry, it's the manicurist's day off." Out of old habit, Maxi bent to flick the pages of the appointment book. "I can book you in for Tuesday if you like."

Gloria looked down her nose at Maxi. "Can't *you* do it? You don't look busy."

Maxi raised her head from the book and stiffened her shoulders. "I don't work here. I'm just keeping an eye on things for Peg 'til she gets back."

Gloria threw a look over at Lily, who was likely watching the exchange from the back. "Still trying to impress Jason and his mother, I see. Don't waste your energy. Take it from someone who knows. He's not worth it."

Maxi's hands curled into tight fists. How dare she talk about Jason that way? A string of oaths escaped before she could check herself.

"I can see New York's sophistication hasn't rubbed off on you." Gloria sneered. "Don't bother with an appointment. I'll come back another time — when the stench clears."

She turned and stalked out the front door, letting it slam behind her. With great deliberation, Maxi unclenched her hands and took a deep breath. She'd like nothing better than to smack the smug smile off Gloria's overly made-up face.

"Is it me, or do you two have a history of some sort?"

Lily's voice behind her made Maxi start. She blew out the breath she'd been holding. "Sorry about that. I shouldn't have let her get to me." She paused. "I keep forgetting you've only lived here a few years. You missed the great high school escapades."

"You want to talk about it? I don't have any ice cream, but I think there's soda in the lunch room."

Maxi grinned, remembering the time she'd been upset about Jason and Susie

Marshall, and Lily had cheered her up with chocolate sundaes. "Soda will do fine. Thanks."

"So what's with this Gloria person?" Lily asked a few minutes later as she handed Maxi a cola from the fridge in the break room.

Maxi popped the top of her can and joined Lily at the scarred metal lunch table. "We went to school together, but never got along. She was in the popular crowd. You know, a new boyfriend every few weeks, until she ran out of eligible males. I don't know what the guys saw in her."

"Blonde, built, and available. Say no more." Lily sipped her orange soda. "I take it Jason was one of her conquests."

Maxi frowned. "Not back then. But apparently he broke up with her a few months ago." She was amazed how much the thought of Jason and Gloria together made her see red. "I can't believe he'd go out with her after all the mean things she did to me in high school."

"Like what?"

Maxi flinched. The pain of Gloria's last stunt still stung, and she didn't relish reliving it. "Let's just say I was the butt of her very public jokes."

"Why does she hate you so much?"

Trust Lily to get right to the nitty-gritty. Maxi sighed. "For one thing, I caught her cheating on an exam and snitched on her. And two, she wanted Jason. In the worst way." Maxi took a long gulp of soda and fought the tension curling up her spine. "At the time, he wasn't interested. Jason and I were best friends, but everyone assumed there was more to it. Gloria was flat out jealous."

Lily shook her head. "Wow. I thought high school in a small town would be simpler. But it sounds worse than mine." She drained her can. "So why'd he go out with her now?"

"I don't know. Maybe a rebound thing after he and Susie broke up."

Lily rose and rubbed her belly. "Could be. Susie was really torn up when Jason ended their relationship."

Maxi snapped to full attention. "Jason ended it?" Maxi had assumed Susie had broken his heart.

"Yup. Things were getting serious between them. Susie wanted to get married, but as soon as she raised the subject, Jason bolted. Word around town says he has an aversion to commitment."

Of course. It all made sense now. A girl like Susie would expect marriage after dating for two years.

Lily winced and seemed to go pale, but she recovered quickly.

Maxi was sure the baby had just kicked her too hard. She threw her empty can in the trash and followed Lily into the shop. "They're right. Jason is leery of marriage. It has something to do with his father leaving when he was young." She shook her head. "Funny, I thought Susie would be the one to change that."

Gloria slammed the door to her BMW and jammed her keys into the ignition. That trash Maxi North was back in town and had somehow wormed her way into Jason's life again. Just when she was about to make her move to get him back. She didn't need Maxi distracting Jason when *she* was trying to get his attention.

The engine purred as Gloria pulled away from the curb.

She'd had to contend with Jason and Maxi's friendship all through high school. When Maxi had finally left town for good, no one had been happier than Gloria. Happier still to hear they'd had some big falling out before she left.

Then Gloria had to bide her time until Jason's relationship with Susie Marshall ran its course. It hadn't been too hard to get Susie to push Jason for marriage. A few strategic suggestions and Susie had bridal gowns blinking in her brain. Gloria knew Jason would head for the hills at the mere mention of the idea. Her plan had worked to perfection. He'd dropped Susie like a grenade about to detonate, and once they'd broken up, Gloria had taken full advantage of a very lonely Jason.

True, she hadn't been able to keep his interest for long, but their brief time together had only increased her feelings for him. As well as her determination to win him back.

Gloria gripped the steering wheel with iron fingers. There was no way she'd let Maxi North's unexpected arrival ruin her plans.

She would keep Maxi away from Jason — no matter what it took — because one way or another, Gloria *would* become Mrs. Jason Hanley.

10

Maxi hummed to herself as she made her way to the nurses' station near her mother's room. On her way to the hospital, she'd stopped in the Kingsville camera shop to get the pictures of Lily's hairdo printed. Maxi's pulse had quickened as she studied the results. They'd turned out even better than she dared hope. With Lily's exotic looks, the photos would make a wonderful addition to her portfolio.

Residual excitement lingered as she waited for the nurse to update her on her mother's condition. Finally a woman came to tell her that Mama had improved greatly in the last twenty-four hours, and she'd be able to go home in the next day or two.

Sure enough, when Maxi poked her head in the room, her mother's color looked much better. Maxi bent to kiss her cheek. "Hi, Mama. How are you feeling today?"

Her mother struggled to sit upright in the

bed. "Much better. How are you, dear?"

"Good, thanks." Maxi rearranged the pillows behind her mother's back and then pulled up a chair beside the bed. "There's something I need to tell you, though." She couldn't put it off any longer.

A frown creased Mama's forehead. "What is it?"

"We're going to have to stay with the Hanleys for a while until repairs are done to the roof and the soot is cleaned out."

Tears edged her mother's eyes. "So we didn't lose the house?"

"No. The damage is repairable. Jason is helping with that."

"What about the insurance? Won't they handle it?"

Maxi hated the lines of worry on her mother's face.

"Eventually, but you know how much red tape is involved. Jason's going to start on things, and when we get the money from the insurance, we'll reimburse him." No use worrying now whether the insurance would pay. Truth was on her side. Neither she nor her mother had started that fire, and if arson was involved, they could prove their innocence.

Her mother smiled. "Sounds like you've got it all worked out. I should have known better than to worry. God will take care of us. He always does."

Maxi bit back the sarcastic remark that burned on her tongue. She wouldn't ruin her mother's optimism with her own negative thoughts. Nothing Maxi said would change Mama's unwavering view of the Almighty. Maxi sighed, wishing she could regain the simple faith of her youth. It would be nice to lean on God for help with life's problems. Truth was, ever since Drew's senseless death, Maxi didn't feel entitled to call on God for anything.

She spent another twenty minutes with her mother until Mama's lids began to droop. She left her mother to rest, with the promise to pick her up as soon as the doctor released her.

Maxi had just turned onto the road to Rainbow Falls when her cell went off. She glanced at the display. Jason. This was the first time he'd initiated contact with her since the kiss. Looking in the rearview mirror, she slowed her speed and pulled off to the side of the road before answering the call.

"Maxi. Thank the Lord. Can you come over to Lily's right away?" Panic infused his voice.

Her hands stiffened on the wheel. "What's

wrong?" It wasn't like Jason to show fear. He was a fireman, trained to handle emergency situations.

"Lily's not feeling well. I think she might be in labor."

"Labor?" Was that why Lily seemed so pale when she left the shop earlier? "Did you call Doc Anderson?"

"Yeah. But I can't reach him. I called for an ambulance, and they're tied up with a multi-car accident. They'll be here as soon as they can. And Nick's in Bismarck today. He's not answering his cell. I suggested the hospital, but Lily won't hear of it. Not without Nick."

"Is she having regular pains?"

"I don't know. She's moaning a lot."

Maxi let out a relieved sigh. Jason was likely panicking for nothing. If he couldn't tell whether or not Lily was having contractions, it couldn't be too serious. Maxi pictured him pacing as he talked and had to grin at the thought of Jason alone with a pregnant woman who might be in labor.

"Calm down, Hanley. Everything will be fine. I'll be there in a few minutes."

Maxi wasn't laughing half an hour later when she saw her friend's pain firsthand.

No wonder Jason had sounded so panicked on the phone. Up in the master bedroom, Lily writhed on her bed, emitting gut-wrenching moans with each contraction. Maxi wiped Lily's sweat-soaked face with a cold cloth and then laid it on her forehead.

Lily reached over and clutched Maxi's arm, fear evident in her dark eyes. "This is happening too fast, too soon. I'm scared. I should have let Jason call for an ambulance sooner."

Maxi's pulse sprinted to a dizzying rate. Her friend needed someone — a doctor, a mid-wife — anyone who knew something about delivering a baby. But Doc Anderson still wasn't answering his phone. Probably off on an emergency call. "If Jason and I help you downstairs, we can get you into the car and drive you to the hospital."

"I don't know if I can . . ." Lily's fingers clamped like a vice around Maxi's wrist.

Maxi tried to ignore her friend's panic and stay rational. Provide calm assurance.

"Sure you can. First we'll get you sitting up." Puffing and straining, Maxi struggled to lift Lily's upper torso and push some pillows behind her. When another contraction hit, a scream exploded from Lily's chest, resonating through Maxi's frame. The blood drained from Lily's face, and for a second,

Maxi thought she might pass out. Maxi murmured soothing platitudes while Lily endured the pain. When the death grip on her hand eased up, Maxi knew the contraction had ended.

"Thirsty," Lily croaked from between lips that were beginning to crack at the corners.

Maxi rearranged the sheet over Lily's extended belly and patted her hand. "I'll go get some ice chips. Be right back."

Guilt washed over her at the relief she felt to be out of the room. Like a prisoner executing a jailbreak, Maxi made her way down the stairs and into the kitchen.

Jason was pacing the length of the room when she entered. Lines of worry wrinkled his brow. "How is she?"

Maxi swallowed hard, trying to quell her own anxiety and not make matters worse. "I'm pretty sure she's in advanced labor."

Her hand shook as she opened the freezer and took out the ice trays. How could this have come on so fast? Lily had been fine earlier. Or had she? She had seemed spent when she left Peg's. Had Maxi's photo session contributed to the early onset of labor? Maxi attacked the cubes with the kitchen mallet. Each crash of the hammer jarred her arm up to her elbow. "Did you reach the doc yet?"

He shook his head. "No. I left another message. You'd think he'd have some way of getting hold of him. Ambulances tied up, and the only doctor in town out of contact with a pregnant woman in labor."

His exasperation would've been comical if Maxi didn't want to scream. She had no idea what to do for a woman in labor. "What about Nick?"

"Can't reach him either. The last thing he said was that he'd have his cell on. I don't understand it."

Maxi tried to think clearly, to focus on a logical solution. "Lily's in too much pain to move her now. She couldn't even sit up for a minute." She dumped the ice chips in a bowl. "You said you called the Kingsville Hospital, and they're going to send an ambulance as soon as it's free?"

"Yeah, they're all tied up with some car accident." Jason scrubbed a hand over this face as he walked. "I put in a call to the guys at the fire station. They're in the same boat as the ambulance drivers."

"We need help. Who else in town has experience delivering a baby? Is there a midwife or anything?"

Jason's eyes slid away from hers. He jammed his hands deep into the pockets of his ripped work jeans. "Well . . ."

"What is it?" She fought the urge to shake the words out of him.

"I've had some training with the birth process — as a fireman, I mean. We worked with dummies and watched videos, so nothing firsthand."

She could see the fear in his eyes. A bubble of hysterical laughter rose in her throat. He could dash into a burning building without blinking, but assisting a birth scared him to death. She took a breath to control herself. His training was all they had to go on. "What do we do? Boil water? Rip sheets?"

He smiled at that. "No. We'll need lots of towels. Some sterilized scissors and a clamp. And something clean to wrap the baby in."

A wave of dizziness struck as the stark reality of the situation became evident. Could the two of them actually bring a baby into this world?

She and Jason? Alone?

For the first time in years, Maxi began to pray.

11

Darkness was falling when Jason finally heard from dispatch. The ambulance was now en route. Estimated time of arrival half an hour. Jason pressed his lips together as he pocketed his phone. They didn't have half an hour.

"Jason." Maxi's frantic voice reached him in the hallway where he'd taken the call in order to hear better. Lily's screams during the contractions told him the pain had become almost intolerable.

He rushed into the room, where Maxi sat by Lily's side, one hand holding hers, the other wiping her perspiring brow.

"I think she's getting weak."

The fear in Maxi's eyes steadied him. These women needed him to be calm, to guide them through this. He took a deep breath and squared his shoulders. "Everything's going to be fine," he said in his most soothing voice. "It shouldn't be much longer now."

He took his place at the foot of the bed where Lily lay draped in a sheet. He approached the situation as he would a victim in a fire.

Be impersonal and professional, kind but firm.

He could do this. He *had* to do this.

Jason lifted the sheet to check on her progress. Adrenaline kicked in at the sight of the top of the baby's head. Suddenly this emergency became very real. "I can see the head. Lily, you need to push down on the next contraction."

He looked up to make sure both women had heard him. Lily's hair lay plastered against her head, soaked with sweat. But she nodded her understanding. Jason's heart thumped loudly in his chest as he recalled the next steps in the training manual.

"Maxi, when the contraction starts, help her lean forward and support her from behind. She'll have to push for as much of the contraction as she can. And rest in between."

"Easy for you to say." Maxi scowled and took her place.

In the distance, a phone rang, but no one was in a position to answer it. The next contraction had begun. As instructed, Maxi helped Lily move forward, urging her to push. Lily grunted with exertion, her face crimson. The minute and a half contraction seemed to last forever.

"OK, let her rest," Jason told Maxi when it subsided.

Lily fell back, panting, while Maxi wiped her face with the damp cloth. A cold bead of perspiration slid between Jason's shoulder blades as he waited.

Two more contractions followed. He couldn't tell if they were getting anywhere. The baby hadn't budged. Jason's tightly held control began to slip as doubts crept in. Was he doing the right thing? What if the baby got stuck? They had no way to monitor the baby's heart rate. No way to tell if it was in danger.

He shook his head as if to shake loose the negative thoughts. He had to be strong for these women. They were depending on him to get them through this crisis. He bowed his head and prayed for strength and guidance. If anything happened to Lily or the child, he could never live with himself.

Lord, bless Lily and her baby. Cover them with your grace and protection. Guide me with the right steps to deliver this child safely.

He opened his eyes when Lily groaned,

signaling the next contraction.

"Come on, Lily. You can do this. Help her, Maxi."

With Maxi's support, Lily pushed until she was worn out and then fell back on the pillows almost unconscious. What would they do if she actually passed out? Jason stood to pace the room until the next contraction. He looked at his watch. Nick should be home soon. What kind of scene would he arrive to? Miracle or disaster?

He felt Maxi's hand on his arm. "Why don't we switch this time? You can help Lily better up there."

Maxi's face was so pale her freckles stood out in stark contrast. Her eyes met his, and he nodded. "Say a prayer, Max," he whispered. "This isn't looking good."

"I've been praying all along."

Lily's scream mobilized them both into action. Jason took Maxi's place beside Lily. He used his strength to raise her ravaged body. "Come on, Lily. Your baby needs you to push. You can do this."

With tears and sweat running down her face, Lily pushed until Jason heard Maxi's cry. "The baby's coming. One more time should do it."

Thank You, God.

Again, instructions swirled in his head.

135

"Once the head's out, we have to stop and clear its mouth. Make sure the cord's not wrapped around the neck. Then wait for the next contraction before any more pushing."

"Got it." Maxi swiped an arm across her forehead.

Five minutes later, the lusty cry of Lily's baby filled the room. The sound was sweeter than anything Jason had ever heard. His breath whooshed out of his lungs as his spine turned to gelatin. Maxi held up the squalling red bundle, tears streaming down her face.

"It's a girl, Lily. You have a beautiful baby girl."

A hundred pound weight lifted from Jason's shoulders. Tears stung his eyes as he looked at the miracle of life in Maxi's arms.

Thank You, Lord, for Your help. We couldn't have done it without You.

Lily lay back limply while Jason went to cut the cord and clamp it off. With a clean towel he wiped the infant's face. Maxi wrapped her in a fresh sheet, and then, as if holding a priceless work of art, carried her over to Lily. She laid the baby in her mother's arms, and the howling stopped immediately.

"See, she knows her mama," Maxi whispered.

Despite her ordeal, Lily beamed at the bundle while tears dripped down her cheeks. "Hello, beautiful girl."

Jason watched them for a minute, amazed at the transformation in Lily. How could she seem on her deathbed one minute, and Madonna-like the next? All part of the miracle of childbirth he supposed. He walked over to kiss Lily's cheek and then stepped outside to give the women some time alone. He'd leave the rest of the details to the paramedics.

Relief spread through his body replacing the adrenaline, and sudden exhaustion set in. He blew out a long breath as he descended the stairs on stiff legs.

They'd done it. The baby and Lily were alive.

He offered another prayer of thanks. Then he headed outside to wait for the ambulance.

Maxi's high-strung nerves gave way to immense relief when the paramedics arrived mere minutes after Annabelle Maxine Logan made her grand entrance into the world.

Nick showed up five minutes later. He'd been frantic when he arrived. He'd lost his cell phone at the conference, had a flat tire on the highway, and when he tried to call from a payphone, no one had answered. Then, greeted by the sight of an ambulance pulling into his driveway, sheer panic had set in.

Maxi had done her best to reassure him, but her words fell on deaf ears. He'd rushed right past her into the room where the paramedics had started to examine Lily.

The tears streaming down Nick's face as he looked at his daughter for the first time brought a lump to Maxi's throat. With a quiet click, she closed the door to give the family some privacy and let the paramedics handle the aftermath.

She leaned against a wall in the hallway and took in a few deep breaths to steady herself. The band of tension across her shoulders released and sagged like over-stretched elastic. Her head floated somewhere up near the ceiling as if detached from her body. Helping that tiny body emerge from its safe cocoon, hearing the first breath enter her lungs, followed by a loud wail — the whole thing had seemed like a miracle.

Maxi pushed away from the wall and headed down the stairs to the main level, wondering where Jason had gone. She and Lily owed him a huge debt of gratitude. Without his presence, things may not have turned out so well for the Logans. Maxi would definitely want him around whenever she gave birth.

The thought gave her a jolt so hard that she stopped dead at the end of the stairs and gripped the ornate newel post. She'd never given much consideration to having children. She assumed that once she found the right man, the decision would become self-evident.

But now Maxi's throat felt like sandpaper as a sudden realization broke through her consciousness like rays of sun breaking through the clouds. Sharing this ordeal together, right on the heels of almost dying in the fire, had brought things into sharp focus for her. She knew with absolute certainty that her long-standing crush on Jason had morphed into something a lot more serious.

Something that bordered on real love.

She pushed the idea away as soon as it formed. She could not deal with her feelings for Jason now. First things first. She needed a cold drink, and she needed to find Jason.

Armed with a glass of iced tea, she found him a few minutes later on the front porch, sitting alone on the top stair, staring out at the night. For a moment, she hesitated, wondering if she should leave him be. But instinct told her to go to him, that he felt as overwhelmed as she did by the birth.

Quietly, she pushed through the screen door and onto the porch. Without a word, she sat down on the step beside him, their shoulders almost touching. He didn't move or acknowledge her in any way. In the dim light of the moon, she saw traces of moisture on his cheeks.

Her heart squeezed with some untold emotion. She wanted to reach out and hug him, yet something held her back. "You were amazing in there, Jace. I couldn't have handled it without you."

He scrubbed a hand over his face. "Ditto."

She stretched out a hand, longing to touch him, to feel the strength of a physical connection. At the last second, she pulled it back. "You're going to make a terrific fireman. If you ever need any testimonials, I'd be happy to give one." She wanted to tease him out of this grave mood, lighten him up. After all, they should be celebrating. They'd just been part of a miracle, bringing a new life into the world.

"You know, I've seen a lot of things," he said at last, his voice quiet. "Been involved in a few serious fires. Seen some horrific accidents. But that was the scariest thing I've ever been through. How do women do that?"

Maxi shook her head. "I don't know. I only hope I'll be as brave as Lily one day when it's my turn."

Jason rocketed up from the stairs as if someone had poked him with a giant needle. He leapt onto the grass below and ran his fingers through his already messy hair. When he looked over at her, raw fear shone in his eyes. Her mouth gaped open. What had spooked him so badly?

"If everyone's OK in there, I have to get going." He slapped his pants pocket and then pulled out his keys.

She set her glass on the step and rose. "Are you sure you're OK to drive, because I can give you a ride —"

"No, thanks. I'm fine." He was already halfway across the lawn. "Tell Lily and Nick I'll see them tomorrow."

With a heavy heart, Maxi watched him leave, his truck pealing out of the driveway, realization dawning as to the source of his panic. The mere mention of her becoming a mother one day had been enough to send Jason packing. Had he maybe pictured the same thing she had? The two of them sharing the birth of their own child one day? It would explain how freaked out he might be

— knowing how he felt about becoming a parent.

She sank onto the top step of the porch and blew her damp bangs off her forehead. She swallowed to contain the threat of tears that seemed so near the surface tonight.

Thank goodness she hadn't, in a rare moment of camaraderie, blurted out anything about her feelings. They would have to stay locked away for good. If she hadn't believed it before, Jason's reaction tonight had made his position crystal clear. He would never be ready for marriage or a family.

She straightened her spine against the porch post. This was exactly what she needed. One more reminder that her future awaited her in New York — far away from Rainbow Falls, white picket fences, and Jason Hanley.

12

A nagging feeling of worry shadowed Maxi the next day, dampening her usual good spirits. When she arrived at the Kingsville Hospital to pick up her mother and visit Lily and Annabelle, who'd been taken in by ambulance the night before, she was determined to keep an upbeat attitude.

Maxi hadn't seen Jason since he left Nick and Lily's in such a rush. When she got home, his truck hadn't been in the driveway, and though she'd barely slept all night, she never heard him come in. There had been no sign of him this morning. She left a couple of messages on his cell phone, but he hadn't returned her call. She left word with Peg to call her as soon as she heard from him.

Lily, Nick, and the baby were all huddled in the one tiny hospital bed when she arrived. Maxi hesitated in the doorway, feeling like an intruder, until their faces brightened when they saw her.

"Come on in, Aunt Maxi," Lily said, beaming. "We were hoping you'd come by."

Maxi brought in the gift bag and balloons and set them on the side table. Little Annabelle's pink face, topped with a mop of dark hair, peeked out from her blanket.

Nick got off the bed and came over to wrap Maxi in his arms. "How can I ever thank you and Jason for what you did last night?" Emotion roughened his voice.

"By being the best dad ever. Be kind and supportive, no matter what Annabelle does." She cleared her throat and pulled away from him.

"Come and hold your honorary niece." Lily held out the tiny bundle to her.

Nerves made Maxi's hands unsteady as she took the precious bundle in her arms. The smell of talcum powder and newborn baby drifted up to her. Little Annabelle squirmed once and then settled in with a sigh. Maxi thought she had never seen a more wondrous sight as that tiny face, with bow lips puckered to match the slight frown between her almost invisible eyebrows.

"She's so . . . perfect."

"I know." Lily beamed at Nick. "Definitely worth all the pain."

Maxi handed the baby to Lily, who looked

up with a question in her eyes. "I have a favor to ask you."

"Sure thing."

"If you have some free time, could you pop in to the shelter?"

"The shelter? Why?"

"The women there really appreciate another female to talk to. And there's a new girl, Dora Lee Cooper. She's only nineteen with a two-year old boy, and she mentioned that she'd always wanted to be a hairdresser. I thought if you didn't mind, you could talk to her about it."

Maxi could tell by Lily's enthusiasm how much this meant to her. "No problem. I can do that."

"Good." Lily's smile brightened the room. "You could be a real inspiration to her."

Maxi snorted. She'd never considered herself a role model. But for Lily's sake, she'd give it a try.

"Hey, where's Jason?" Nick asked. "I was hoping he'd come by so we could thank him in person."

A niggle of unease surfaced again. "I don't know. I assumed he went to work."

Nick frowned. "No. He wasn't at the house this morning. Maybe he's at the fire hall."

Maxi shrugged, trying not to let worry get

the best of her, but failing. She knew in her gut something had upset Jason on a deep level last night.

The question remained. Where on earth was he now?

The dumpster situated below Maxi's bedroom window was filling up quickly with all the debris. Jason had almost finished throwing out the pieces of ceiling and drywall that had collapsed into the room. Even with a mask covering his nose and mouth, he found breathing a chore. The rancid odor of burned wood and drywall made it even worse. Particles of dust, along with remnants of ash, managed to get behind the mask. He knew his face and clothes were covered in soot. But he didn't care. He needed this house repaired — and Maxi out of his home — as soon as possible.

He ripped the ruined linens off the bed and tossed them out the window into the dumpster, followed by the soggy mattress. No point in trying to save them. He'd moved most of the furniture out of the room. Now he had to dismantle the bedframe and tear out the waterlogged carpeting. The clothing he would leave for Maxi to deal with.

He paused to wipe the sweat out of his

eyes, already blurry from lack of sleep. He'd spent the night at the fire station in Kingsville, but sleep had eluded him. Lying on the narrow metal cot, he replayed the evening's events over and over again. The fear that he could have done something wrong and lost both Lily and the baby overwhelmed him. Most terrifying of all was the thought of Maxi ever going through a similar experience. He could never stand to see her in that kind of pain.

Ever.

"Do you realize half of Rainbow Falls is looking for you?"

Jason jumped and banged his knee hard on the metal bed frame. Maxi stood scowling in the doorway, arms crossed over her chest like a shield, her face a thundercloud.

"Do you always have to sneak up on a person like that?" He lifted his hardhat, tore off his mask and bent to rub the injury. He stood and shoved the hardhat back onto his head.

"I thought you had to wait until the investigation was over before you could start this?"

He could tell by her tone she was mightily ticked off at him.

"I checked with the chief this morning. Since the fire started in the barn, Steve said it's OK to start cleaning in here."

With the pain in his knee subsiding somewhat, he hobbled across to his tool chest, pulled out a screwdriver, and attacked one of the bedposts with a vengeance.

"Here, let me hold that for you." Maxi had moved into the room and grabbed hold of the frame. Her icy tone did not invoke a trusting attitude.

"I'm sure you have better things to do. Isn't your mother getting released today?" He could feel the waves of anger rolling off her. Her nearness was as jarring to his system as the clang of metal on metal.

"She's already settled in your guest room taking a nap."

"So what are you doing here?"

She reached over and banged down on his helmet. "Are you kidding me? Peg is worried sick about you. You never came home last night and never even called to say where you were." Maxi's gaze could've bored holes right through his chest.

Guilt washed over him. He'd been so busy stressing and avoiding Maxi, he'd forgotten to let his mother know he was OK. "Sorry. I'll call her in a minute."

Maxi grabbed the screwdriver out of his hand. "You and I need to talk, Hanley. I want to know what crawled under your skin last night on Lily's porch. Something made you take off like a swarm of angry bees were after you."

He yanked the tool back, avoiding her eyes. "I was a little overwhelmed by the whole birth thing. Can't a guy have some space?" The frown on his face felt like permanent grooves had formed.

"You're lying."

Ripe anger burned in his chest. He banged the screwdriver against the metal, and a zing raced along his arm. "Don't tell me how I feel. You have no idea."

"I have a very good idea. You're scared, Jason Hanley. Scared to death."

In a flash, he dropped the tool and lifted her off her feet. Adrenaline surged as he carried her to the hallway and set her down with a loud thud, feeling the reverberation through both arms. "Go home. Before I lose my temper completely."

She stared at him, the combination of anger and anguish riveting. "I have no home at the moment, remember?"

The air crackled with tension. He should apologize, but he couldn't seem to get a civilized word out of his mouth. Which only made his mood worse.

She crossed her arms. "Anyway, I'm meeting the insurance agent here in fifteen minutes, so you're stuck with me."

Great. Just great.

"Well, keep out of my way. And quit trying to psychoanalyze me." He slammed the door shut and stalked back to the bed.

The door flew open so hard it hit the wall inside the room.

"You are an insensitive, overgrown bore, you know that?" Maxi stomped away.

Jason gaped at her retreating back, anger pumping through him. He raced after her, but seconds later, he stopped dead in his tracks as the awareness of what he wanted to do when he caught her hit him.

He wanted to kiss her senseless again.

Bracing his hands on the doorframe, he breathed heavily, trying to slow his heart rate back to near normal.

Count to ten, Hanley. Get a grip on yourself.

How did Maxi always manage to push every one of his buttons? Make him so mad he could combust.

Because you're in love with her, you dope.

The truth hit him like a load of drywall falling on his head. His legs buckled, and he slid down the wall to the floor. His uneven breathing rasped in his lungs. Suddenly, everything about their relationship began to make sense. He finally understood why no other girl could keep his interest. Why he felt half-dead without Maxi around. Why her cold shoulder over the past two years had hurt almost as much as his father's desertion.

He scrubbed his hands over his face. The last thing he wanted was to fall in love. The last thing he needed was this terrible knowledge. How would he face her again and keep her from guessing his feelings when she always managed to see right through him?

He closed his eyes and leaned his head against the wall. He'd have to find some way to keep his emotions to himself. Because there was no way in heaven he was going to act on them. He knew Maxi well enough to realize that when she fell in love, she would want the whole package — the ring on her finger, the husband, the home, and of course, children. Which brought him right back to thinking about Maxi, in labor, having their child.

A wave of nausea gripped his stomach. No matter what he felt for Maxi, he could never trust himself to be a reliable husband and father. Could never risk turning out exactly like his deadbeat father. He'd never risk hurting Maxi that way.

Ever.

13

The next day, Maxi followed up on her promise to Lily and went out to Logan House to see Dora Lee Cooper. She rang the bell and waited on the doorstep, half-hoping no one would answer. What did you say to an abused woman anyway?

"Who's there?" The hesitant female voice seemed to echo out of the brickwork.

Maxi noticed the intercom and pressed the button to answer. "It's Maxi North. A friend of Lily and Nick. I'm here to see Dora Lee."

She sensed the hesitation on the other side of the massive wooden door, but a few seconds later, it opened a crack. A dark-skinned woman with multiple cuts and bruises on her face peered out.

"Hello." Maxi smiled, trying to appear trustworthy. The woman seemed to make a decision and opened the door wider.

"Come in. I'll get Dora Lee." The timid

woman stared at the floor while she closed and locked the door. Then she hurried up the main staircase.

Annoyance flared in Maxi's chest at whomever or whatever had robbed this woman of her self-confidence.

While she waited, Maxi wandered into the tasteful living room, admiring it anew. Painted in a soothing shade of sage green, the room exuded a relaxed, homey atmosphere, somewhat reminiscent of her favorite room in the farmhouse. Comfy sofas faced the brick fireplace. One corner of the room hosted a television and a play area for young children. Maxi picked up a discarded stuffed lamb and placed it in the toy bin.

Her mind turned to the disconcerting events of the previous day, the fight with Jason and the meeting with the insurance agent. Maxi had been so incensed by Jason's abnormal behavior she'd barely been able to concentrate on what the adjuster said. The insurance settlement would take some time to come through, pending a decision on what caused the fire. An unspoken implication remained that if the verdict was arson and if they did not find the culprit, there would be no settlement. Maxi couldn't think about that yet. For the time being, the repairs to the barn would have to wait, unless she could come up with the money some other way.

Her anger and frustration turned back to Jason. What was the matter with him anyway? The miracle they'd shared helping deliver Lily's baby was cause for celebration, not for acting like an ill-tempered adolescent.

Men. She would never understand them.

"Sorry about the wait. Robbie didn't want to close his eyes today."

Maxi turned to see a tall, blonde woman standing in the entrance to the living room. Her untidy hair had escaped its pins and hair ties. Large wet patches stained her baggy, blue T-shirt, presumably from a struggle with her son. Her worn out appearance tugged at Maxi's instinct to fix people.

She smiled. "You must be Dora Lee. I'm Maxi North."

The girl came forward to shake Maxi's hand. "Nice to meet you. Lily's told me a lot about you."

"Nothing bad I hope." Maxi hoped a joke would put her at ease.

"Only glowing reports about what a brilliant hair stylist you are."

Maxi motioned to the sofa, and they both moved to sit down. "Lily said you were interested in becoming a stylist yourself."

Dora Lee pushed some stray wisps of hair off her tired face. "I've got to find some way to make a living for me and my boy. Other than waitressing, I have no experience." She paused as if gauging how much to say. "I got pregnant in my senior year of high school. I did manage to finish the year, but once I had Robbie, it was next to impossible to find work and pay for a babysitter. So I moved in with Dennis, Robbie's father." Her face hardened. "But we can't stay there anymore. And I need to find a way to support myself."

Though Maxi could see no evidence of Dora Lee's mistreatment, she recognized the pain in the girl's eyes. Not all wounds were physical. "Hair stylists don't get paid a whole lot, especially in the beginning. You have to really love it to keep it up."

Dora Lee smiled, transforming her face into something very attractive. "I do love it. When I was little, it's all I ever wanted to do."

Maxi pursed her lips, taking in the girl's bone structure and the length of her hair, which would fall well past her shoulder when free of impediments. A win-win idea crept into the creative side of Maxi's brain. She could help Dora Lee, and, in the process, get some more material for her portfolio. "Tell you what. I'll give you a few tips, if you'll let me use you for a project I'm working on."

The girl looked skeptical. "What type of project?"

"I'm putting together a portfolio of interesting hair styles for my job in New York. Would you consider being one of my models?"

Dora Lee frowned. "I don't think I'm model material."

"Leave that part up to me. How's tomorrow? I'll bring everything we need."

Dora Lee shrugged. "OK, I guess."

"Don't worry. It'll be fun, and if you don't like how the pictures turn out, I won't use them."

Maxi had no doubt the results would be fantastic, and for the first time in weeks, she looked forward to the next day.

Exhaustion crept through every one of Jason's muscles — his body's silent rebellion after working all day at Nick's, then pulling a five-hour volunteer stint at the fire hall. He shifted into park and slammed out the door and onto his driveway. Maxi's car was nowhere in sight. He blew out a sigh. Maybe he could escape to the basement and sleep for the next forty-eight hours straight.

The look on his mother's face when he entered the kitchen sent that idea up in smoke. She sat at the table, tears staining her cheeks, with Bernice holding her hand.

Tension tightened his stomach muscles. "What's wrong?"

"I'll let you two talk." Bernice squeezed Ma's hand and then wheeled her chair out of the kitchen, throwing a sympathetic glance at Jason on her way by.

Ma swiped at some strands of hair on her forehead. Real fear gripped him. Was his mother sick?

"Sit down, son. I have some news you're not going to like."

Slowly Jason lowered himself into the chair across from his mother. Every drop of moisture vanished from his mouth, making speech impossible.

Please, God, don't take her from me. She's all I've got.

"I had a visitor today." Ma's eyes swam with pain. For the first time he could remember, she looked much older than her age. Taking a deep breath, she continued, "Your father's back in town."

Jason jerked upright on the chair. In all the years he'd been gone, Clint Hanley had never once tried to contact them. The hatred and bitterness Jason had worked so hard to overcome rose to the surface in a steaming mass of anger. He clenched his fists on top of the table. "What does *he* want?"

She pulled a tissue from her pocket and wiped her nose. "He wants to see you."

Jason stood up so fast the chair crashed over. "Now, after twenty years with no word, he suddenly wants to talk? Sorry, not interested."

He stalked into the living room and began to pace like a man trapped in a burning building. His mother followed and stood in the doorway.

"I told him you wouldn't want anything to do with him. But he insists he's not leaving until he talks to you."

"Then he'll be waiting a very long time." Jason fought to contain the fury that threatened to explode within him. He wanted to put his fist through the wall, smash all the glass figurines off the mantel. Anything to ease the awful pressure in his chest.

"There's something else you need to hear. Please sit down a minute."

The despair on his mother's face broke through the haze of Jason's anger. He was so busy focusing on his own issues, he'd forgotten how hard this must be for her — seeing her former husband again after so long. For her sake, he stifled his rage and sat beside her on the couch.

She took one of his hands in hers. "I . . . I'm not proud of what I'm about to tell you." She hesitated, eyes downcast. "The truth is your father did try to contact you over the years." She took a deep breath. "I wouldn't let him see you."

Jason's mouth fell open as he struggled to make sense of her words.

"At one point, Clint even wanted to come back. You were about five by then. We'd adjusted to life on our own, and I couldn't bring myself to trust him again, so . . . I refused."

Knots formed in his stomach, twisting his insides like his mother's mangled tissue. His father had wanted them after all. Had wanted to come back, but his mother had turned him away. To be fair, he tried to see things from her perspective. "Can't say I blame you for not taking him back. But why wouldn't you at least give him visitation rights?"

He watched the struggle play over her tired face. Finally she looked down at their clasped hands. "I guess it was spite, pure and simple. He left us, and I wanted to punish him. Show him he couldn't just waltz back in like nothing had happened. I wanted to hurt him as bad as he'd hurt me." A lone tear trickled down her cheek. "Trouble is, I didn't think about what it would do to you."

Jason clenched his jaw, grinding his teeth together so hard he thought they might crack. His mother had denied him a relationship with his father. How different would his life have been if Clint had been part of it?

"Because of my selfish decision, you may never find true peace or happiness. Can you ever forgive me?" She was sobbing now. This woman who had given him everything yet denied him his father. His heart wrenched as he put his arm around her shaking shoulders. He would not let her feel guilty for his dysfunctional attitude.

"Of course I forgive you. You did what you thought was best at the time. Who's to say you weren't right?"

Ma sniffled and wiped her nose with the tissue she held in a death grip. "So you don't hate me?"

His kissed her cheek. "How could I hate you? You gave up your life for me." He thought of his father and a nerve jumped in his jaw. "No, the only person I hate is Clint."

"You won't even consider talking to him? For your own peace of mind?"

"No." Jason could not suspend his deeply

ingrained resentment. If Clint had really wanted them back, he could've tried again. He wouldn't have given up so easily. "And I don't want him coming around here upsetting you. We've made it fine without him all these years. We don't need him now."

Jason sat with his arm around his mother for several more minutes, making a silent vow to protect her from any more pain Clint Hanley could dish out.

As far as Jason was concerned, the door to the past would remain firmly closed.

14

Maxi took a second look at the image on the screen and lowered the camera. Dora Lee peered at her from her spot on the couch in the living room of the shelter where Maxi had finished capturing the girl's makeover.

"Well, what do you think?" Dora Lee bit her lip.

"They're gorgeous." Maxi grinned, unable to believe her eyes. Dora Lee's before and after photos just might be her ticket to swaying Philippe's decision on the partnership at *Baronne's.*

She handed the camera to Dora Lee who took one look and promptly burst into tears.

"I'm pretty again." She threw her arms around Maxi in a ferocious hug. "It's been so long since I've felt good about myself."

Laughter bubbled up and erupted as Maxi hugged her back. She'd taken a frumpy young mother in sweats and transformed her into a goddess any modeling agency would die to have on board. This was Maxi's gift to share with the world — the ability to take the ordinary and turn it into the extraordinary. And no one appreciated it more than Dora Lee.

Leslie, the timid woman who had answered the door the other day, smiled for the first time. "Pretty? You're stunning."

Maxi wished she could perform the same miracle for Leslie. Unfortunately, the lacerations on Leslie's face needed time to heal. Maxi had tried hard to ignore the injuries to Leslie's face and arms, not wanting her anger to be misconstrued by the fearful woman. Maxi couldn't do anything to lessen the scars, but she had helped the woman feel better with a small makeover.

Leslie's chemically straightened hair had long since outgrown its style. With a new cut, she immediately seemed to gain more confidence. Helping these women made Maxi feel like a true fairy godmother.

"How can I ever thank you?" Dora Lee asked.

"By letting me use these photos for my portfolio."

"You really think they're good?"

"They're better than good. They could be the key to a huge promotion." Maxi grinned at the girl. She might only be a few years older than Dora Lee, but Maxi felt like her mentor.

"You've only had one lesson, but I can tell already you have an aptitude for hair. You should be able to make a career for yourself with the proper instruction."

Dora Lee frowned. "I don't know how I'd manage that. Daycare on top of tuition is more than I can afford."

Leslie looked up from tending to her young son on the floor. "Some community colleges offer free daycare to students. You could check into it."

Dora Lee brightened. "This has all happened so fast. I haven't had time to think straight."

"What did your boyfriend do to you, Dora Lee?" The question slipped out before Maxi could check herself. The haunted expression on Dora Lee's face made her wish she could learn to keep her mouth shut. "I'm sorry. You don't have to answer that."

"It's OK. The therapist says I should talk about it." Dora Lee stood to pick up some kids' books from the floor. "It started with shouting, insults, and names. Then it escalated until one day he broke my arm. Dennis was always careful not to hit my face. He made sure the bruises could be covered by clothes." She straightened and placed the books on the shelf, her expression hard. "I took it because I had no job and nowhere to go. But the day he hit my baby was the last straw." She placed her hands on her hips, her stance combative. "I got a restraining order and came here."

Maxi looked up from packing her gear. "Do you worry he might find you?"

A shadow flickered over her delicate features. "Yes." She handed one of the styling brushes to Maxi with trembling fingers. "Until I find a new place to live, there's not much I can do. Except pray."

Maxi hoped prayers would be enough to keep this woman and her son safe.

Half an hour later, Maxi hummed as she drove out of the driveway at Logan House. For the first time in a week, she felt a glow of optimism spread through her. She left with the promise to return in the next couple of days to provide Dora Lee with some more tips that might help her when she started school for her cosmetology degree. Helping Dora Lee made Maxi feel alive inside, rekindling her enthusiasm for her craft.

Maxi's good mood led her right to Lily's driveway. She couldn't wait to report on Dora Lee's progress and to share her newfound enthusiasm with her best friend. She hopped out of her car, smiling at nothing in particular. When she noticed Jason's truck on the road, the smile morphed into a frown. It had been several days since she'd seen him. She'd hoped he would've gotten over his snit by now. Instead, he seemed determined to avoid her at all costs.

Maxi slammed her car door shut and strode up the walkway toward the house. She would not let Jason and his irrational mood swings ruin this happy moment for her.

Then she heard the shouting.

Loud male voices erupted from somewhere outside. Were some of the neighbors fighting? She continued up the steps until one voice stopped her cold.

Jason.

Chills raced down both arms. She couldn't ever remember Jason raising his voice like that before. Instinctively, she followed the sound around the side of the house and into the backyard. Her feet faltered at the vision before her. Jason stood in his work jeans on the back patio, hands clenched at his side, his face a picture of rage and hatred. A gray-haired man with a neatly trimmed moustache seemed to be the object of Jason's anger.

"If you'd let me explain," the man said, "maybe you could understand . . ."

Jason lunged forward as if to strike the man but checked himself before any physical contact. "I told you. I don't care what you have to say. Get out of here now and don't ever bother me or my mother again."

Maxi's mouth fell open in disbelief. No matter what this man had done, he didn't deserve such rude treatment. Jason's behavior was completely out of character.

She edged closer to the scene. The two men were so intent on each other, they didn't even notice her.

"I'm not the only one at fault, you know. Your mother played a part in this as well."

Maxi swore she could see steam blowing out of Jason's nostrils. He looked exactly like an enraged bull ready to charge its victim.

"Don't you dare say one word about my mother," he spat. "Get out of here now before I do something we'll both regret."

The man held his ground for a moment, standing toe-to-toe with Jason. Then his shoulders sagged, and he stepped back. "Fine. But I'm not leaving town until you hear my side of the story."

Maxi was grateful not to be the recipient of the glare Jason gave him. It sent shivers down her spine — even at ten feet away. The stranger turned and headed right toward her, allowing Maxi a good look at his face. Who was this person that had Jason so riled up?

He gave Maxi a brief nod as he passed her and made his way around the side of the house. Maxi started as understanding broke through her confusion. Jason's rage made sudden sense. Only one man could cause this type of reaction.

Maxi's heart squeezed with the pain Jason must be feeling as she watched the hurt and anger he'd repressed all these years now erupt like a flash fire. Jason grabbed a hammer from his tool chest and hurled it across the lawn. It hit the ground with such force that grass and dirt hurtled in all directions.

She shook a little at the violence evident in him, but despite her trepidation, she couldn't leave him alone. He needed her — whether he'd admit it or not.

With quiet resolve, she took a few tentative steps toward him.

The hammer hit the earth, spewing debris in its wake, but the action did nothing to relieve the emotion coursing through Jason's body. His arms and legs quaked with the force of his rage. He wanted to destroy something, rip something to shreds. Drive his car through a fence, or over a cliff. Better yet, he'd like to drive Clint Hanley over a cliff.

"Jason." Maxi's soft voice penetrated the red haze around his brain.

"Go away, Maxi." The last thing he needed was her to be anywhere near him in this state. He felt naked, his emotions stripped raw.

"I'm not going anywhere."

The stubborn words only increased his irritation.

"That was your father, wasn't it?"

He turned so fast he nearly tripped over her. "How did you know that?"

Did anyone else in town know? He would *not* be the subject of small town gossip.

"You have his eyes."

Instead of helping, the quiet sympathy on her face only made him angrier. "This is none of your business. Just leave it alone." At the hurt brewing in her eyes, he felt like he'd kicked a puppy, but he was beyond caring. He wanted to maim everyone, make the world feel the way he did.

"Would you like me to get a beer?"

The unusual question jarred him out of his thoughts. "What did you say?"

"Do you want to get a beer?"

"You know I don't drink anymore."

She shrugged. "It's what they do in the movies when someone's upset. How about a coffee then? Or an ice cream sundae. I know from personal experience it helps take the edge off."

"Ice cream." Despite the anger, he barked out a harsh laugh. As if ice cream could help this situation.

"Don't laugh at me." Maxi's thin brows shot together in a frown. "You don't know if you don't try it."

"Believe me. Ice cream can't fix this." He walked over to retrieve his hammer and brought it back to his box. He scrubbed a hand over his face. He doubted he'd get any more work done today. How Clint had tracked him down at Nick's house he'd never know.

"How about a ride out to Rainbow Falls? It's a good place for talking or thinking."

He looked over at her, his heart rate starting to come down a notch. Maybe it was a better option than hurtling off a cliff. He released a long breath. "Fine, but you'd better drive."

Maxi glanced over at Jason's stony face as he sat rigid in the passenger seat of her father's old Toyota. She was glad he'd agreed to come with her, but now that they were getting close to the falls, she had no idea what to do. Surprisingly, she found a silent prayer on her lips.

Lord, Jason's dealing with a lot of pain right now. Please help me find the right words to comfort him. And if possible, help him let go of the anger and hatred he's harboring against his father.

She pulled the car into the small parking lot and turned off the engine.

"Come on. Let's walk."

They got out of the car, and she led the way toward the sound of falling water. Robot-like, he followed her.

"So what's your dad doing back here after all these years?" she asked when she couldn't stand the silence anymore.

"I have no idea. Other than trying to mess with me and my mom." His scowl left a ridge in his forehead.

"Must've been quite a shock."

He didn't reply.

Dumb, Maxi, dumb. Think of something to say. "Why don't you tell me what's going on in your head?"

He glanced over at her. "I think that was pretty evident before."

"Yeah. I was glad you didn't grab that hammer 'til after he took off." She was gratified to see a faint twitch to his lips. They walked on. "He obviously wants to talk to you about why he left."

"And I don't want to hear it. His excuses don't mean a thing." He reached down to pick up a pinecone and threw it into the air. It hit the water and skipped a few feet before sinking.

They continued to a spot where a fallen log served as a bench overlooking the cascade created by the waterfall. The soothing rush of water always made Maxi feel better.

"Let's sit down."

"I'll stand, thanks." He moved to the edge of the river bank.

She pushed her hands into the pockets of her cotton pants and followed, considering her next words with care before she spoke. "Maybe your father realized what a terrible thing he did and wants to make amends." She thought of her own father and how she'd always wished he would come to her, apologize for the hurt and anger he'd heaped on her, and ask for her forgiveness. She would've given anything for that.

"It's too late for apologies. Twenty years too late." The terseness in his voice made her wince.

"It takes some people longer than others

to ask for forgiveness, if that's what he's here for. Some people never get there." She swallowed hard. "What if your father died and you never got the chance to reach some sort of peace between you? Wouldn't you regret it for the rest of your life? I know I do." Hot tears burned the back of her eyes. Whether she wanted to face it or not, this was the tragedy of Charlie's death. That she would never get to hear him say he was sorry. That she would never get to tell him how much she regretted her part in Drew's death.

She felt Jason watching her as she struggled to contain her emotions. This was not about her. She'd lost her chance to reconcile with her father. Maybe her job right now was to help Jason figure out how to reconcile with his.

Jason closed his eyes and exhaled loudly, rocking on his heels. "We're quite the messed up pair, aren't we?"

"Yes, we are." She glanced at him staring out over the water and hoped her next point wasn't hitting too low below the belt. "Doesn't your newfound faith include a tall order of forgiveness?"

A nerve jumped in his jaw. Coins jangled in his pocket as he fiddled with them. A soft breeze blew the hair over his forehead, and her heart ached with tenderness. She longed to gather him close, to hold him and ease his pain. But she didn't dare, afraid her actions would reveal too much.

She startled when he reached out to grasp her hand. Then in one quick movement, he drew her to him. At first, she stiffened at the close contact but soon allowed herself to relax into his arms, giving him the comfort he needed.

"How do I let go of all this hatred inside?" he whispered into her hair.

The feel of his warm breath on her cheek made her pulse quicken. "I'm not sure. But maybe hearing his side of the story will help you decide if you can."

He sighed deeply, his chest expanding under her. "I'll think about it. That's all I can do right now."

"It's a start." She pulled back to look at him. The pain on his face made her want to weep. "You're entitled to your feelings, Jason, no matter what they are. If you can't change them, then accept it and move on."

Wow, that sounded insanely mature. Maybe she should take her own advice. Apply it to her own mixed-up life.

"Thanks." He gave a thin smile. "That helps."

"I'm glad."

Their eyes locked, and for one heart-stopping moment, Maxi couldn't breathe. The intensity of Jason's gaze held her riveted until he slowly lowered his mouth to hers. Currents of electricity raced through her veins as their lips joined. Like a flash fire, the heat flared between them. He wrapped strong arms around her, pulling her feet off the ground, while his mouth devoured hers.

When they finally pulled apart, Maxi rested her head on Jason's chest, trying to get her breathing under control. Regret and sorrow choked her airways. She hadn't brought him here for this reason.

"This isn't a good idea," she whispered. "I'm going back to New York soon. I don't want to start something we can't finish."

She felt the walls go up around him. Literally, his chest muscles solidified, one by one, until he set her away from him. The look in his eye was unfathomable. His mouth, soft on hers a moment ago, hardened into a solid line. "You're right. Let's forget this ever happened."

And he stalked off toward the car, leaving her heart shattered into tiny fragments.

15

Gloria slammed out of the *Cut 'N Curl,* making the bell almost fly off its pins. Usually she enjoyed getting her hair and nails done, but not today. The only thing anyone in this town talked about anymore was Maxi North. That and Charlie's unfortunate death and the terrible fire at the North farm. All the old biddies at the hairdressers seemed obsessed with the topic. She, for one, was tired of hearing about it. She wished Charlie North hadn't been stupid enough to get himself killed and that Maxi had never returned to Rainbow Falls.

Gloria got great satisfaction from the sound of her high heels tapping out the rhythm of her annoyance as she strode down Main Street toward the drug store. Maxi North had been a thorn in her side all through high school. Maxi's low opinion of her had kept Jason from ever giving Gloria a second glance. A fact proven when he hooked up with her once Maxi had moved away and their "friendship" had cooled.

Now Maxi was back and staying at the Hanleys'. That thought, more than anything, rankled Gloria. She needed a plan to get Maxi out of Rainbow Falls for good.

As if she'd conjured him up from her imagination, Jason walked out of Dave's Hardware Store and stepped onto the sidewalk in front of her. There was no polite way he could ignore her, and Jason was nothing if not polite. Her heart picked up speed in her chest at the sight of his rugged profile.

Pleased her blonde tresses looked their best just coming from the salon, Gloria put on her brightest smile. "Why, Jason Hanley. It's been too long."

He turned to look at her. "Hello, Gloria."

Not letting his lack of enthusiasm dissuade her, she hooked her arm through his. "How is the fireman training going? You know I admire you for having such noble career goals."

He shot her a sideways glance. "It's coming along. Thank you."

"When will you be a full-fledged firefighter?"

She knew men loved to talk about themselves, and women who showed an interest in their affairs proved practically irresistible to them.

"I have two more courses in the fall, and I'll be done."

"Wonderful. I can't wait to see you in your uniform." She winked at him.

He only frowned.

"Are the rumors true? You're planning to propose a fire station in town?"

His frown deepened. "Where'd you hear that?"

She waved a hand to show off her perfect French manicure. "Through the proverbial grapevine. Are you saying it's not true?"

"I've been looking into it."

She beamed at him. "Well, I, for one, think it's a brilliant idea. I'll be sure to mention it to Daddy and get him to approve any loans you may need."

The fact that Owen Johnson was the head of the bank often proved beneficial to Gloria. Why didn't Jason seem more interested? More enthused about the help she could offer him?

He stopped on the sidewalk beside his truck and pulled his arm free from hers. "If and when I need a loan, I'll handle it myself. Have a nice day." He nodded to her and then loaded his purchases into the back of the truck.

Gloria swallowed her annoyance at his attitude. "See you again real soon," she called.

He gave her one long look before hopping into the driver's seat. A look that made her pulse trip as she recalled their fevered kisses. She'd loved Jason Hanley since high school, and nothing would stop her from getting him back. As she watched the truck pull away from the curb, the seed of a plan began to take shape.

A brilliant plan that might accomplish everything she wanted in one shot. As well as solve another bigger problem that had been niggling at the back of her mind for several weeks now.

She smiled to herself and continued on to the drugstore.

Wailing a hammer into wood was a great stress reliever, Jason decided. Upstairs in Maxi's farmhouse, he'd almost completed the framework for the new window. Tomorrow the contractors would come to shingle the new roof, now that it was framed and ready. The knot of tension — the one that should be easing up, knowing Maxi and her mother would soon be able to move back into their home — still screamed in Jason's neck. He took a break from hammering to rub it.

The sound of tires on the gravel below pulled Jason to the window. Maxi's car jerked to a stop in front of the house, stones spewing from under the wheels. The knot cinched tighter in Jason's neck. What was she doing here? He'd come to the farm to avoid her.

She jumped out of the car, obviously embroiled in a heated conversation on her cell phone. She gestured with her free hand and then ran it through her hair, which she now wore in a sleeker style. Jason watched for a minute longer then frowned. Judging by her erratic hand movements and frantic pacing, something was wrong. He huffed out a loud breath. Despite his annoyance at her, he couldn't prevent himself from going down to see if she needed help.

"I'll be back as soon as humanly possible, Philippe."

Jason heard the frustration in her voice as he stepped out onto the porch. With her back to him, she didn't know he was there.

"Look, I'm doing as much as I can from this end. I don't know what else you want me to say." She stopped dead in her tracks. "If that's the way you feel, why don't you give the partnership to Sierra right now and save us both a whole lot of trouble."

She stood for a moment, almost vibrating with rage. Then, in a pose that would rival a major league pitcher, hurled her phone across the field.

Jason struggled to contain the urge to laugh. Right at that moment, she turned to see him watching her from the porch. He schooled his face to make sure he wasn't smiling.

She frowned, hands on her hips. "Well, don't just stand there. Help me find my phone."

Stifling a grin, he set off after her. It took them several minutes on their hands and knees in the long grass to find it.

"I take it there's trouble in New York." He held out the phone in one hand and extended the other to help her to her feet.

Maxi pocketed the device. "That's an understatement."

"Wanna talk about it?" The last thing he wanted to hear about was her yearning for the big city, but she probably needed to vent.

"My boss wants me back. *Now.*"

Jason frowned as they walked toward the house. "Did he threaten you?"

"Not in so many words. He hinted that Sierra was showing more interest in the partnership than me. And if I was serious about it, I'd better start showing him."

His stomach clenched. "So you're heading back then?"

"How can I? I can't leave Mama in limbo."

"She's OK with us for a while." He hated giving her a way out, but then again, she'd go one day anyway.

She glared at him. "Are you trying to get rid of me, Hanley?"

He sighed. No matter what he said, he couldn't win. "Just trying to help. If you need to go back for a few days, Bernice will be fine with us."

A war of emotions played over her face. He knew she was tempted by his offer, but before she could answer, the sound of an approaching vehicle pulled her attention away.

"You expecting someone?" he asked.

She didn't answer but shaded her eyes to watch the car turning down the long driveway. She noticed the rental plates at the same time he did, and her face drained of color.

The vehicle pulled to a stop behind Maxi's Toyota. A lean, blond man in a fancy suit and sunglasses stepped out of the sleek vehicle. Jason stiffened. This must be the hotshot boyfriend. He glanced at Maxi to see her reaction, not knowing what he'd do if she threw herself into the guy's arms. Or worse.

He was gratified that she didn't seem the least bit happy to see him. In fact, she looked a little green around the edges.

"Lance. What are you doing here?" She took a hesitant step forward to meet him on the driveway.

"Hey, honey. I came to see how you're doing." In a slick move, he whipped the glasses off and bent to kiss her cheek.

Jason disliked him immediately.

Maxi's face flamed as she pushed away from him. "Lance, this is my good friend, Jason Hanley. Jason, this is . . . Lance."

Jason shook his outstretched hand, pleased to note he was a good two inches taller than Lance with much more muscle. The guy might be rich, but Jason could take him in a fight.

Lance stepped back to look at the house. "You weren't kidding when you said you came from a small town. More like a farm."

Maxi jutted her chin out the way Jason loved. "It *is* a farm. I grew up here."

Blond eyebrows winged upward. He scanned Maxi from head to toe taking in her denim overalls and tie-dyed T-shirt. "Getting back to your roots, I see?"

"I'm here to help with the renovations. And to feed the chickens." She gestured toward the coop in the field behind them.

Jason's lips twitched as Maxi's infamous temper built. "Speaking of renovations," he said, "I have work to finish inside. I'll let you two catch up. Nice to meet you . . . *Lance.*"

"Same here."

"Holler if you need anything, Max." *Like someone to throw Lance off the property.*

Then he turned and headed into the house, fully prepared to spy on them from the upper window.

Maxi swallowed her mortification at Jason's rude behavior, hoping Lance hadn't caught on to his undertones. To her relief, Lance seemed oblivious.

"What are you doing here?" she asked again.

Lance frowned. "You don't seem too happy to see me."

"I'm just surprised. I told you there was no need to come." The fact that he would override her wishes and show up here unannounced did not win him any favor.

"I wanted to see the problem for myself." He glanced at the hole in the roof. "Now I understand the reason for the delay."

"Yeah, and the barn's completely gone." She waved in the direction of the remaining half wall. "If we want to sell the property as a farm, we'll have to rebuild it."

She shuffled from one foot to the other, feeling at a distinct disadvantage next to Lance's designer suit.

He ran a finger around his tight shirt collar. "It's been a long drive from the airport. Could I maybe get a cold drink?"

She hesitated. "Have a seat on the porch, and I'll see what we have." She felt bad for not inviting him in. Even worse for being embarrassed by the un-chicness of her parents' home compared to his ultra-modern condo in the city.

He frowned slightly but agreed. Soon she reappeared with two glasses of iced tea and sat down beside him on the wooden deck chairs.

After a long gulp, Lance set the glass on a side table. "I thought you'd want to know what's going on at the salon."

She stiffened in her seat. "How do you know what's going on there?"

"I *am* a client, remember? That's how we met."

"Yes, but you're *my* client."

He reddened a bit and shrugged. "I couldn't wait forever for a haircut, so I went

185

to someone else."

Maxi couldn't have felt more betrayed if he'd said he was dating another woman. "Who?" she demanded, her gut already telling her exactly who had cut his hair.

"I thought you'd want me to get some feedback for you, so I went to Sierra."

She glared at him. "Traitor."

"Hey, that's not fair. Don't you want to know what I found out?"

She crossed her arms over her chest. "Fine. What's the ice princess up to?"

He leaned forward with his elbows on his knees. "She's stealing your customers. And telling Philippe they're hers now."

Maxi's stomach clenched. She should've known Sierra would take advantage of her absence.

"Her main coup is Mrs. Hoffman."

She gasped. Mrs. Hoffman, one of the wealthiest women in Manhattan, had been a loyal customer since Maxi's first week at *Baronne's.* The fact that she would jump ship hurt Maxi's feelings, not to mention her pride.

"There's several more, too. I didn't catch all their names."

Maxi gripped the arms of the chair to keep her temper in check. "I can't believe this."

186

He leaned closer, his face intent. "Maxi, if you want this partnership, you need to come back. We'll have to do major damage control. If it's not already too late."

"*We'll* have to do damage control?" She narrowed her eyes, her suspicious nature taking over. "Why do you care so much about this?"

A flash of hurt passed over his features. "We've been going out for six months now. I know how much you want this promotion. Am I wrong to care about you — about your career?"

Maxi bit her bottom lip, doubts swirling through her.

He reached over to take her hand in his. "I've booked you a ticket on my return flight tonight. Come back with me."

His gray eyes beseeched her while she sat open-mouthed trying to process everything he'd said about their relationship, about Sierra's treachery. Still, Lance had presumed too much, booking her a ticket without consulting her. She couldn't leave her mother yet. Not with so much up in the air.

Maxi pulled her hand free and lurched to her feet. "I'm sorry, but leaving right now is not an option." Before he could reply, she jumped down the stairs toward the driveway, knowing he would follow.

She turned to face him beside the rental car. His grim features told her he was less than happy with her. "Look, I appreciate your concern, Lance, I really do. And I'm sorry you came all this way for nothing —"

"Not for nothing. I also came for this."

Without warning, he pulled her against him and clamped his mouth down over hers. Maxi froze at the unexpected assault. They'd only ever shared the briefest of kisses, mainly because Maxi hadn't been ready for anything more. But Lance's frustration now came through loud and clear. In that instant, Maxi knew there could never be anything between them but friendship. Her heart and her kisses belonged to Jason. She planted her palms against his chest and pushed him away. "Please don't."

He took a step back and gave a harsh laugh. "Well, I guess that answers my question, doesn't it?"

Heat stung her cheeks. "I'm sorry, but I'm not ready for this."

Lance pulled his sunglasses out of his breast pocket and jabbed them on. "You'd better figure out what it is you want, Maxi. Maybe you're sabotaging your shot at this partnership because you'd rather be somewhere else." He lifted his face toward the upper portion of the house. "With someone else."

She followed his gaze upward to the second story window where Jason stood staring down at them. Her stomach sank to her feet.

Great. He must've seen the kiss. Could this day get any worse?

"Good-bye, Maxi."

As Lance got in the car, she tried to think of something to say to help the situation, but nothing could. "Good-bye, Lance."

He backed out, and with a spray of gravel, he was gone.

Jason picked up the broken pieces of the pencil he'd snapped in two, like he wanted to snap the neck of Lance What's-his-name. So much for Maxi not being serious about the guy. Not after a lip lock like that one.

That's what you get for spying, Hanley.

Jason grabbed the hammer and began to swing, hitting nails already firmly in place. Dents formed in the wood before he realized what he was doing.

"Hey."

Maxi's voice from the doorway startled him. He hadn't even heard her come up the stairs. Afraid his emotions would be evident on his face, he bent to retrieve a new pencil

189

from his toolbox.

"Where's Lance?" he asked, trying to appear casual.

"Probably headed back to the airport."

Jason rose and turned to face her. She stood small and quiet in the doorway.

"You going with him?"

"No."

He schooled his face to hide his relief but curiosity got the better of him. "Why'd he come all this way just to turn around and go back?"

She took a step inside and leaned against the wall as if afraid to come too close. "He wanted me to go with him. But I can't leave yet."

Her eyes were wide and vulnerable, locked on his, causing his hands to sweat. He watched her for a minute and then nodded. "So let's get to work then." He handed her a hammer and bent to pick up the measuring tape.

"I broke up with him."

Jason's hand stilled on the tape measure, his heart pounding double time in his chest. It seemed like she was trying to tell him something. Something he wasn't sure he was ready to hear. He swallowed. "Good. Seemed like a lightweight to me."

Her face remained blank for a minute

until she broke out in a long laugh. "You never change, Hanley."

"Shut up and hold the tape for me."

16

At Logan House the next day, Maxi laid the last styling device on the coffee table, and took a sip from her mug while waiting for Dora Lee to come downstairs. Anticipation buzzed through her system along with the caffeine. She hadn't felt this eager about hairstyling since taking classes herself. Just knowing she could help Dora Lee change the course of her life for the better gave Maxi an immense sense of satisfaction.

Don't get too attached, an inner voice warned. Dora Lee and little Robbie would be moving away from Rainbow Falls as soon as arrangements could be made for their safe integration into a nearby community. And she would be heading back to her job soon anyway.

Against her will, her thoughts drifted to Jason and the amazing kiss they'd shared a few days before at the falls. She knew her rejection of his affection had hurt his pride, but it'd been for the best. For both of them. Jason's cool acceptance of her breakup with Lance only reinforced her decision.

Footsteps on the stairs alerted Maxi to Dora Lee's approach. She entered the living room with little Robbie glued to her shoulder. She looked exasperated.

"Sorry," she shrugged. "He won't go down for his nap."

Maxi smiled at the boy. His white blond hair with a huge cowlick in the middle of his forehead made him incredibly endearing. "I guess Robbie doesn't want to miss the fun. How about we put a movie on for you while I teach your mommy to cut hair?"

The little boy stared at her with his big blue eyes. Then he nodded. "Fish" he demanded and popped his thumb back in his mouth.

"Fish it is," she agreed. If only she had a clue who or what Fish was, she'd be golden. She held out her hand. "Come and help me find it."

The boy wriggled down from his mother and ran to the pile of movies. At first grab, he came up with a case with a cartoon fish on it.

"Ah, Fish. Looks like fun." Maxi popped the DVD in the machine and turned on the TV. Soon Robbie was settled in a chair, his attention riveted to the screen.

"I bet he's asleep in five minutes," she told Dora Lee.

"Thank you. I run out of patience with him sometimes."

"All mothers run out of patience sometimes, don't they? Isn't it part of the job?" Maxi smiled and took another quick sip of her coffee. "Ready to get started?"

Dora Lee's fatigue seemed to vanish. "You bet."

The woman picked up the techniques Maxi showed her with amazing aptitude. Even though they were using a dummy head for practice, Maxi was confident Dora Lee would be working with live models very soon. As soon as Maxi could convince her to take some real classes.

When they were almost finished, Leslie came in carrying her son. She paused to chat for a minute and then continued back to the kitchen to make the boy a snack. At the sound of footsteps in the hallway a few minutes later, Maxi looked up, expecting to see Leslie again.

"Hello, Dora Lee."

The deep masculine voice made the hairs on Maxi's arms rise. No men were allowed inside the house, except Nick or supervised workmen. A burly stranger, badly in need of a shave and some clean clothes, stepped into the room.

The comb fell from Dora Lee's fingers and bounced on the floor. "Dennis," she whispered. "What are you doing here?"

The terror in Dora Lee's eyes kicked Maxi's instincts into high gear. Her pulse sprinted as she searched for a plan of escape.

The man curled his lip into a sneer. "What do you think, darlin'? I'm here to get my son." The foul stench of alcohol permeated the air around him.

Anger mixed with the fear and adrenaline in Maxi's system. She would not allow anyone to harm that precious boy. With shaking fingers, she picked up the long scissors from the table in front of her and stepped in front of Dora Lee and the boy sleeping on the couch behind them, prepared to defend her new friends if necessary.

Dennis turned his bloodshot eyes to her and, without blinking, pulled a gun from his pocket. "I'd put those down if I were you."

17

Maxi's glance darted from Dora Lee to the gun in Dennis' hand. "You're not touching him." She prayed she sounded more confident than she felt — that the man wouldn't notice her knees shaking.

Dennis waved the gun and clicked off the safety. "I'm taking my son one way or another. Even if I have to kill the both of you to do it."

Maxi's mind whirled, adrenaline singing through her veins like a surge of electricity. She had to stop this now.

Dora Lee stepped out from behind Maxi. "Dennis, no. You can visit him whenever you want. I swear. Just don't take my baby."

In that instant, while Dennis shifted his focus to Dora Lee, Maxi leapt forward. She knocked his hand down and struggled to wrest the gun from him, but she was no match for his size or strength.

Grunting with exertion, the man flailed

out his hand, hitting Maxi and sending her to the ground with a heavy thud. Pain shot through her forehead as she connected with the edge of the coffee table. Before Dennis could aim the weapon, Dora Lee attacked him, hitting him over the head with a lamp she pulled from a table. The man crashed to the ground, moaning. The gun skittered across the floor under the couch.

Maxi scrambled to her feet and grabbed a blow dryer from the table.

Dora Lee squatted beside her as Maxi bound the semi-conscious man's hands together. The reek of alcohol became so strong she had to hold her breath while she repeated the process on his feet. Once they were sure he couldn't move, Dora Lee picked up her terrified son, clutching the now awake and wailing boy to her chest.

Relief trickled through Maxi's muscles as she gave silent thanks for her self-defense training in New York. She pulled out her cell phone and punched in 9-1-1.

Jason found driving to be his best time for thinking. Today, as he guided his truck along Main Street, his mind mulled over the situation with his father. Deep down he knew Maxi had a valid point. He'd been given the chance to get to the bottom of his father's rejection, and he should take it. If, for no other reason, than to let Clint Hanley know just what his leaving had done to him and his mother. The toll it had taken on both their lives.

Now that he'd made up his mind, he would wait for Clint to approach him again. He didn't want to seem too eager. And Clint needed to suffer a bit in the process.

As he turned onto Hickory Lane, the beautiful Johnson manor came into view and Jason thought of his encounter with Gloria Johnson the other day. The mention of her father and the bank loan didn't sit well with him. Was it his imagination or did her comment contain a thinly disguised threat?

He shook his head. Gloria Johnson was one big heap of trouble. Lucky for him, he'd come to his senses sooner rather than later and ended their relationship when he did.

Looking back now, he could see that he'd gone out with Gloria because he was so ticked at Maxi for ignoring him. What better way to get back at her than to date one of her worst enemies?

Real mature, Hanley.

Jason's phone vibrated as he slowed for a red light.

"Hey, Nick. What's up?"

"Jason. Thank God. Can you get over to the shelter right away? I've got the baby right now and can't leave." Nick sounded panicky.

Jason frowned, keeping an eye on the traffic light. "Is something wrong?"

"Chief Hillier called to let me know there's been some trouble there. One of women's boyfriends showed up . . . with a gun."

Jason blew out a long breath. "Geesh. What do you want me to do?"

"The situation's under control, but the women are pretty shook up." Nick paused and Jason's pulse thudded. "Jace, Maxi's there."

His heart leapt in his chest like a wire had short-circuited. "I'm on my way."

With a grunt, he tossed the phone onto the passenger seat, and as the light turned green, he peeled through the intersection. His mind flew in a hundred directions as he pushed the truck to its limit. Nick hadn't said anything about anyone being hurt, so she must be OK.

Please God, let her be OK.

Five minutes later, Jason pulled up in front of Logan House. Maxi's car sat in the driveway with the chief's cruiser parked behind. His stomach tightened. What would he find inside?

Jason knocked on the door, surprised to be greeted by a dark-skinned woman with a young boy on her hip. Her face bore several newly-healing cuts.

"Hi. I'm Jason. Nick asked me to come and make sure everyone's OK."

She nodded, her chocolate brown eyes solemn. "We're all fine, praise God. If it weren't for Maxi, I don't know what would've happened."

Jason frowned. "Why? What did Maxi do?"

"She jumped on the man with the gun."

Jason snaked a hand through his hair. "Where are they?"

"In the living room. If you'll excuse me, I need to put my son down for a nap." She gave a timid smile before sliding off to the stairs.

Jason strode through to the living room and peered inside.

Chief Hillier stood in full uniform, scratching something on a pad of paper. Maxi and a young blonde woman with a child in her arms sat on the sofa. Officer Joe Connell pushed a slimy looking man in handcuffs toward the doorway.

"Hey, Joe. Everything under control?"

"It is now. Excuse me while I take this

one to the car." He gave the guy in cuffs a shove.

Jason stepped aside and let them pass. The man kept his gaze glued to the floor. He was at least six feet tall and husky, maybe two-hundred-and-twenty pounds. How had Maxi gotten the best of him?

Jason stepped farther into the room, his eyes trained on Maxi as she answered the chief's questions, trying not to think how easily the situation could have gone horribly wrong. That Maxi could have been shot, or even killed. The vision of her body lying bleeding on the floor filled his imagination. He shook his head to clear the picture.

At last, Mike Hillier flipped his notebook closed. "Thanks for your help, ladies. We'll do our best to make sure he won't bother you again." Mike tipped his police cap to the blonde woman. "I'm going to get some extra security cameras and an alarm system installed here. Nick's a great guy but a bit too trusting in this instance."

The woman rose, her son in her arms. "Thank you, Chief. I appreciate your help."

"You're welcome. But the real thanks go to both of you. Your quick actions averted a potentially deadly situation." He adjusted his belt. "I'll be in touch."

Mike turned and nodded to Jason on his

way out of the room.

Maxi hugged her arms around her torso, her eyebrows rising as she noticed Jason. "Jason, what are you doing here?"

He forced himself not to rush to her side. "Nick asked me to make sure everything was OK after the chief called him." The boy squirmed in his mother's arms. Jason fought back a surge of anger at a man who would expose his child to this type of violence. "Are you both OK?"

Maxi nodded. "We're fine. Just shaken up."

The woman shifted the boy on her shoulder. "If you don't mind, I'm going to get Robbie a drink and see if he'll go down for another nap."

"Sure." Maxi stuffed her hand in the pockets of her jeans. "I'll call you tomorrow."

The blonde nodded and hugged her son as she exited the room.

Maxi turned her full attention to Jason. "Nick must feel terrible about what happened. He wants this to be a place of refuge, free of violence." She pushed her bangs off her face, revealing a smear of blood on her forehead.

In an instant, Jason moved to her side. "You're bleeding. Let me see." He took hold of her chin and brushed her hair aside to find a gash on the left side of her temple.

"It's nothing." She tried to move away. "I hit the corner of the coffee table when I fell."

He plucked a tissue from the box on the table and dabbed it to the wound. The need to lash out burned in his chest. "What were you thinking, jumping the guy like that?"

Her hazel eyes blazed in response as she pushed his hand aside. "I had to do something. I couldn't let him take the baby."

The fear he'd felt driving over, not knowing what he'd find, came rushing back. He let it swirl in his gut until it turned into something he felt more comfortable with. Hot anger. "Who let him in anyway? I thought this was supposed to be a safe house."

She raked her hand through her red mop. "I don't know. He showed up out of nowhere . . ." Her voice broke. She turned and charged down the hall to the kitchen.

Banking his frustration, he followed her. She lifted a pitcher of water from the fridge. Without a word, he took the container from her unsteady fingers, set it on the counter, and pulled her into his arms.

"You could've been killed."

It took all his concentration not to crush

her in a fierce embrace. Instead, he willed his arms to be gentle. Maxi's frame trembled, telling him she was far more shaken than she'd ever admit. She leaned against him for only a moment before pulling away. "I should see if Dora Lee and Leslie are all right."

"They're fine. But you're not." He tugged her back against him and absorbed her tremors. They remained there locked together in silence for several minutes. It took every ounce of willpower not to kiss her. But she'd made it clear she wanted nothing more than friendship. Deep down, he knew she was right.

When she seemed steadier, he made her sit at the table and poured her a glass of water. After she'd finished the last drop, he helped her to her feet.

"Come on. I'll follow you over to Nick's. He won't stop worrying until he sees for himself you're in one piece."

18

"It's your father, isn't it?"

Jason wished his mother would leave him to his eggs in peace. At 5:00 AM, with a sleepless night behind him and an early shift ahead at the fire station, he was in no mood for his mother's badgering. He'd wanted to grab a coffee and go, but Ma had insisted on making him a hot breakfast.

"What about my father?" Jason's brain still wasn't functioning, even after his first jolt of caffeine.

"The reason for this snarly mood you're in lately."

"I'm not snarly."

"Call it what you want, but you're not yourself." Ma set the frying pan back on the stove, poured herself a cup of coffee, and then came to sit beside him at the table.

"I'm fine."

The fib slipped out before he could think of another answer. He was nowhere near fine. He had no idea what to do about his feelings for Maxi. Her return to Rainbow Falls had become sheer torture, making him long for things he had no right to want.

Like a family of his own.

He pushed his chair away from the table as though he could push away all his baggage.

"You hardly touched your eggs."

The disappointment in her voice made guilt curl in his stomach. "Sorry, Ma. Just not hungry."

He grabbed his cell phone, his keys, and his thermos of coffee and set out the door. She followed him to the driveway in her slippers and robe and laid a hand on his arm before he could get into his truck.

"If it's not your father, then what's eating at you? You can't sit still for more than two minutes."

He tried to curb his impatience, knowing her concern came from a place of love. "I don't know, but I'm sure it'll pass."

At least he hoped it would. As soon as a certain redhead went back to New York.

Her brows rose. "It's Maxi, isn't it? That girl has you all tied up in knots like a hogtied calf. Come to think of it, this all started after the fire. When you saved her life."

A jolt of anxiety made Jason's head snap

up. He needed to get that idea out of her head right away. "Stop messing in my business, Ma, or I'll have to get my own place. I don't need this constant pestering."

Avoiding the hurt in her eyes, he wrenched open the driver side door. "I'll see you at dinner."

And before she could say another word, he threw his truck into gear and roared away.

Relieved to find herself alone, Maxi poured a cup of coffee and sat down at Peg's kitchen table. She'd hardly been able to sleep a wink all night. The scene at Logan House replayed in her mind like an endless tape on rewind. Her head ached as she relived the terror, which hadn't hit her fully until after the danger was over. Her life could've ended last night, and that thought shook her to the core.

What would she have to show for her life? What accomplishments, relationships, or good deeds could she claim at the pearly gates?

Nothing came to mind. But the list of her mistakes and regrets would stretch from one end of eternity to the other.

What was her purpose in this world? Catering to the rich, pampered women of

Manhattan? Suddenly Maxi found herself wanting to ask God for help. Would He listen or just bang the gavel and pronounce her guilty? Guilty of wasting the precious gift of life.

Tears burned hot behind her closed eyes. Her mind spun in circles, like a wheel stuck in the mud, spinning and spinning, getting nowhere fast. The past loomed behind her, mocking her with its ever-present pain, while the future hovered ahead, shrouded in fog. She couldn't go backward or forward until she got herself unstuck.

She drained her cup and rose to rinse it in the sink. Her mood plummeted further as she stared at the water circling the drain. Around and around before finally gurgling away. Like the thoughts chasing around her head.

Thoughts of Jason.

Once again, he'd helped her through a crisis. He'd offered her comfort, but had she shown any appreciation? No. She probably owed him an apology and a thank you. Unfortunately, that would have to wait until later. Doc Anderson had found a nice long-term care facility about forty miles away in Glenville, and she'd promised to take her mom to check it out.

Footsteps echoed in the hallway, alerting

Maxi to Peg's arrival. She was dressed for work in what Maxi called her uniform. Black pants and a white blouse.

"How are you doing this morning?" Peg gave her an odd look as she opened the fridge.

"Still shook up a bit. Couldn't sleep much last night."

Peg set the jug of milk on the counter. "Any idea what's got Jason in such a state?"

A thousand thoughts buzzed through Maxi's brain, none of them suitable for sharing. Instead she shrugged. "I think he's upset because I jumped the guy with the gun."

"That was a mite foolish, but it's more than that."

Heat flared in Maxi's cheeks. "What are you getting at?"

Peg folded her arms in front of her ample chest. "You know I love you like a daughter. But the pair of you are about to drive this body mad." She tapped her toe against the linoleum. "I think Jason's full of feelings for you he doesn't know what to do with. He's so jam-packed with frustration, it's oozing out of his pores."

Maxi didn't have the energy for Peg's theories this morning. "You're wrong. I think his bad mood has more to do with his father being in town."

"He told you about that?"

"I ran into them mid-fight. I thought Jason was going to kill him." She shuddered remembering the hatred contorting his face.

Peg sat down heavily on a kitchen chair. "So they've seen each other. I wondered when that would happen." She raised weary eyes to Maxi. "Do you know if Jason is going to see Clint again?"

"I tried to convince him to. He said he'd think about it."

Peg nodded. "It's more than I could get him to do. Guess we'll have to give him some time." She rose from the chair, looking to Maxi like a woman old before her time. She turned and pierced Maxi with a dark stare. "You, on the other hand, are running out of time. You'd best figure out if you want my son or not. If not, make a clean break and get on with things."

For the first time, Maxi sensed harsh criticism from this woman she loved, yet the truth of her words seared Maxi's heart and settled like a weight on her shoulders. It had never occurred to her that if she rejected Jason, she could lose Peg as well.

As per Lily's directions, Jason found Nick in the little office at the back of the Good

Shepherd Church, his fair head bent over his desk, intent on the task before him. Trying to ignore the legion of wasps swarming in his stomach, Jason knocked on the open door.

Nick looked up. "Hey, Jason. Come on in."

Jason took one step inside the door and stalled. Suddenly, spilling his guts to his friend and spiritual mentor didn't seem like such a great idea. "You look busy. I can come back later."

"It's nothing that can't wait." Nick rose from the desk and came around to where the guest chairs sat. "What's up? Some snag with the renovations?"

Jason shifted from one foot to the other and fiddled with the collar of his shirt. "No. This is personal. If you have a few minutes."

"I always have time for you." Nick smiled and closed the office door. "Have a seat."

Jason perched on the edge of the hard-backed chair while Nick moved the other chair to face him. Not too close, but more intimate than across a desk. Jason leaned forward, his arms on his knees, his hands clasped in between. For some reason, he couldn't seem to open his mouth and verbalize his confused thoughts.

Nick bowed his head over his hands to

murmur a quiet prayer. "Lord, in Your wisdom, allow Jason to trust me to help him. Give him the courage to say what's on his mind, and grant me the understanding to counsel him wisely. Amen."

Jason had prayed many times with Nick, but now these simple words brought a lump to this throat. He took a deep breath and plunged in. "You once told me you had a bad relationship with your father."

If Nick was surprised, he hid it well. "Yes. My father was a drunk who beat my mother and me. That's why I started the shelter. I wanted women and children to have a place to go in times of crisis."

Jason's knuckles whitened from clenching them so hard. "How did you ever get past the hatred?"

Nick took a moment before answering. "I won't lie to you. It wasn't easy. I hated my father for more years than I care to remember. It took a lot of soul searching and prayer, but I finally got to a place of peace." He paused. "It wasn't until my mother was on her deathbed, though, that I truly let it go. Mom told me that she had forgiven him, and she couldn't die in peace unless she knew I had forgiven him, too."

Jason bent his head over his knees and ran his hands through his hair. "I thought I'd gotten past the hatred until my father came back."

"Back? When?" Nick sounded surprised. Guess the grapevine hadn't gotten to him yet.

"A few days ago."

"Have you spoken to him?"

"Once."

"Is he here to make amends?"

Jason raised his head to look at Nick, not bothering to disguise the disgust on his face. "As if that's possible. How can you make up for a lifetime of absence and indifference?" Even as he said the words out loud, he remembered his father hadn't really been indifferent, had in fact tried to see him.

"Maybe you're afraid to let go of the anger and hatred," Nick said. "Maybe if you heard your father out, you'd have to forgive him. Holding on to the negative feelings is a lot easier than letting down the barriers and risking a relationship with a man you don't trust."

Jason jumped to his feet. A nerve twitched in his jaw. He walked to the window behind the desk to look out over the church gardens. Nick was right. Anger was easy. Letting it go was the hard part.

"Don't you think you owe it to yourself to get the full story? Even if you decide you can't forgive him, make peace with it, and move on with your life. One way or the other, it will be over."

Jason turned and gave him a half smile. "That's nearly word for word what Maxi told me."

Nick grinned back. "Smart girl." He rose from the chair as well. "How are things with you two anyway?"

Jason sighed. "That's the other thing I need advice about."

Nick clapped a hand on Jason's back, seeming to sense the restlessness in him. "Why don't we take a walk out in the garden? I find nature has a way of helping me find clarity."

The two left the office and exited into the back garden. They walked in silence for the first few minutes. Jason felt a small measure of calm returning with the warmth of the sun on his shoulders and the buzzing of bees around the roses.

"So you need advice about Maxi?" Nick finally asked.

How did he begin to tell Nick about his feelings? Once he said them out loud, they'd be real. "Yeah. It's been driving me crazy. I can't think straight sometimes, especially with her living in our house right now."

"Sounds like you're in love with her."

The simple statement hung in the air and then drifted overhead with the summer breeze.

"I think I might be." Jason glanced over to see Nick's reaction.

Nick's expression remained neutral except for the slight upturn of his lips. "I take it this poses a problem for you?"

They paused on the walkway before a small pond with a stone fountain in the center. The gurgling of water instilled a sense of serenity within the oasis the garden provided. The perfect spot to bare one's soul.

Jason turned to look at Nick. "I've always been afraid to get too close to a woman. In case I hurt her the way my father hurt my mother. I've never allowed myself to think of Maxi as anything more than a friend. But for some reason, in the past few weeks, everything's changed. I'm not even sure how it happened."

Nick chuckled. "Love's like that. It sneaks up on you sometimes. I know it did with Lily and me." He motioned them over to a wooden bench with a view of the fountain. "How does Maxi feel about all this?"

"I have no idea. I think she's as confused as I am." Jason picked a daisy from the plant to his left and began to pull the petals off.

"Trouble is, she's set on leaving for New York as soon as she can get things settled with her mother."

"And you don't want to live in New York."

"No. I've always loved Rainbow Falls." He hesitated and looked Nick in the eye. "I'd like to push for a fire station here in town. Contribute to the safety of the community. Be a better citizen than my father was."

Nick's face showed surprise and delight. "What a great idea. We sure could use one around here." He crossed one leg over the other and shifted on the bench. "You know, just because your father had problems, doesn't mean you'll turn out the same. Believe me, for a long time I worried I'd be physically abusive like my own father, but that couldn't be further from the truth. With God's help, I will never lay a hand on Lily or Annabelle."

Jason found it comforting that Nick understood the demons haunting him. "So you're saying I'm not destined to abandon my family?"

"I'm saying you're more likely to be a wonderful husband and father, knowing how important a man is to a family. And God is our Father — the one we should model for our children." Nick stood and Jason followed him as they continued down the path. "I've always thought love was a risk well worth taking. My one mistake with Lily was not telling her I loved her soon enough. I almost lost her because of it. But I realized I'd rather tell her the truth and face rejection than to regret for the rest of my life that I never tried."

Nick's blue eyes burned with an intensity Jason seldom saw unless he was preaching a Sunday sermon. "How would you feel if Maxi went back to New York and you never saw her again?"

An uncomfortable sensation churned in Jason's stomach. "Terrible."

"I think you have your answer, my friend. Tell Maxi your feelings and let God's plan unfold as it will."

Jason's foot faltered on the stone pathway. His pulse sped up at the thought of what Maxi might say. But Jason knew Nick was right. He had to know one way or the other.

"Thanks, Nick. I knew talking things over with you would help." He pumped his friend's hand in a strong handshake.

"So you're off to see Maxi?"

Jason shook his head. "There's one other matter I need to clear up first."

19

"I need you to do me a favor, dear." Mama sat ramrod straight in the passenger seat of Maxi's car. The drive back from Glenville had been fairly quiet after an unsatisfactory visit to the nursing home.

"What's that, Mama?"

"I need to pick up your father's ashes from the mortuary. If it's not too far out of your way."

Maxi jerked in her seat. "What are you going to do with them?"

Her mother gave her a sad smile. "I think I'll have them buried on the property. He loved that farm so much. It seems fitting to leave him there."

Unbidden tears burned beneath Maxi's lids. With everything that had happened, she hadn't let herself fully accept that her father was gone. "Sure, Mama. We can stop and get the ashes."

She didn't bother to point out that they

would be selling the property, and Mama wouldn't be able to visit his burial spot whenever she wanted. First things first.

Twenty minutes later, Maxi sat beside her mother's wheelchair in the lobby of the Rainbow Falls Mortuary, waiting while the clerk retrieved her father's remains. Mama sat in perfect tranquility, her hands folded on her lap, while Maxi jiggled and tapped and shifted in the guest chair. Unable to contain herself a moment longer, she jerked out of her seat to pace the lush green carpeting that muffled her harried steps. The unnatural stillness made Maxi want to scream. The scent of flowers and vanilla-scented candles seemed bent on suffocating her.

"Maxine, come and sit with me." Mama's soft voice beckoned Maxi back.

Reluctantly she returned to the chair flanked by a mahogany side table topped with an expected box of tissue. Everything about this place, with its air of death and grief, made Maxi cringe.

Bernice reached out and took her hand. "You haven't accepted your father's passing yet, have you?"

The question jarred Maxi. Her throat felt thick and dry. "I guess not. I still picture him out on his tractor in the fields."

"I know you two hadn't got on the best in recent years, but I want you to know he loved you very much."

Maxi flew to her feet, the blood rushing from her head. "That's not true, Mama. He hated me for letting Drew die." The words were out of her mouth before she had time to check them. She bit down hard on her bottom lip, not sure whether to control the trembling or to keep her from blurting out something worse.

"Charlie didn't hate you. You were his only daughter. He loved you."

Maxi shook her head in denial. Tears blurred her vision of the painting on the opposite wall. "He always blamed me. I know it was my fault. I should never have left the house that night when I was supposed to be watching Drew."

"You thought he was asleep. How could you know he'd sneak out to his treehouse with matches?"

"If I'd been home . . ."

"If you were home, he would've waited until you were asleep. You know how Drew was once he had something in his head." Pain laced Mama's sigh.

Maxi swiped at the dampness on her cheeks. She'd never considered that possibility before. "He was a stubborn one, wasn't he?"

Her mother smiled. "Not unlike his older sister." She wheeled over to take Maxi's hand in hers. "The truth is, dear, your father forgave you long ago. Charlie actually blamed himself for leaving the matches out where Drew could find them. For taking me away on a romantic evening when he should've been home on the farm where he belonged."

Maxi tried to believe her mother's words. "He never told me any of this. Just called me a whore for running off to meet a boy."

Not any boy either. Jason Hanley whom Charlie loathed. Jason personified irresponsibility to Charlie, yet he'd never even bothered to talk to Jason.

"Your father was wrong to say that. It was his own anger and guilt speaking." Mama's pale eyes grew watery. "He regretted it more than you know, except his stubborn pride would never let him apologize to you. Pride was your father's biggest flaw. Other than his drinking."

Maxi sagged onto the nearest chair and faced her mother. "How did you put up with it, Mama? How did you ever forgive him?"

One lone tear traced a path over Bernice's pale cheek, but she smiled at her daughter.

"I forgave him because I loved him. It's that simple."

Maxi jerked upright as the truth slammed into her with the force of an airplane hitting a brick wall. *I forgave him because I loved him.* Could it really be that easy?

Mama patted her arm. "I know you can forgive your father, Maxine, because it's the right thing to do. And because deep down you loved him."

Fresh tears flowed down Maxi's cheeks. Her voice croaked out as a whisper. "All I ever wanted was for Daddy to say he was sorry. So I could tell him I was sorry, too."

Mama brought Maxi's hand to her lips and kissed it gently. "You just did."

Jason wiped his sweating palms on his jeans, took a deep breath, and knocked on the door of Clint Hanley's room at the Rainbow Inn. The walls in the hallway needed painting, and the scent of pine freshener clung to the air, not quite masking the musky odor of the stained carpeting. Several seconds passed with no response, and Jason dared to hope Clint was out. He was about to turn away when shuffling footsteps sounded inside.

"Who is it?" came the gruff voice.

"Jason."

After a brief moment of silence, the lock turned, and Clint slowly opened the door. Today, without the red haze of anger to cloud his vision, Jason took a critical look at his father. Clint stood almost the same height as Jason, his frame much slimmer. His black hair had turned mostly gray, even his mustache. Clear blue eyes had faded with time, or maybe the spark of life within had dulled. His unbuttoned shirt revealed a wrinkled white undershirt beneath. Red suspenders hung limply at his side. Clearly Jason had awakened him from a nap.

"May I come in?" Jason kept his tone even.

Animation returned to Clint's face. "That depends. You planning on perpetrating any violence?"

A reluctant smile tugged at Jason's lips. "I don't think so."

Clint swung the door wide and invited Jason in. "Don't mind the mess. I wasn't expecting company."

Takeout food wrappers littered the small table in the corner of the room. The bed linens sat in a tangled ball in the middle of the bed. The lingering smell of greasy food hung in the air. Clint moved to pull a pair of pants and a tie off one of the side chairs. "Have a seat. Give me one minute to straighten up."

In silence, Jason sat on the uncomfortable chair while Clint hastily rearranged the bedding, picked up the trash, and disappeared into the adjoining bathroom. Seconds later he reappeared, wiping his face with a towel. Jason watched as his father pulled over a second chair and took a seat. He put down the towel and fixed Jason with a solemn stare. "So what brings you by?"

"I've decided to hear your side of the story."

Clint's eyebrow rose a fraction of an inch. "I'm not going to ask what changed your mind. Whoever or whatever it was, I'm grateful."

Jason folded his arms over his chest, not prepared to soften yet. "Why don't you start at the beginning? Why'd you leave mom and me?"

Clint lowered his head for a moment, and Jason thought he was going to try to weasel out of the truth. Then he raised his eyes to Jason's in a direct gaze, his face set in an expression of resignation. "I'm not going to make excuses for my behavior. Nothing can excuse what I did." He sighed. "I was young and selfish. The realities of living with a wife and a child wore me down, little by little. One day, my boss called me in and told me he had to let someone on the sales team go.

Said there wasn't enough work to keep two insurance agents on, and I was being laid off. I begged him to reconsider because I had family to support. But since the other man had four children, there was no choice. On the way home, I stopped at the bar in the hotel for some liquid courage before I faced your mother. But after a few too many, instead of going home, I left town."

Jason curled his hands into fists. What kind of coward disappeared on his family? His disgust must've shown on his face.

"I know what you're thinking, and you're right. It was a low-down, lousy thing to do." Clint hung his head. "Once I sobered up a few weeks later and realized the mess I'd made, I went back and tried to make it up to Peg. But she wouldn't have anything to do with me. She thought there was another woman involved." He held out a hand, palm out. "But I swear there wasn't."

Jason grudgingly decided he was telling the truth. "Go on."

"I tried everything I could think of to make amends. Nothing worked. She wanted no part of me. Even threatened to get a restraining order if I didn't leave her alone." Clint fiddled with the tab of a soda can. "Finally I settled in Bismarck, taking odd jobs, and I kept trying to see you. Peg wouldn't return my calls. When I came to town on my days off, she would never let me in the house."

A toxic swirl of emotions swam in Jason's stomach. Disbelief, anger, and resentment all warred to gain the upper hand. "You could've gone to court. Demanded visitation rights."

Clint pressed his lips together. "If I'd had the money for a lawyer, maybe. I didn't have a steady income, so there was nothing I could do. Finally after about a year of trying to outwit your mother, I gave up."

So he did give up on me after all.

Jason shifted in his seat to ease the pressure in his chest. "What happened then?"

Clint stood and walked to the grimy window. "I'm not proud of my life after that point." He shoved his hands deep into the pockets of his pants. "Alcohol became my comfort and my mistress. I gave her all my money and all my time. In return, she gave me nothing but ill health and a stint in prison."

"You were in prison?"

Clint nodded and shot a glance over his shoulder. "For the past eighteen years. Serving time for armed robbery." He slumped forward as if the weight of his actions wore him down. "I got out two months ago."

Silence sat between them like a stone as Jason stared at Clint's back. It was worse than he'd imagined. His father was a criminal. An ex-con.

Clint turned to face Jason. "I know I have no right to expect anything from you, but I had to see you at least once and explain myself." He walked toward Jason, knelt down until their eyes were level, and fixed him with a sincere look. "I'm sorry for everything, son. All the hardships you endured because of me. All the pain. But I want you to know I've always loved you. Not being able to see you all those years almost killed me."

Spasms gripped Jason's gut. The words he'd always longed to hear from his father, the words he'd imagined every night as a child, now filled him with panic. The room seemed to shrink, taking the air out with it. Jason jerked to his feet.

He looked once at his father, unable to comprehend the tears in the man's eyes — tears that matched his own anguish. "I have to go."

He lurched toward the door, wrenched it open, and stumbled into the hallway. Without a glance behind him, he dashed down the hall to the staircase and kept running.

20

While Mama waited in the car, Maxi carried Charlie's remains home. His ashes were encased in an elegant pewter urn engraved with his name, date of birth, and date of death. Maxi set the container on the mantel over the fireplace, a temporary resting place, and ran her hand over the etching in the vessel. The weight of guilt in her chest eased for the first time in eight years. She would never forget the role her carelessness played in the events of the horrible night her brother died, but now she saw the bigger picture and realized others had played their own parts as well. The burden wasn't solely on her shoulders.

And according to her mother, her father had forgiven her. Could she really believe that?

Her fingers trailed over the mantelpiece and came away dust free. Someone had been in to clean the layer of soot off everything, she noted, inspecting the room further. Jason must have hired a crew. Maxi frowned. She must owe him a lot of money for supplies and labor. She'd have to repay him from her savings. What was left of them.

Maxi sighed. What a mess her life was in. Mentally she ticked off the problems: Philippe was hounding her to go back, Sierra was stealing her customers, the farm was eating her nest egg of savings with no sign of ever being sold — eating up the investment money she would need for a partnership if she were offered it — and they were no closer to finding a place for her mom to stay. As for Jason . . . well, she wouldn't even go there.

Maxi straightened her shoulders, pushed the negativity aside, and went to help her mother get some things from the bedroom. She would take her mother to Peg's and then come back and see what she could do about fixing the upstairs. Maybe some physical labor, like painting the new drywall, would distract her from her problems and bring her closer to returning to New York.

Jason stomped up the stairs of the North farmhouse, looking forward to some intense physical exertion to release the pent-up emotions swirling inside him. He'd expected his talk with Clint to make him feel better. Instead he was even more confused, not sure how to deal with an ex-con for a father.

He entered the bedroom, then froze at the sight before him. Maxi stood near the top of a stepladder, her hair stuffed under a spattered ball cap, paintbrush in hand. Her denim overalls sported more yellow paint than the wall. When she turned toward him, he stifled a grin at her speckled face.

She gasped, shock registering over her features, as she pulled out the earbuds attached to her mp3 player. "Jason, you scared me. I didn't hear you come in." In one lithe step, she jumped down from the ladder. Music blared from her dangling earbuds.

"No wonder with your player set at fifty decibels."

She shrugged and grinned. "I like my music loud."

"So I noticed." He walked around the paint tray to inspect her job. "Not bad. But why are you here painting?"

She dropped her brush in the can. "Restless, I guess. Needed something to keep me busy. This seemed like a good idea." She swiped a hand across her cheek, smearing another streak of yellow. "How about you?"

He pulled a clean brush out of his pant pocket. "Same thing."

Her eyes, which seemed more green than hazel today, sparkled with mischief, reminding him of the impetuous girl she used to be. "How about a race to see who can paint the most?"

"How is that fair? You have a huge head start."

"I'll spot you half a wall."

He laughed aloud, amazed at how great the sound felt. Seemed like he hadn't laughed in months. "I'll see your ante and raise you one paint roller."

"You're on."

The next two hours passed in friendly competition. Jason would never admit that his arms burned from the exertion of rolling color up and down the walls. If he kept up this pace, he wouldn't have to go to the gym tomorrow. He sneaked a glance at Maxi who barely seemed bothered. She hummed off-key to whatever song blared on the mp3 player as she studied a spot on the wall and then rolled viscously to cover it. Jason smothered a grin. This easy camaraderie reminded him of their former happy times. Times he missed more than ever.

When the whole room had a new coat of sunshine yellow, they plopped the rollers and brushes in the tray.

"I win." Maxi raised her fist in victory and

did her version of a happy dance.

Jason's heart pumped a little faster. She looked adorable covered in paint. Suddenly he didn't want this time together to end. He turned away in apparent nonchalance to pour the remaining paint from the tray into the can. "To prove I'm not a sore loser, I'll treat you to dinner." Nerves rolled in his stomach, awaiting her response.

He turned to find her kneeling beside him on the newspaper. "Dinner? As in a date?"

Her face was too close. His fingers twitched, suppressing an urge to wipe the paint off the corner of her lower lip. "What if I said yes?"

Their gazes met and held. "Then I'd say yes, too."

A bubble of elation rose in his chest. He hadn't felt this way since . . . since Susie Marshall agreed to go out with him. But this was even better. He smiled into her eyes. "Great. I'll finish here. You go get cleaned up, and I'll meet you in half an hour."

Butterflies — no dragonflies — battled for footing in her stomach as Maxi waited on Peg's front patio for Jason to finish getting ready. Was she actually going on a date with him after all these years? What if she couldn't think of something to talk about? What if he found her boring? What if she spilled a drink and ruined her lime green sundress, which had fortunately been in the dryer at the time of the fire?

Seated on a wicker chair, she clasped her hands together in her lap to keep from ruining her hairdo. For once, she didn't resemble a Tinker Bell look-alike. She'd even put on strappy, high-heeled sandals and dangly pearl earrings.

The screen door opened beside her, and her pulse rate kicked up two notches. Jason stepped out, looking so incredibly handsome that Maxi's heart stuttered. He wore a dark brown jacket and a cream-colored dress shirt set off by a striped tie. He'd tamed his wild chestnut locks into a sleek GQ style, making him seem very sophisticated all of a sudden. And even more dangerous than his former motorcycle-riding persona.

"Hi." She jumped to her feet and smoothed down her dress.

His gaze moved over her with appreciation. "You look amazing. I've never seen you wear high heels before."

Her hand flew to the gold chain that decorated her throat. "There's a first time for everything, right?"

Like this date.

"I guess so." He smiled and held out his hand to her.

Maxi hesitated for a moment, not sure what she was supposed to do. Where had the smooth, confident city girl disappeared to? She swallowed once, willing her nerves to dissipate, and placed her hand in his. The warmth of his skin heated hers. He made a mock bow and led her down the walkway to his truck where he held the passenger door open for her and then helped her in.

"Where are we going?" she asked when he started the engine.

He only grinned as he shifted into reverse. "You'll see."

Twenty minutes later, they parked in front of Chez Marie's, the most expensive French restaurant in Kingsville. This didn't seem like Jason's style, but she wasn't about to complain. She'd released her seatbelt, about to open her door, when he put a hand on her arm.

"Wait here for a minute. I'll be right back." He hopped out before she could answer.

She crossed her arms and frowned out the window. What was he up to?

She tapped a toe on the floor of the truck and kept glancing out the window toward the stained glass doors to the restaurant. Finally, Jason bounded out, his arms full of paper bags bearing the name "Chez Marie."

French take out? What kind of date was this?

Jason laughed as he opened the door and placed the bags in the backseat. "Don't look so miserable. Let yourself be spontaneous for once."

"I can be spontaneous. As long as I know what I'm getting into." She realized she was pouting and deliberately relaxed her lips.

"Trust me. You're going to have a good time."

The truck roared to life. Jason guided it back down the road the way they'd come.

"What? Now we're going home?"

Jason laughed, little lines wrinkling his eyes. "You're such a control freak. Relax."

It took all her might to keep her mouth shut for the rest of the ride. She would not ask him where they were going, even if it killed her. Ten minutes later, when Jason turned down the road towards the falls, she knew. He was taking her to eat by the water. Her insides softened to warm liquid at such a romantic gesture. He'd remembered how much she loved that spot.

Jason parked near the path to the falls. After he helped her down, he reached into the backseat for a blanket, a picnic basket, and the bags of takeout.

"Is this OK?" He suddenly looked unsure. "Those shoes might not do well on the grass."

"I'll be fine. If not, you'll have to carry me as well as the food." She grinned at him, and he laughed back.

They walked at a slow pace as far as the path would take them, then branched off over the grass to Maxi's favorite fallen log in front of the cascading falls. Overhead, the sun had already dipped behind the trees. Bits of crimson peeked out through the branches, casting an almost magical glow over the oasis. She breathed deeply, taking in the smell of pine tree mixed with the earthy scent of loam. When Jason spread the blanket on the ground, Maxi kicked off her sandals and sat down with a sigh.

"This is perfect." And it was. So much better than sitting in a stuffy restaurant. For a brief moment, she thought of her many dinners with Lance in New York at all the high-end eateries and knew she much preferred it here.

"Glad you approve." He knelt beside her, opened the basket and took out paper plates, cutlery, and a bottle of sparkling apple cider.

"You thought of everything."

He gave a lopsided smile. "I was lucky Ma had this bottle kicking around." He popped the cork and poured a half glass each. "To life, with all its ups and downs."

"Cheers." She sipped the tart liquid enjoying the burst of flavor.

Jason opened the bags of food and, with amazing skill, fixed a plate of pasta and salad for each of them. Maxi balanced her plate on her lap and took a bite, not even minding the awkwardness of sitting on the ground in a dress. They ate in companionable silence for a while until Maxi broke the quiet.

"We brought Charlie home today."

Jason choked. "What?"

She laughed at his horrified expression. "His ashes. In an urn."

"Oh. How was that?"

She sobered. "I don't think I actually realized he was dead until today."

"Must've been hard to face the finality of it."

She dabbed her mouth with a paper napkin. "Hard, but necessary." She glanced over at him. "It's funny though — Mama took it really well. She seems to have accepted his death and the changes it means to her life."

"Bernice is one strong lady."

Maxi nodded and sipped her drink. "We had a good talk about Charlie. She told me he didn't blame me . . . for Drew's death. That he actually blamed himself."

He finished his meal and wiped his hands on a napkin. "I always suspected as much, but I knew you'd never believe me."

The burn of sudden emotion lodged in her throat, and she had to put down her fork. He knew her so well, sometimes better than she knew herself. "I guess my own guilt wouldn't let me believe you."

"And now?"

She felt his gaze on her face as she stared out over the water and didn't dare look at him, afraid the empathy on his face would bring about a torrent of weeping. "Now, I think I can start to let it go."

"I'm glad." The huskiness of his voice made tears sting her eyes. She blinked hard to push them away.

They sat in silence for a few moments, their shoulders lightly touching.

"How about you?" she asked after recovering her equilibrium. "Have you decided if you'll talk to your dad?" She glanced over in time to see untold emotions cross his face.

His mouth hardened. "I saw him today."

Her eyes opened wide. "And you didn't mention it until now?"

"Didn't feel like talking about it." He moved to his knees on the blanket and began to push the trash into the paper bag with unnecessary force. The muscles corded in his arms beneath his rolled up sleeves.

She reached out a tentative hand and laid it on his arm. "Feel like talking now?"

He stilled for a brief moment. "Not yet. I need time to think about everything he told me."

She bit back her disappointment. "Well, I'm proud of you for at least giving him a chance. No matter what happens, I don't think you'll regret it."

He raised his head to look in her eyes. A mixture of dark emotions swirled in their blue depths. Before she could catch her breath, he reached out and pulled her into his arms, his mouth claiming hers. He tasted like apples, sweet and sour at the same time. His hands slid down her bare arms creating a cascade of tingles along her spine. Then, as suddenly as he'd initiated the kiss, Jason ended it. He sat with an abrupt jerk and blew out a deep breath.

She sat more slowly, still reeling. "I'm not complaining, but what was that about?"

He stared out at the water, not looking at

her. "For always giving me good advice."

Her lips twitched. "With that incentive, I'll come up with some more in a minute."

He turned his head to look at her then. "You're not mad?"

"Should I be?"

"I think I've been giving you mixed signals lately."

Unease churned the food in her stomach. *Please don't let him go back to being just friends.* She swallowed. "I'll admit I'm a little confused. Exactly what *is* happening here, Jason?"

He got to his feet and reached out a hand to pull her up beside him. Without her heels, she was at a disadvantage height-wise. She willed her breathing to slow down, refusing to second-guess what he might say.

"I'm not sure. I do know I've never felt this way before . . . about anyone. And if you're willing, I'd like to see where this . . . relationship . . . is heading."

Relief spilled through her tense muscles. It wasn't a declaration of love, but it wasn't a rejection either. "I'd like that very much."

The furrows in his forehead relaxed, and he expelled a loud breath. "I was hoping you'd say that."

He lowered his mouth to hers again, and her body sighed at the familiar feel of him.

Joy swirled through her as their kiss deepened into something more than purely physical. As though their souls united.

When they finally drew apart, Jason looked down at her with such a tender expression Maxi thought she might explode with joy. How long had she waited to see that look in his eyes, a look just for her? He pushed a strand of her hair behind one ear. "I guess we should clean up here before it gets too dark."

She hadn't even noticed that the light had faded to dusk. A faint pink haze colored the sky. An absolutely perfect night. "You take the trash, and I'll fold the blanket."

She hummed as she packed up the picnic basket and stole quick glances at Jason as he moved, picking up the garbage. He was so lithe in everything he did. She could watch him forever. The muffled sound of her cell phone ringing brought her back to reality. For a moment she was tempted to ignore it. She wanted nothing of the real world to intrude on her evening with Jason.

Then she thought of her mother. What if she needed her? With a sigh, she fished the device out of her small handbag and looked at the display.

Her heart sank to her toes when Philippe's ID blinked at her.

"Hello, Philippe." She tried to keep her voice cheerful.

"Maxi, I want you back in New York tomorrow. Not a minute later."

21

Jason whistled as he polished the mirrors on the fire engine at the Kingsville station the next morning. Nothing could dampen his mood today. Not even that phone call summoning Maxi back to New York.

For the first time in his life, he was truly in love.

In love with Maxi North.

Even if she did return to New York, Jason was determined to make this relationship work. He'd make it work because he wasn't giving up now. Call him selfish, but he wasn't ready to relinquish these feelings that acted like a drug, running rampant through his system.

He bent with the rag and began to shine the chrome trim. With this energy, he could probably finish his chores in record time. And then he could plan his speech for Maxi. He was driving her to the airport later that afternoon. Even though she only intended to stay for a few days to put out some fires so to speak, Jason wanted to make sure Maxi knew how he felt about her. In absolute terms, with no doubt involved. He intended to tell her he loved her and make sure she had a very good reason to hurry back.

As for the future, he'd worry about that later. They'd take it one day at a time and make decisions as they went. That is, if Maxi felt the same way. His hand stopped mid-stroke over the hubcap. What if he'd misread her reactions? What if . . . ?

No, he was pretty good at reading female reactions, and he knew Maxi felt something for him. The question remained — was it strong enough for her to want a future with him?

He stood up, stretched his back, and inhaled deeply. He'd find out when he kissed her good-bye. He'd see then whether it was a "see you again soon" type of kiss or an "it's been nice knowing you" kiss. Every instinct told him she was as invested in this new relationship as he.

"Hey, Hanley." The voice of one of the other firefighters broke through the haze of his thoughts. "There's someone here to see you."

A huge grin spread across his face. Maxi

couldn't wait to see him. She'd come all the way into Kingsville. Maybe she'd changed her mind about going to New York after all.

Adrenaline surged through his limbs as he tossed the rag into the dirty laundry pile, took a quick glance at his reflection in the side-view mirror, and then bounded through the station to the inner office. His smile of anticipation slid away the moment he saw the woman in the blue dress standing at the reception desk. What was *she* doing here?

"Gloria?"

She turned. "Hello, Jason."

Something about her seemed different. She wasn't her usual flirtatious self. In fact, she appeared subdued, almost guilty. Alarm bells rang in his ears — alarms that had nothing to do with the fire station. "Is something wrong?"

His first thoughts turned to Maxi. His hand clenched into a fist at his side. If Gloria had done something to Maxi, he wouldn't be responsible for his actions.

Gloria twisted a crumpled tissue between her fingers. "Is there somewhere we could talk? In private?"

A cold ball of fear lodged in his chest, but he refused to let her see his discomfort. He kept his voice low and smooth. "There's a room down the hall. It should be empty right now."

He led the way to the small utility room that served as a storage/meeting room. A rectangular table and four mismatched chairs took up most of the dingy space. He pulled a chair out for her and then took a seat on the other side of the table. Wariness told him to keep a safe distance between them.

"What can I do for you, Gloria?" He couldn't help the coldness in his voice.

She lowered her fake lashes, still twisting the tissue. "I have some news I need to tell you."

He frowned, paying more attention to her trembling chin and shaking fingers. This news couldn't be good. "What is it?"

She bit down on her bottom lip, which had started to quiver. If he didn't know the kind of hateful person she could be, he might almost feel sorry for her.

"I don't know how to tell you this . . ."

Wisps of fear curled through his veins as he waited.

At last she raised misery-filled eyes to his. "I'm pregnant," she whispered.

Initial relief spread through his tense muscles. It had nothing to do with him or Maxi. "Wow. I'm sorry." He felt the stirrings of sympathy for her. "Does Marco know?"

Stunned surprise spread over her features. "Marco?"

"Yeah, you know, my former best friend you cheated on me with. I assume he's the father, unless you've moved on to someone else."

The hurt expression on her face pricked at his conscience. Even though she deserved it, he probably didn't need to rub her nose in it at this particular moment.

She shook her head. "I never slept with Marco."

His brain refused to comprehend what his ears had just heard. "Don't lie to me, Gloria. There's no point at this late date."

"I'm not lying."

The quiet dignity of her words rang with truth. Icy fingers of panic began a slow climb up his spine. His breathing slowed to almost nothing. "Then who's the father of this baby?"

Seconds passed like hours as Jason watched a lone tear slide down her heavily made-up cheek, leaving a trail in its wake. The tear reached the edge of her jaw, hung suspended there for a moment, then plopped onto the table below.

"You are."

22

"I'll be back in a few days at most, Mama." Maxi flew by her mother's wheelchair in the Hanleys' living room to toss another pair of jeans into her bag on the couch.

"Don't worry about a thing, dear. I'll be fine with Peg and Jason."

Something about Mama's lighthearted tone made Maxi straighten to scrutinize her mother. The usual lines of worry and tension had disappeared from her mother's face. She wore a smile which brightened her pale eyes and made her seem years younger. Maxi hadn't seen her this content for a long time.

Peg poked her head out of the kitchen. "We'll take good care of her. In fact, I might put her to work at the shop. Our new receptionist isn't working out so well."

Mama beamed. "I'd love to help. I haven't felt useful in years. And I'd get to hear all the good gossip first hand."

"It's settled then. You go solve the world's problems in New York, and we'll be here when you get back." Peg gave Maxi a sly wink. "Just don't stay away too long. That boy of mine will drive me crazy with you gone."

Heat rushed into Maxi's cheeks. Had Jason told his mother about their date? About their kisses? In one jerk, she yanked the zipper closed on the duffel bag. "I'm sure he won't even notice I'm not here." She tried to keep her tone light.

"Oh, he'll notice all right."

The two older women grinned at her. Discomfort made her fumble with the strap of her bag before she hauled it over her shoulder. "I'll wait for Jason outside." She bent to kiss her mother's cheek. "Stay well, Mama."

Maxi tried to escape Peg's knowing look, but the older woman blocked her exit and pulled Maxi into a bear hug. "I haven't seen Jason this happy in ages," Peg told her in a low voice. "Hurry back now. We'll miss you."

Maxi swallowed a lump of emotion. "Me, too."

Out on the little cement patio, Maxi breathed in the fresh air to calm her nerves. Why was she dreading this trip so much? Maybe she was afraid that while she was gone Jason would come to his senses and decide it was all a huge mistake. Maxi didn't want her absence to change the fragile momentum of this new turn in their relationship.

She carried her bag down the walkway to the lawn and set it by the driveway. Jason would be here in about five minutes to pick her up, and she needed to figure out what to say to him before she left.

Her sneakers squeaked on the grass as she paced. Nerves jumped in her stomach when she recalled their good-night kiss in the truck after their date. She could still feel Jason's arms around her, smell his subtle aftershave, and taste his warm lips. The enclosed front seat of his truck had become their private refuge. She hadn't wanted to leave, fearing reality would rush in and break the spell between them.

Now in anticipation of seeing him again, the same weak-in-the-knees sensation swept over her. At the same time, a bubble of joy threatened to burst up through her throat.

A taste of her dream was not enough. She had to find a way to let Jason know how much he meant to her before she left, give him something to look forward to when she came back. Despite her fear, she planned on telling him she was falling in love with him. He needed to know that she had a serious stake in this relationship, and that she would definitely be coming back to Rainbow Falls, at least until she could figure out how to make all the pieces of her life fit together.

Because even if she had to take a mallet to them, she'd make them fit.

Just then Jason's truck roared into the driveway and slammed to a halt. He jumped out without turning off the engine. The scowl on his face threw a momentary damper on Maxi's plans. The bubble of joy deflated like a leaky balloon.

"Hey." He barely glanced at her as he picked up her bag and hefted it into the back of the truck. He opened the passenger door and waited for her to get in. The blank expression on his face caused prickles of alarm to skittle down her back. If she wasn't sure Peg was watching from the window, she'd have laid a huge kiss on that handsome face to make him smile.

"You OK?" she asked instead.

"Great." His face was carved in stone. "Let's go."

In the time he took to round the end of the truck, Maxi tried to think of what she could have done to make him angry. True, he wasn't thrilled she was going to New York, but he swore he understood and that he was OK with it. What else could have happened?

The truck vibrated with the force of Jason's door slamming shut. He didn't even bother to put on his seatbelt but threw the vehicle in reverse and gunned out of the driveway.

After a few miles of silence, Maxi took the bull by the horns. "What's up with you? Bad day at the station?" She prayed that's all it was.

"You could say that."

His terse answer did nothing to help her. She opened her mouth to ask another question when he shot her a dark look. "I don't want to talk about it. Let's get you to the airport."

Maxi swallowed hard. Why did this somehow feel personal?

Very personal.

The hour-long drive to the airport felt like five. Maxi stewed the whole time, wondering what had happened to make Jason so miserable. Had he decided their relationship was not what he wanted after all? She found herself lifting a silent prayer for him not to close his heart. Not after she'd finally had a taste of what romance Jason-style could be like.

God had answered when she'd prayed for

Lily and the baby. Maybe he'd listen to her now. Her mind raced as she tried to form the right words, to put her plea into some semblance of clarity. All she could manage was *Please, God, please.* A few miles outside Bismarck, Jason suddenly pulled over to the shoulder of the road and shut off the engine. He sat staring over the steering wheel, not looking at her. Dread squeezed Maxi's stomach. This didn't seem like a romantic stop over before leaving. Something else was going on.

Courage failed her, rendering her silent. She couldn't bring herself to ask what was wrong. He'd have to bring it up himself.

Finally he heaved a huge sigh and turned to look at her. The abject misery in his eyes scared her more than any display of temper ever could.

Her palms slicked with sweat. "Jason? What's wrong?"

"I'm so sorry, Maxi."

She tried to swallow, but the lump in her throat prevented it. "Sorry about what?"

He was breaking up with her. She knew it.

He scrubbed a hand through his hair. "This . . . whatever it is between us . . . isn't going to work out after all."

Searing pain sliced through her chest,

more intense than the stab of a knife. She clutched her hands together in her lap to keep them from shaking. "Why? Did I do something wrong?"

He turned to focus on her face, which she knew had gone white. "No. It's nothing to do with you. It's me —"

Fear morphed into explosive anger. "Don't you dare say 'It's not you. It's me.' That's the oldest brush-off in history." Her hands itched to slap some sense into him.

Then she saw the sheen of moisture in the corner of his eyes. Her breath lodged in her lungs, her mind whirling with horrible possibilities. Was Jason sick? Or worse, dying?

Jason straightened against the seat, hands clenched on the steering wheel. "Gloria's pregnant with my baby."

Maxi's mouth dropped open. She blinked once, then twice. Nothing could have prepared her for that statement. As her mind struggled to grasp what he'd said, white noise buzzed in her ears, muffling every sound. Jason's lips moved, but she couldn't hear a word he was saying. The air in the cabin seemed suffocating. She had to get out of the car. She needed air, or she'd die right here in the front seat of his truck.

The handle stuck, then the door flew open, and she almost fell out onto the gravel. Blindly she ran down a gulley, then up into a clump of trees. Faster and faster her sneakers flew, as if trying to outrun the panic that throbbed in her temples. A gnarled tree root caught her foot, sending her sprawling onto the earthen floor. Pain shot through her leg. She moaned and lay still, not having the strength to get up, not caring about the dirt on her hair and in her mouth.

Jason had created a child with that . . . woman. How could he have been intimate with her?

Betrayal stung worse than the pain in her ankle. She lay there for several minutes until she heard footsteps pounding toward her. Strong arms lifted her to her feet and brushed the grime from her face.

"Don't cry, Maxi. Please."

She wiped her forearm across her cheek, surprised by the wetness there, and stepped back to stare at him.

A sickening thought crossed her mind. Had he been sleeping with Gloria all the time she'd been here? Surely he wasn't that low. "When did this happen?" Her voice came out as a croak.

Crimson bled up his neck. "Months ago. I realized it was a huge mistake right after it happened. I broke up with her the next day."

Maxi's breath came in choppy gasps. "Why did she wait so long to tell you?"

He raked his hand through his hair. "She says she didn't realize until a few days ago. She took a home test, and it came back positive."

The buzz of anger burned through her. "She's probably been with several guys since then. How do you know it's even yours?"

"She swears there's been no one else since."

"And you believe her? That lying —"

His finger on her lips silenced her. "Yes, I believe her. I've never seen her this upset."

Maxi wrenched away and then forced herself to take in two deep breaths. Forced her mind to slow down and focus on the problem. A child would be a complication, but not one she couldn't handle. She raised her eyes to his. "This doesn't have to be the end. If a DNA test proves you're the father, I know you'll provide for the child. And I understand you'd want to be part of its life. We can work around this."

Instead of looking relieved that she could accept his child from another woman, from one of her worst enemies, in fact, Jason paled. "I'm going to marry her, Maxi."

His quiet voice and steady eyes told her

he was deadly serious. She bit her bottom lip that had begun to quiver. "No. You don't mean it."

His brows shot together in a fierce scowl. "I won't let a child of mine grow up without a father. The way I did."

"You'd still be part of his life. You don't have to marry *her* to do that." Her body shook from repressed emotion, a toxic blend of anger, hatred, and betrayal.

"Yes, I do. I never planned on having a child, but now that it's a reality, I *will* be a father in every sense of the word. My child will have the family stability I never did."

"Stability?" Her tone bordered on hysterical. "You think you'll have stability with that man-hopper?"

The veins in Jason's jaw popped from being clenched so hard. "I'll make it happen."

Shallow breaths moved in and out of her lungs. She knew that look on his face, the inflexible set to his chin. He'd made up his mind and nothing would change it. Defeat crept over her like fog over water. "Well, I guess Gloria got what she wanted all along. She finally got you."

Maxi started to limp toward the road.

He caught up with her in two seconds and grabbed her arm. "Please believe me. This is not what I wanted. But it's the way it has to be. I'm so sorry, Max. I have no choice."

At that moment, she felt his anguish as keenly as she felt her own. "You always have a choice, Jason. You're just making the wrong one."

Their eyes remained locked for one heartbreaking moment where hope leaked out of every pore and drifted away on the breeze. Jason lifted one finger to touch her cheek, but she moved aside and shook her head. "Don't." She bit down hard on her bottom lip, determined not to give in to the torrent of pain that threatened to erupt.

Her gaze dropped to the fullness of his lips — lips she would never again kiss — noting that they also trembled. But the stubborn set of his jaw told her he wouldn't change his mind.

"Come on. You're going to miss your plane," he said.

Her daydreams of a life with Jason swirled up and evaporated into the clean country air. Suddenly the noise, crowds, and pollution of New York became the exact distraction she needed to once again escape the pain of Jason's rejection.

This time permanently.

23

Seated in Philippe Baronne's office the next day, Maxi fought to clear her mind of every thought, every emotion, to keep her mind a blank slate.

She'd cried herself out on the flight to La Guardia yesterday, much to the apparent consternation of the flight attendants. But at least they'd left her alone, curled up in her window seat for the duration of the flight. When the plane landed, she walked out of the airport with her carry-on bag and hailed a cab, feeling like a person underwater, where everything appeared muffled and slow moving. Once she got to her apartment, the crushing depression magnified. There was no way she could face Philippe in this condition. So she'd called, told him she was in New York as promised, but felt ill after her trip. Although annoyed, Philippe had grudgingly agreed to meet with her the next day. A twelve-hour reprieve. Could she pull herself together enough in that time to convince her boss of her suitability as a partner?

Now, after waiting in his office for twenty minutes, Maxi didn't know how much longer she could keep up the façade of calmness. If Philippe didn't come in soon, she'd crash and burn like the Hindenburg.

"Maxi, there you are. At last." Philippe burst through the door in his usual exuberant style, dressed impeccably in a gray pinstriped suit. He bent to kiss both her cheeks. "I trust you are well?"

The question made her want to laugh out loud. Only the fact that she would appear unbalanced made her choke back the response. "Fine. What did you want to see me about so urgently?"

He paused to look down at her with narrowed eyes. "You say 'fine,' but I say no. Not fine. You have dark circles, and you've been crying." His expression changed to concern. "Your *maman* is worse?"

Maxi's gaze slid to her lap. "No, in fact she's doing much better."

"Then what is wrong, *chérie*?"

Part of her longed to pour out her problems to him, the other part knew it would be professional suicide. She lifted her chin. "Nothing I can't handle. Now, why did you summon me here?"

One eyebrow rose a fraction. "You need to ask?" With the grace of a gazelle, he slipped around his desk and into his leather chair. "I'm supposed to make a decision about the partner, and I have heard nothing from you. Forcing me to ask, are you still interested in the partnership, or should I simply award it to Sierra?"

Even though Maxi knew he was baiting her, irritation prickled under her skin. Her temper roused to life, breaking through the fog of depression for a brief moment. "Of course I'm still interested. And what do you mean you haven't seen anything from me? Didn't you get the pictures I e-mailed to you?"

"*Quoi?* What pictures?"

Unease stirred in her chest. "Two stunning women, among others. Lily, a gorgeous brunette, brown eyes, an elegant up-do. The other a young blonde, model-like, with a trendy cut *'a-la-Maxi.'* I sent them to you over a week ago."

Why hadn't she followed up with him to make sure he'd received them?

Philippe's chiseled face, normally as easy to read as a tabloid cover, now froze. "It cannot be . . ."

"What's wrong?"

Without a word, he pulled open a drawer and took out a file folder. His well-manicured fingers pulled out two eight-by-ten headshots.

Relief spread through her stiff limbs. "You did get them. I think they're some of my best work." She pulled the shot of Dora Lee toward her. "Especially this one. I couldn't believe the transformation." She looked up to see his reaction, but his forehead, wreathed in wrinkles, did not ease her mind.

"What's wrong? You don't like it?"

Without a word, Philippe rose and walked to the window. "I should have recognized it. I wondered how Sierra's work had improved by such a degree."

Maxi shot out of her chair as a red-hot burst of anger spurted through her system. "Are you telling me Sierra is taking credit for these?"

His silence told her everything.

"How is that possible?"

"I do not know. She submitted these as part of her portfolio."

Maxi paced the room as her brain whirled with possibilities. Sierra must have intercepted the e-mail before Philippe had seen it. The desire to rip Sierra's honey hair out of her head rose like an inferno inside her. Not only had the viper stolen her clients, she'd stolen her photos as well. Maxi gripped her hands together to keep from hurling one of Philippe's statues across the room.

"I can prove they're mine. I have the pictures on my camera. I can —" She paused to gain a measure of control. "Sierra must be really insecure to stoop this low. Hacking into your e-mail account." Maxi crossed her arms over her chest and tapped a foot on the carpet. "The question is, Philippe, what are you going to do about it?"

He turned to give her a thoughtful stare. Maxi waited, certain he'd throw Sierra's sorry butt out of the salon. For starters, Philippe didn't tolerate dishonesty or manipulation, never mind hijacking his personal e-mail. She smiled smugly to herself. The partnership had just been handed to her on a silver platter.

"I will have to consider the situation and give you an answer in the morning."

Disbelief made Maxi's jaw drop. Once again the fuse to her temper licked to life with white-hot ire. "What is there to consider? She stole my clients and my portfolio." Maxi hated the way her voice rang with a hint of hysteria. "You're not going to let her get away with it?"

Philippe's mouth formed a grim line. He

walked to his desk and sat down, an action Maxi knew was a form of dismissal. "I will talk to you in the morning."

Betrayal by someone like Sierra was not unexpected. But this cool dismissal by her mentor cut deeply. Coming so close on the heels of Jason's rejection, Maxi's wounds sat open and raw. She swallowed her hurt and stiffened her spine, allowing anger to form a covering of armor-like steel around her. "Just so you know, I'll be contacting my lawyer. To protect my interests in this . . . matter. You may be willing to forgive Sierra, but I most certainly am not."

Slamming Philippe's door on the way out did little to release the pressure valve of her temper. Maxi stalked down the hall, her footsteps rattling on the tiles like gunfire. She almost hoped she'd run into Sierra. At this particular moment, she felt capable of anything. A good physical fight might ease the tightness in her chest.

The object of her ire happened to breeze in the double glass doors of the salon as Maxi entered the foyer. Maxi zeroed in on Sierra's confident sashay, and bee-lined toward her with single-minded purpose. She stopped inches from Sierra's surprised face.

"You stole my clients and my portfolio

pictures," Maxi hissed through clenched teeth.

Sierra recovered her poise quickly. "I don't know what you're talking about." She moved to go by her, but Maxi clamped a steely hand on her arm.

"You know exactly what I'm talking about. And now Philippe knows, too. Tomorrow my lawyer will be here to make sure we're all on the same page."

A sheen of perspiration formed on Sierra's perfect nose. "You're insane."

The superiority of her tone broke the last thread of control. The urge to strike out at her tormenter burned hot in Maxi's veins.

Love your enemies and pray for those who persecute you, a voice in her head whispered.

Maxi froze, her body vibrating with repressed rage. She forced herself to breathe in and out, and to think about the potential consequences of attacking Sierra. She dropped her hand in disgust. No, she wouldn't stoop to physical violence. Instead she curled her hand into a fist so tight that her nails pierced her palms.

"You won't get away with this." Each breath puffed out through her widened nostrils. Then before Maxi could act on her baser impulses, she stormed out through the main glass doors. Not bothering to wait for the elevator, she tore down the stairs to the lobby below.

A bubble of pain lodged in her chest as she strode down Fifth Avenue, but she would not allow it to burst in a torrent of tears. She was done with useless crying.

From now on, Maxi would take fate into her own hands.

24

A jackhammer thundered outside Jason's bedroom window. The pounding in his brain matched the intensity of sound coming from beyond the wall. Jason grimaced as he turned over in bed and pulled the pillow onto his face, making matters worse. The familiar scent of Maxi's perfume lingered on the pillowcase. He probably should've gone down to the cot in the basement. Like the bottom-dwelling creature that he was.

After a few minutes, it registered that the noise emanated from the kitchen. His mother was wreaking havoc with the pots and pans, which meant something — or someone — had royally ticked her off. It had been a long time since Jason had gotten so drunk. Now he remembered why he stopped drinking altogether. Nothing was worth the after effects. Not even the momentary dulling of the pain.

Because the torment always returned in

the morning. Along with one heck of a hangover.

The door to his room flew open and crashed against his wall. Pain shot through his temple into his left eye.

"Are you planning on getting up anytime soon?" Ma stood in the open doorway, hands on her hips. "It's after nine in case you're interested. Nick's already phoned to see what's wrong."

Jason groaned and tried to sit up. The throbbing in his head spiked exponentially. "Do you have to yell?"

Her mouth settled into a thin line. She crossed her arms. "It's been some time since I've seen you in this condition. I thought you'd sworn off liquor."

He swung his legs over the side of the bed and dropped his head into his hands, elbows resting on his knees. "I had . . . have. Got any aspirin?"

Instead of going down the hall to the bathroom, his mother sat beside him on the mattress. He opened one eye. Ma sat on the end of the bed, a worried expression on her face.

"Did you and Maxi have a fight before she left?"

A fight? He squelched the sick urge to laugh hysterically. "You could say that."

"Must've been pretty serious to make you hit the bottle."

He was in no shape for this type of conversation, but he knew his mother. She'd never let up until she had the truth. He sighed. "I ended our relationship."

"What do you mean, *ended*? You'd hardly begun."

He scrubbed a hand over his stubbly jaw. "There's a lot you don't know, Ma. If you get me some aspirin, I'll tell you the rest."

And break your heart in the process. Just like I broke Maxi's. Seemed he was destined to take after his father after all.

Ma rose slowly from the bed. "All right. But you're going to tell me everything. And we'll find a way to fix this."

After she left the room, Jason reached for his discarded jeans and pulled them on over his boxers. When he was little, he'd always believed his mother could fix anything. If only that were the case.

For the first time since the whole Gloria mess started, Jason bowed his head and prayed. Prayed for forgiveness. Prayed he was doing the right thing.

Later that afternoon, after coming up with a plan for one measure of atonement, Jason signed his name with a flourish on the bank documents before him. He'd taken steps to secure a loan to buy the North property. Sold his beloved Harley to use the proceeds, as well as the balance of his savings account, for a good down payment. He pushed aside the pang of loss. Responsible fathers didn't ride motorcycles anyway.

Jason laid down the pen on the bank manager's desk and took a deep breath. Maxi would probably hate him even more when she discovered he was buying her family home. But selling the farm was one of the major hurdles she needed to overcome in order to get back to her life in New York. And Jason could use the property for his own purposes. One day he would offer a parcel of land to the city in exchange for a promise to build the Rainbow Falls Fire Station. It was the perfect location. In the meantime, he'd keep the homestead as his own. Remodel it to suit his tastes and live there.

With Gloria and his child.

Here his plan hit a snag. He doubted Gloria would be thrilled about living out in the country in a refurbished farmhouse. But if she wanted him that bad, she'd have to take his choice of housing as part of the bargain.

It would kill Maxi, however, to know that

he and Gloria would share her old home.

No matter. The decision had been made. Bernice would get the proceeds of the property and be able to repay Maxi for the repairs she'd paid for out of her own pocket. Then Maxi would have the money she needed to buy her share of the partnership at the salon. She could move on with her life. And he could face his sentence with a semi-clear conscience.

Jason stood and shook hands with Owen Johnson. "Thank you for taking care of this, sir."

The portly man with a florid face beamed at him. "It's the least I could do for my future son-in-law." He gave Jason a quick wink.

Jason tried to muster a smile because it was expected, but his lips refused to move. "Thanks, again. I'll be in touch."

A cool breeze blew Jason's suit jacket out behind him as he stepped out of the bank and made his way down Main Street, his hands pushed deep into his pant pockets. With some time to kill before meeting with the real estate agent, he paused in front of the window of Norton Jewelers to look at the winking diamonds on display. He should probably seal his engagement to Gloria with some type of ring. The thought caused his stomach to clench in rebellion. Blood pounded a loud tempo in his brain. Pounding out the truth.

He wanted to buy a ring for Maxi.

Jason's shoulders slumped. He had to let go of that fantasy and focus on his child. For the baby's sake, he needed to find some way to make a life with its mother. No matter how impossible the challenge seemed.

He continued walking toward his truck parked in front of the hardware store. His footsteps slowed as he made out the familiar figure of Nick Logan leaning against the hood of Jason's truck, arms folded over his chest. A spasm of guilt and shame rushed through Jason's system. What would his friend think of him now?

"Afternoon, Jason." Nick pushed away from the truck, his blond hair ruffled by the breeze.

Jason nodded, lowering his gaze to the sidewalk. "Hey, Nick." He headed right around to the driver's door and unlocked it. "How are Lily and the baby?"

He almost choked on the word *baby.*

"Doing great. You should drop in and see them. I know Lily'd like that."

"I'm at your house all the time working. I see them then."

"True. But not much time for friendly

conversation. We'll have you over for dinner one night." Nick shifted position, eyeing him over the cab of the truck. "Actually, I'd like to speak to you about something."

Jason glanced down the street at the people moving along the sidewalk. "Sure. Give me a call when you've got some free time." He pulled the door open, anxious for escape.

"How about right now?" Nick's clear gaze held a challenge.

Jason tried not to squirm. "Can't. Got things to take care of."

"Fine. I'll ride along with you then." Nick pulled open the passenger door and climbed in before Jason could get a word out.

Seeing no other option, Jason got in his side, plugged the key in the ignition, but didn't bother to turn on the engine. He stared straight ahead out the window. "Guess you've heard."

"Yup."

Jason gripped the steering wheel until his knuckles ached. He couldn't find the words to begin, so he stayed silent.

"Seems you've got yourself quite a dilemma." Nick's quiet voice held no anger, no recrimination. He simply stated a fact.

"I'm handling it."

"Word is you're going to marry Gloria."

"That's right." Jason couldn't help the defiance in his tone — not after having to defend his decision to his mother and Maxi and . . . everyone. "It's the right thing to do, Nick."

When Nick released a long breath, Jason dared to glance over at him. Sympathy swamped Nick's blue eyes as he shook his head.

"I'm not sure what's right in this situation. I do know you're not in love with her. You love Maxi, and I'm pretty sure she loves you, too. Has for a long time."

Jason jerked in his seat. "How do you know that?"

Nick blew out a breath that lifted a lock of hair off his forehead. "May Maxi forgive me for this, but I've been listening to her moan about you for years. How she wished you'd see her as more than a friend."

Jason's mind swirled. "Why didn't she ever say anything?"

"It's complicated. But I'm sure you have some idea about that, or you would have said something, too."

A prickle of irritation itched his neck. "I didn't know I loved her until recently."

Nick quirked a brow. "Really?"

Jason scowled. "OK. Fine. Maybe I didn't want to know. Wasn't ready to know. But that doesn't change anything. I'm going to be a father now, and I have to take responsibility."

"I expect you're dealing with a lot of guilt at the moment. Maybe this is your way of punishing yourself for your mistake."

Jason clenched his fingers tighter on the wheel, mainly so he wouldn't lash out at his friend with misplaced anger. Anger at himself for being so stupid. "I never wanted to be a father. But since it's now a reality, I will do right by my child."

"Unlike your father."

Jason turned to glare at Nick, who didn't blink.

"You want to punch me right now. I get that. It won't help though. Trust me."

Jason sagged as the anger seeped away. His hands fell away from the wheel. "I'm sorry I let you down, Nick. Sorry I let Maxi down, my mother down, God down." He swallowed to push the ball of emotion back.

Nick laid a hand on his arm. "You know none of us, including God, loves you any less. Well, maybe Maxi, but she'll get over it eventually. Everyone makes mistakes in life. It's how we handle our mistakes that defines who we are."

Jason swiped at the moisture rimming his lashes. "Which is why I'm marrying Gloria and raising my child, like a responsible adult."

Nick sighed. "Have you even talked to God about it, Jason? Laid it at His feet and asked what He would have you do?"

Jason stiffened. "No." In fact, he'd barreled through with his decision, sure he was doing the right thing. Didn't want to hear otherwise.

Nick smiled, his expression sad. "Isn't this the time you should be doing that? Like I said before, I don't have the answer to your dilemma. Only God can give you that. Just know I'm here for you, as your pastor and as your friend, anytime you need me."

Jason clenched his teeth together until his jaw ached, and then turned and nodded. Nick had a valid point. "Thanks. I'll keep that in mind."

At 7:00 AM the next morning, Maxi rose and showered and then repacked her small bag. Sometime during the sleepless night in her apartment, cold calculation had replaced the anger in the pit of her stomach. She was tired of waiting for outcomes, tired of taking what fate threw at her, tired of waiting for prayers to be answered. Today, she would create her own destiny.

By nine o'clock, she had phoned her

lawyer, a colleague of Lance's, whom she trusted as much as she could trust anyone. He agreed to meet her at *Baronne's*. She then booked a seat on the afternoon flight back to North Dakota. Once she'd taken care of business at *Baronne's,* she needed to go home and deal with a few outstanding issues there.

Keys in hand, she opened the door to leave her apartment when her cell phone rang. She drew in a sharp breath. Could it be Jason calling to say he'd changed his mind? That he couldn't live without her?

Disappointment crashed through her system when she read the display. It was Myra Goodwin, her real estate agent.

"Well, hello there. Have I got good news for you." The woman was inordinately cheerful for such an early hour.

Maxi gave a harsh laugh. "I could use some good news. What is it?"

"We have a buyer for your property. A firm offer, slightly above the asking price." Her voice could not contain her enthusiasm. "I took the paperwork to your mother, and of course, she accepted it. Thought you'd like to hear the news right away."

An offer? Maxi pinched the bridge of her nose. "What about the possible arson charge? And rebuilding the barn?"

"That's the best part. Because of the offer, I spoke with Chief Hamilton and the report has come back. Insufficient evidence for arson. The most likely cause is combustible rags your father left in the barn. They've ruled the fire accidental. And the client doesn't want the barn rebuilt anyway."

Maxi's brain whirled, trying to take in all the information at once. One glaring fact jumped out at her. She found it very hard to believe this "magical offer" had happened the moment she'd left for New York. Suspicion dampened her response. "Who is this mysterious buyer?"

Ms. Goodwin's perkiness waned for a moment. "Since you're not a party to the contract, I'm not at liberty to relay that information. You'll have to speak to your mother about that. But I can tell you that most of the monies will be paid in cash. Mr. Johnson at the bank has assured me he is personally handling the approval for the small loan necessary to purchase and to renovate the home."

Maxi stiffened. Gloria Johnson's father? What did he have to do with this? The president of the bank didn't usually get involved in real estate deals, did he?

Unless it had something to do with his daughter.

"You don't seem too excited." Myra sounded hurt. "I thought you'd be thrilled we'd sold without needing the repairs."

"I have an idea who put the offer in, and you're right, I'm not thrilled at the prospect. I'll call you when I get back to discuss this further."

She disconnected before Myra could reply. What was Jason up to now? Whatever it was, she'd get to the bottom of it. But first she had someone else to put in her place.

With a sharp click, she closed the apartment door behind her and headed to *Baronne's,* mentally preparing for more than one battle that day.

25

Jason allowed himself a brief moment of happiness as he walked back from the east pasture of the North farm — correction, soon to be his farm — and let the pride of ownership color his view of the land. The lush greenery, waving fields of wheat, and rich black earth provided a great backdrop. It reminded him of a landscape painting, except that he could smell the mixture of manure and earth in the air, feel the warm breeze in his hair, and the soft give of the dirt beneath his boots. He allowed his mind to wander for a minute, daydreaming of what else he could do with all this land besides giving a portion to the city for a fire station, which wouldn't happen until he'd paid off the loan on the property.

Maybe he would run a small farm here as well. He could continue to grow the crops Charlie had started. Maybe plant a large vegetable garden. Keep up the chicken coop. A smile teased his lips at the prospect until he turned to look at the now-repaired homestead. The reality of just who he'd be coming home to each night slammed into his brain with the force of a fireman's axe.

How could he face sleeping in the same bed as Gloria every night, having to make love to her, when he'd only be thinking of Maxi? The air squeezed out of his lungs, making it difficult to draw a breath. He shoved his fists into his pockets. He couldn't think about that right now or he'd go crazy.

The sound of tires crunching over the gravel in the driveway filled the air. Who would be coming out here? The real estate agent? A hand over his eyes shaded the blinding sun, allowing him to make out the beat up Oldsmobile slowly approaching the house. He didn't recognize the car. Curious, Jason walked toward it. He reached the steps to the porch as the car door opened. His father stepped out.

Jason's stomach muscles tightened. He hadn't seen Clint since the day at this hotel room, and he still wasn't sure how he felt about him. The whole ordeal with Gloria had side railed his thought process.

Clint took some tentative steps toward him. "Hello, son."

Jason dipped his head in silent greeting.

"Hope I'm not disturbing you. Peg said I could find you here."

Jason thought about telling him to leave, that he was too busy right now. But he knew it would be putting off the inevitable. Might as well hear him out and gauge his emotions as he went. At least now he didn't want to kill Clint the moment he saw him. It was progress of some sort.

"I can spare a few minutes. Come on up."

Jason mounted the stairs to the porch and motioned to the wooden chairs. Clint seemed to hesitate as if he shouldn't be there.

"Isn't this the old North property?"

"Not for long. I signed the contract to purchase, and Mrs. North accepted it today."

Clint's eyebrows winged upward. "You're buying this whole place?" His hand swept out gesturing toward the fields beyond.

"Yup. I hope to offer some of the land to the city — if they'll agree to build a fire station on it."

"A fire station?" Clint lowered himself slowly into the chair and smoothed out the creases in his slacks.

Jason braced himself for criticism.

Instead, approval glowed on Clint's face. "That's a mighty fine idea. God knows

282

Rainbow Falls needs one." He paused. "How are you going to manage all this?"

"I don't have all the details yet. But the fire chief is helping me drum up funding and support. Have to wait and see how it all plays out." Jason gave a rueful grin. "I'm also thinking about learning to be a farmer."

Clint whistled. "You got gumption, boy. I don't think I'd have the nerve."

The note of pride in Clint's voice gave Jason a warm feeling in his chest. He glanced over at his father. Clint had cleaned up quite well. Despite living in the fleabag motel, his hair was tidy, his moustache neatly trimmed. His clothes, though probably secondhand, were clean and pressed. "What are you doing for work?"

Clint looked out over the railing. "Mostly odd jobs for cash. Not too many places willing to hire an ex-con."

Jason nodded, staring out over the acreage. "I can ask around and see if there are any handyman jobs or cleaning needed at the fire hall or the church. Can't promise anything though." He didn't know where this offer had come from but found himself wanting to help his father. If Jason got him some legitimate work, it might help him get something better in the future.

"You'd be willing to recommend me?"

The naked hope on Clint's face made Jason cringe.

"Yeah, I could do that." He paused. "If you're willing to stick around a while."

Clint bent over his knees with his arms resting on his legs and twisted his hands together. When he spoke, his voice was gruff. "I didn't think you'd want me in Rainbow Falls. I planned on seeing you and then moving on somewhere else." He glanced over at Jason. "You wouldn't mind me living here? Working here?"

Jason pondered his question for a minute but knew in his heart what felt right. "I'd like you to stay. To see what kind of relationship we can figure out. I haven't had a father most of my life. I used to hate you for that." He swallowed hard. "But I've realized in recent days that everyone makes mistakes. I hope someday I'll be forgiven for mine. The least I can do is try to forgive you yours."

Clint swiped a hand over his eyes. "You'll never know how much that means to me, son."

Jason fiddled with the keys in his pocket. "Now that I'm going to be a father, it's changed my perspective on things."

"A father? You're kidding. With that cute little red head?"

A spasm of pain hit Jason in the stomach.

How he wished it were he and Maxi, married and having this baby. "No, another girl." He took a deep breath. "I hope you'll come to the wedding. It's going to be a simple ceremony in the next week or two."

Clint didn't reply, and when Jason turned to see why not, his father's stare bored right through him. "You don't love this girl, do you? You got her pregnant, and now you feel you have to marry her."

A flash of the old anger rose in Jason's chest. "It doesn't matter how it happened. My child will have a real family. He won't be a burden on his single mother, with no male role model in his life. If it kills me, I'll give him a normal family."

A mixture of sadness and what seemed like chagrin crossed Clint's face. "I know you're trying to do the right thing, son. And I admire you for that." He reached over and patted Jason's knee. "Whatever you decide, I'm happy to be part of your life. It's more than I deserve or expected."

Jason cleared the blockage in his throat. Every time he wanted to be mad at his father, Clint came up with the words to make him stop in his tracks.

Clint stood, stretched his back and smiled down at Jason. "I only hope I can make up for being a lousy father by being a terrific grandfather."

Maxi sat in the late afternoon shadows on the Johnson's wrap-around porch, partially obscured by the draping foliage of a large weeping willow.

The Johnson home had always been the envy of most of the town's residents. The stately structure reflected the prestige and position of the bank manager. Maxi remembered the late Mrs. Johnson had enjoyed playing hostess for many social functions at the estate while she was still alive, functions that Maxi and her family had never been invited to attend.

Now as she waited for Gloria, Maxi wondered what it would've been like to grow up in this beautiful house, pampered by two adoring parents, given everything she'd ever wanted, instead of living on a farm, largely ignored by her father and tormented by three brothers. Was it any wonder Gloria felt entitled to receive her heart's desire when she'd been given it her whole life?

Maxi rose from the white wicker chair, setting her jaw to remind herself what she was here for. She looked at her watch, then wiped her moist palms on her brown suede pants. She hadn't changed out of her best suit, vowing for once not to be intimidated by Gloria's wealth and air of superiority. She didn't expect Gloria to roll over and give Jason up. That was never going to happen. But Gloria's actions would reap some negative consequences, even if it only meant she'd find herself on the receiving end of Maxi's sharp tongue.

Just as Sierra had been today.

Maxi smiled to herself, recalling the brief moment of satisfaction when, intimidated by the presence of the lawyer Maxi had brought along, Sierra had been forced to admit she'd "mistakenly" included Maxi's pictures in her portfolio. The disapproval on Philippe's face had not matched his calm tone when he apologized to Maxi for the confusion and requested to speak to Sierra in private. Maxi wished she could've eavesdropped on that conversation.

She pulled out her cell phone to check for messages, hoping Philippe had come to a decision by now, but no messages appeared. Returning her phone to her purse, Maxi resumed her seat in the shadows of the porch. No matter what action Philippe now decided to take, at least she'd stood up for herself and hadn't allowed Sierra to get away with the fraud she'd intended.

Maxi drew in a deep breath, focusing her thoughts on another, more personal fraud she needed to deal with.

Fifteen more minutes passed, and she was about to give up her vigil when Gloria's BMW finally pulled into the long driveway. She screeched to a halt and got out with a swing of her long, blonde hair. Humming off-key, Gloria grabbed her purse and bags from the backseat and practically skipped up the stairs to the front door, her yellow skirt blowing out behind her. Maxi waited, motionless, while the woman fumbled with her keys to unlock the ornate front door. When Gloria bent to retrieve her packages, Maxi rose on silent feet, stuck her hands into her pockets, and stepped out of the shadows.

"Hello, Gloria."

The other woman gave a squawk of surprise and dropped one of her shopping bags. Her startled expression twisted into one of extreme displeasure. "You're trespassing on private property."

Maxi chose to ignore the remark. "I have a few things I need to say to you. I'd appreciate five minutes of your time." How did she manage to sound so civilized when her insides rolled with a mixture of nerves and anger?

Gloria stepped away from the door and set the rest of her belongings on one of the wicker chairs. She straightened and crossed her arms over her chest. "I take it you're not here to congratulate me."

"Not quite."

"I didn't think so. Jason and I are expecting a baby and getting married in less than two weeks' time. Nothing you do can change that, so go ahead. Say what you have to."

Maxi's stomach clenched as though someone had punched her. Hearing Gloria say it out loud felt like someone had rubbed vinegar into the raw wound of Maxi's heart. She took a deep breath and blew it out. "You've always been a bully, Gloria. All through high school, I suffered through your cruel jokes, your lies, and harassment. I guess I was as much to blame for keeping the game going. Until you did the meanest thing of all." Maxi's voice cracked. She stopped to shore her courage again. She would not break down in front of Gloria, no matter what it took.

Gloria at least had the grace to look embarrassed.

"Your article in the school newspaper was unforgivable. At the time, I was too grief stricken to do anything about it. Maybe I even believed it somewhere deep down. It's taken me years to forgive myself for that night, and now that I have, I want to tell you what a lowlife you were to print those lies about my brother's death."

Maxi had the brief satisfaction to watch Gloria pale beneath her fake tan.

"Is this all you want to do? Dredge up the past? I haven't got time for this." She made a move to open the door.

Maxi stepped in front of her, blocking her way.

"I'm not finished yet." She met Gloria's furious glare with a steely gaze of her own. "All those so called 'pranks' pale in comparison to what you're doing now to Jason."

Gloria's mouth fell open. "What I'm doing to him? He got me pregnant, and somehow *I'm* the villain?"

She was a good actress, Maxi had to give her that. Playing the outraged victim to the hilt. "You can drop the act with me. You may have Jason fooled, but I'd bet my entire savings account you're not pregnant at all. Or if you are, it's not Jason's baby."

Fear leapt into the other woman's eyes. "You can't prove any of that," Gloria sputtered. She pushed Maxi aside and went to grasp the door handle.

"You're right. I can't prove anything. That doesn't change the truth though. And the truth will come out eventually. It always does. I just hope you care enough about Jason not to ruin his life in the process."

For a moment, Maxi let herself feel the rage she'd kept under such tight control. She grabbed Gloria by the upper arm and jerked her around. "I'll be watching you. And if you hurt Jason, you'll regret it. That's a promise."

They stood nose-to-nose, anger and hatred mixing in the air between them. Maxi fought the urge to smack the lipstick off Gloria's smug lips. In an effort to regain control, she took one long step back.

"What's going on here?"

The loud masculine voice made her jump. Jason stood at the foot of the stairs, a thunderous expression darkening his face. How had she not noticed him arriving? Heat rushed into Maxi's cheeks, blood pounding in her ears. She wished the floorboards on the porch would part and swallow her. She hadn't wanted Jason to know she was back in town, let alone overhear part of her conversation with Gloria. Retreat became her only option. With one quick motion, she jumped off the porch to the grass below.

"Ask her." She jerked her head in Gloria's direction. "I'm sure she'd be more than happy to tell you all about it."

In two strides, Jason caught up to Maxi and grabbed her arm, halting her departure. "What are you doing here? I thought you were in New York."

She could smell the fresh scent of his soap, feel the warmth of his breath on her face. She struggled to maintain her composure and not throw herself into his arms. "I finished sooner than I expected and came back to help Mama finalize the sale of the house." An evil urge took hold. "Tell me, does your future wife know she'll be living on *my* farm?"

The shocked expression on his face told her exactly what she needed to know.

He ignored the question as she guessed he would. "Stay out of this, Max. It doesn't concern you."

The harshness of his tone tore a strip off her already bleeding heart. "You're right. I am so done with this whole situation. You can save yourself a stamp, and don't bother mailing me an invitation to the wedding."

She ripped her arm out of his grasp and took off at a run.

26

Jason ground his molars together and watched Maxi fly down the sidewalk. The sight of her on Gloria's porch, locked in a heated debate with his soon-to-be wife, had shocked him. He thought Maxi would be in the city for a few more days at least.

Jason turned and mounted the stairs to stand before Gloria, wishing he could turn around and go back the way he came. Because she clearly wasn't going to forget a word Maxi had said.

Sure enough, Gloria crossed her arms over her chest and frowned. "What did she mean by that comment?"

He feigned ignorance. "What comment?"

"About living on a farm? You don't live on a farm. You live with your mother."

This was not going well. He didn't want to fight with her right now. "That's right. But we'll find somewhere to live as soon as possible."

Her rigid stance relaxed a fraction. "Good. I've got a few ideas I want to run by you. There's this cute house on Greenmount Avenue —"

"We won't be buying a house." They'd be fixing up a farmhouse. He needed the right time to break that one to her.

She scowled, clearly not happy with the idea. He scanned the house behind him and realized anywhere they did live would be a big come down for her.

"I came by to discuss the wedding date."

She brightened at the change in topic. "Oh, good. I talked to Father Marcus at St. Peter's Church. After my father pulled a few strings, he's willing to marry us next Saturday. That should be enough time to get the bridesmaid dresses and the tuxedos —"

Panic grabbed his throat in a chokehold. "Whoa. Whoa. Wait a minute. Who said anything about a church wedding with tuxedos? City Hall will do fine."

An expression of horror flew over Gloria's face. "Daddy will not allow anything less than a church wedding. Our marriage has to be sanctified by God."

Nausea curdled in Jason's stomach. He wasn't getting married in the church with all the trappings. They'd have a simple wedding. Maybe Nick would marry them quietly with only a couple of witnesses.

Gloria planted her hands on her hips and stamped her foot. "I want a big church wedding."

Jason recoiled at her spoiled behavior. How would he live with her on a day-to-day basis? He took a deep breath and forced himself to think about the only thing that mattered in this situation. Forging a relationship for the sake of the innocent one they were bringing into the world. "I'll talk to Nick and see if he'll agree to perform a simple ceremony in his church."

A storm of emotions crossed her makeup-caked face. She looked like a petulant child unable to comprehend that she wouldn't get her own way. "I could take the baby away and never let you see him."

Jason whirled on her so fast she gasped. His fingers circled her arm in a steely grip. "I would never let you get away with that. I'd hunt you down to the ends of the earth if I had to." Anger had him shaking. He could see fear in Gloria's eyes and felt a twinge of regret.

"OK, fine. We'll do it your way. For now." She pulled her arm away and gave him a scathing look before disappearing through the front door.

He watched her go and then turned and slammed his fist against the portico.

What on earth had she been thinking confronting Gloria that way? Once again she'd come out looking like the shrew and Gloria, the victim.

Maxi gunned the accelerator allowing her self-loathing to express itself through her lead foot. The sight of the local police station brought a splash of cold water to her hot head, and she eased off the gas, mindful she was still within town limits. Running into Jason at Gloria's had unnerved her more than she cared to admit. She needed time to recover her equilibrium before facing her mother and Peg. She decided to head over to the farm to cool down and start packing.

Her tortured thoughts turned to Peg. How was she handling the news that Jason would be marrying Gloria? Maxi doubted she'd take it well. She bit her lip recalling the burgeoning hope on the two mothers' faces as she'd left for the airport and shook her head at how fast the world could change. How hopes and dreams could die in the breath of a word.

The farm seemed desolate as Maxi drove up and parked in front of the house. She took a moment to study her home, the dormer windows upstairs, the friendly wrap-around porch, the lonely window boxes full of her mother's wilting petunias. Even in its neglected condition, Maxi loved the old house. Why was it when she was finally getting rid of this place that her heart squeezed with sadness at leaving it behind?

She swallowed the lump in her throat. No time for silly sentimentality. She had work to do.

With fierce determination, she jogged down to the basement and dug out the stash of old cardboard boxes her mother always kept there just in case they needed them someday.

She hauled a stack up to the kitchen, deciding this was the best room to start in. Her bedroom had nothing left except the dismantled bed frame. The two spare rooms contained only a few pieces of furniture. So the main floor became the area to tackle.

She grabbed a stack of old newspapers from the basket by the fireplace and began to wrap dishes. She placed each item in the box with care, forcing herself to concentrate on the task at hand and not let her mind wander to self-pitying thoughts. Halfway through the second box, a knock sounded on the front door. Maxi jumped and almost dropped her mother's favorite casserole dish. Her heart rushed into her throat, half-hoping, half-dreading that Jason had found her.

She leaned over the kitchen sink to peer out the window. The sight of Nick on the front porch made the air whoosh out of her like a deflated balloon.

The front door creaked open. "Anyone home?"

"In the kitchen," she managed to call. She took a deep breath to settle her system before turning to give her friend what she hoped was a convincing smile. "What are you doing here?"

Nick paused to lean against the doorjamb and gave a sheepish shrug. "Jason called. He was worried about you after the incident at the Johnsons' place. Wanted me to make sure you were OK."

Maxi groaned and tore a sheet of newspaper, getting perverse pleasure from the loud tearing sound. "I suppose half the town knows about our fight by now. Don't people around here have anything better to do?"

"Apparently not."

She slammed some plastic containers into the box.

Nick came into the room and picked up a carton. "How 'bout I give you a hand here, and if you feel the urge to vent, my ears are available." He picked up a glass and wrapped it in newsprint.

Maxi continued to shred sheets of paper, finding a small measure of satisfaction in the destructive action. "I guess you've heard. About Jason and Gloria, I mean." She presumed everyone in town knew by now.

Nick nodded, his sympathetic blue eyes on her. "Yeah. I'm so sorry. Lily's all torn up about it, too. By the way, your presence is required at our house tonight. My wife won't take no for an answer."

Sudden tears stung the back of Maxi's throat. Tears of gratitude for friends like Nick and Lily. "Thanks. I don't think I could face staying at the Hanleys' tonight." She folded the flaps down on a full carton and set it aside.

Nick packed in silence for several moments. Maxi knew he must be dying to ask her questions, but he held back, waiting for her to begin. She loved him for that.

"Jason and I were getting along so great," she said at last. "I really thought he was starting to have feelings for me — as more than a friend, I mean. We even went on a real date. Then he blindsided me with this engagement." She stood back from the table to look at Nick. "I just don't see why he has to marry her."

Nick deposited a wrapped item into the box. "It's the honorable thing to do. And Jason is an honorable guy."

Maxi flung out her arms. "But it's wrong on so many levels. I confronted Gloria, Nick. I saw the truth in her face. She's lying to Jason. Of course, he shouldn't have slept with her, but she's going to make him pay for it for the rest of his life. This lie will turn Jason's world upside down. This *honorable* man will be stuck in a loveless marriage built on mistruth." Was she the only one who could see the reality of the situation? "Doesn't he understand he'll never be happy, and the child will suffer because of it?"

"He can't see it because of his own childhood." Nick's voice was gentle. "He'll have to come to that realization in his own time."

"There is no time. He's getting married next week." The finality of the statement tore away the last piece of the shield she'd placed over her heart. A rush of sorrow and loss raced through her torso. She turned away from Nick's gaze to reach blindly for a glass bowl on the counter. It slipped from her fingers and shattered into a thousand pieces on the kitchen floor. She stood paralyzed amid the debris. "I've made such a mess."

Nick steadied her with warm hands on her shoulders. "It's all right. I'll get a broom."

"My life is as broken as that bowl." Fat tears she'd tried so hard to repress rolled down her cheeks. Tremors seized her body, and she began to sway.

In one swift movement, Nick lifted her into his arms and stepped over the shards of glass. He carried her to the living room and sat her gently on the sofa beside him.

"It's going to be OK."

Taking advantage of the comfort he offered, she buried her face into his shoulder and let go of all the grief inside her. She'd lost Drew, her father, and now, in every real sense, she'd lost Jason, too. Nick said nothing but held her until the tears subsided.

"Does God hate me, Nick?" she whispered at last. "Is that why everything goes wrong in my life?"

He handed her a tissue to blow her nose. "God doesn't hate you, Maxi."

She finished wiping her face and shook her head.

"Maxi, I've known you a long time, and I've seen a pattern with you over the years. Subconsciously, you don't see yourself as worthy of happiness. Your guilt over Drew's death has colored everything in your life with a tainted brush."

She frowned, twisting the tissue in her hands. "That could be true." She gave a huge sigh. "I don't understand why he had to die, Nick. Why did God take Drew from us? What did we do to deserve that?"

Nick's arm tightened around her shoulders. "I don't believe God works that way." His voice was soft. "All kinds of bad things happen in life. Wars, sickness, accidents . . . God doesn't cause them, but He does help us get through them."

They sat in silence for a moment. "You've been angry at yourself — and at God — for a very long time now. Do you think you can forgive not only yourself, but God, too?"

The truth of his words jarred her. "I don't know how." She pushed off the sofa and paced to the fireplace where she stood looking at the urn containing her father's remains. "I've been so angry lately, Nick." She ran a finger over the etchings on the pewter container. "So angry I almost attacked two women who betrayed me. That's not how I want to see myself."

"How do you want *others* to see you?"

The sudden image of Dora Lee came to mind. She wanted to be the person Dora

302

Lee believed she was. "Someone people can look up to and respect."

Nick rose and came to stand beside her. "You're all that and more. Lily and I have chosen you to be Annabelle's godmother, because you're the type of person we'd like our daughter to emulate. We believe in you. Now it's up to you to believe in yourself. And how you choose to react to the bad circumstances in your life determines who you are."

The sincerity of his words reached into her soul and touched the truth within her.

"How do you choose to react to this, Maxi?"

Nick was right. She'd been reacting badly to both of the unfair situations in her life. Like a shrew, spewing anger and hatred in her wake. She bit her lip and then raised her eyes to meet his gentle regard. "I choose to rise above it. Not sink down to their level."

Nick smiled. "Good choice."

Maxi felt a weight lifting. "I told Jason he was making the wrong choice. But I'm doing the same thing. I need to make better decisions in my life. Follow God's plan for me."

"By George, I think you've got it."

Maxi laughed and then reached over to

give Nick a huge hug. "How'd I get so lucky to have you as a friend?"

Nick's cell phone buzzed saving him from answering. Maxi moved back and wiped her face with the remnants of a tissue.

"Hi, honey. Yeah, I found her. We're packing boxes at the farm." He handed the phone to Maxi. "Lily wants to talk to you."

As much as she wanted to hide out and not talk to anyone, Maxi knew she had to speak to her friend. "Hi. How's little Annabelle?"

"She's great. But how are you?" The genuine concern in Lily's voice caused more emotion to well up.

"I've been better."

"I can't believe that Gloria person. Now I know why you dislike her so much."

"Yeah, well, Jason's not blameless in this either."

"It's all so unfair." Lily sighed on the other end of the phone. "Nick told you about staying here, didn't he? Once Annabelle's in bed, we'll have a chance to talk this through and figure out —"

"There's nothing to figure out, Lil. The farm is sold. I'm packing up what I can, and I'm heading back to New York. Philippe is making his final decision today or tomorrow."

"I'm so sorry," Lily said again. A few seconds of silence followed. "Before you go back, can you do me one favor? Drop in and say good-bye to Dora Lee? She's been asking about you."

Maxi pushed the hair off her forehead. How could she have forgotten to call Dora Lee? "Sure. I'd like to say good-bye and wish her good luck. I need to see my mother first, though."

"Great. Then come here for a late dinner. I'll see you then."

Maxi ended the call and handed the phone to Nick with a watery smile. "Guess who's coming to dinner?"

After a quick but uncomfortable trip to the *Cut 'N Curl* to see her mother and drop off some real estate papers, Maxi headed over to the shelter to see Dora Lee. The stark sympathy on her mother's face, combined with the out-and-out sorrow on Peg's, had almost been too much to bear. Not to mention the stares and whispers of the ladies in rollers. Did the whole town know about her feelings for Jason?

Dora Lee greeted her at the doorway of the shelter with an enthusiastic hug. At least one person was treating her in a normal fashion.

"I'm so glad to see you. Come in." Dora Lee literally glowed. She'd kept her new hairstyle and was wearing neat, clean clothing. Not the baggy sweats Maxi had first met her in.

They walked into the living room where little Robbie sat watching a children's program on TV while he played with some toy cars.

"So much has happened. I couldn't wait to tell you. But Lily said you'd gone back to New York." The disappointment on her face made Maxi wince.

"I'm sorry I didn't call. I had to go for a quick visit to settle something." They both sat on the overstuffed couch. "Have they found you a new place to stay?"

Dora Lee grinned. "Yes. And the best part is, I'm able to stay in Rainbow Falls."

Maxi had never even let herself think about that possibility. Maybe that was why she'd kept herself from fully embracing a friendship with Dora Lee. "But what about Dennis?"

Dora Lee put her hand on Maxi's arm. "My lawyer told me that with you and Leslie to give evidence, it won't be only my word against his, and he'll most likely go to prison." She squeezed Maxi in a hard bear hug. "God brought you into my life. You've given me so much. I don't know how I can ever begin to thank you."

When Dora Lee pulled away, tears in the woman's eyes made Maxi jumpy. "I didn't do much except give you a couple of hair-styling tips."

"Are you kidding? You gave me back my confidence. You stood up to Dennis for me. You showed me how wonderful it is to feel good again. I look better. I feel better. My son is even improving. See how well he's playing."

"I'm not responsible for all that —"

"Yes, you are. Directly or indirectly." She laughed. "I'm going to hairdressing school, too. Lily and Leslie have offered to babysit during my class times."

The girl's joy was contagious. For one brief moment, Maxi set aside her own pain and let herself celebrate with this coura-geous woman. "I'm so happy for you. You two are going to be just fine."

"Yes, we are. The only thing better would be having you here to share it." Dora Lee stood and wiped her eyes. "Hey. Don't listen to me. I'm being selfish. You have your great job in New York. By the way, did you get the partnership?"

Maxi stood as well. "I'll find out soon. Within the next day or two."

"Well, I'm sure you'll get it. Those pictures you showed me were awesome."

They walked out into the hallway and paused by the front door, where Dora Lee hugged Maxi again. "I wanted to thank you for everything and wish you all the best. And whenever you come home for a visit, I'd be thrilled if you'd call. Maybe come over for coffee."

Maxi fought to speak from a throat that had gone bone dry. The simple beauty of this girl's friendship floored her. "Of course. I'd love to." She jerked her head toward the living room. "Tell Robbie I'll see him again soon. Maybe we can get some ice cream next time I'm home."

"He'd love that."

Maxi stepped out the open door and looked back over her shoulder. "And don't forget. I expect an invitation to your graduation."

Dora Lee's face shone. "You got it."

Maxi waved good-bye as she backed out of the driveway. She drove away slowly, marveling at the courage and faith Dora Lee had demonstrated. After all the girl had been through, she was picking herself up and starting a new life for herself and her son. If Dora Lee could be that strong, starting over from scratch and facing an uncertain future, could Maxi do anything less?

She smiled to herself, wondering how the tables had turned and the mentor had now become the pupil.

Before she drove to Nick and Lily's for the night, Maxi had one more important stop to make. A visit long overdue. She pulled up to the curb in front of the Good Shepherd Church, cut the engine, and sat trying to gather the will to do what she knew she must.

After several minutes, she pushed out of the vehicle and strode around the building to the cemetery situated behind.

Though she hadn't been here since the day of Drew's funeral, Maxi remembered the exact spot. Of course, the large stone monument topped with a cherub made it impossible to miss. Her steps slowed the closer she came. She bit down on her trembling lip as if to hold the emotion at bay.

The angelic smile of her younger brother stared back at her from the photo her mother had insisted on embedding in the tomb. She wished she'd thought to bring some flowers to lay on the barren grave.

"Hey, Drew. Bet you're surprised to see me here." A breeze lifted her hair from her forehead. "I guess Dad's up there with you now, and he's probably told you all about my . . . mistakes. You know how badly I messed up the night you died and how much I wish I could change what happened." Her voice broke. "But I can't change it. So I have to try to get past the guilt and move on with my life. I don't know if I can forgive myself, unless I know you forgive me." Tears leaked down her cheeks. "Can you forgive me, Drew?"

Her question hovered in the air then blew away on the breeze. Maxi shook her head. Did she really expect her brother to answer? She lowered herself to sit cross-legged on the grass.

"I'm so sorry, Drew. I was stupid and selfish, and I regret it every minute of every day."

She laid her head on her knees and let the sorrow drain out of her along with her tears. Finally she sniffed and wiped her face on her sleeve. "You know, Jason's got himself in a heap of trouble. Looks like we're not meant to be together after all. And I have to learn to live with that." She ran her fingers through her hair. "I guess I need to accept Jason's decision and move forward with my own life. With my career in New York. As long as I know you're OK and Dad's OK, and that you both forgive me, I think I might be able to do that."

With a quiet sigh, she waited in silence and listened to the sounds of nature around her. The lilt of the breeze, the cry of a bird overhead.

A thought whispered through her. Maybe it wasn't just Drew's forgiveness she needed.

She bowed her head. "Lord, I'm sorry for being so angry at You for so long. Please forgive me for that, and for my carelessness with Drew, my anger at my father, my neglect of my mother." She paused. "I need your help to let go of the hatred toward Gloria and Sierra. Change my heart, Lord. Let Your grace soften me, and help me accept your will for my life."

A sense of rightness filled her being. Slowly, a feeling of peace invaded her tense muscles. When she opened her eyes and looked up at the clear sky, she had to blink twice. Though not a cloud or hint of a storm threatened, a double rainbow streaked across the sky.

Maxi smiled through the remnants of her tears with calm certainty that God had placed the arc there as a sign for her. A sign of hope that everything would be all right after all.

For the first time, she believed it.

27

Two days after finding Maxi at Gloria's, Jason pulled his truck into the Johnson's driveway. He stared straight ahead, his mind and senses numb. Beside him, Gloria's inane chatter became a muted din in the background that didn't penetrate the fog he'd created around his brain. Now that they'd obtained their marriage license and made arrangements with Nick to do the ceremony, reality sank onto his shoulders like a two-ton load of bricks.

"I'll guess I'll see you tomorrow."

The change in Gloria's voice pulled him back into his body. She sat looking at him expectantly, waiting for something.

"Maybe. I have an evening shift at the fire station, though. So it may not be 'til the next day."

Her pouting plump pink lips left him cold. "You can at least call me."

"I'll try." His conscience twinged at his

less than enthusiastic response. Somehow he had to try harder to make an effort. He twisted in his seat to face her. "Look, Gloria. I need to be honest here. I can't pretend to be madly in love with you when I'm not."

Her face crumpled, lines appearing on her forehead.

"I want to make this work. But you're going to have to bear with me for a while." He paused. "With God's help, I'm going to try to be the husband you deserve and the best father I can to this baby. For now, let's start by being friends, and hopefully love will grow with time."

She studied him for a moment and then nodded. "I can be patient, Jason. After all, we've got the rest of our lives, don't we?"

She exited the truck and walked up the brick walkway to her porch, where she turned to give him a cheery wave before disappearing inside.

Jason scrubbed a hand over his face, Gloria's words echoing in his head. *We've got the rest of our lives, don't we?*

If ever he needed God's help, it was now. His mother was so distraught, she would barely speak to him. Bernice's quiet disapproval followed her chair every time she left a room. And Maxi . . . Well, Maxi would never forgive him. That was a given.

His chest contracted in a painful spasm at the thought. He rubbed an absent hand over the area before shifting the truck into reverse. A pink piece of paper on the floor of the passenger seat caught his eye. He pushed the vehicle into park and reached over to pick up what looked like an appointment card. It must have fallen out of Gloria's purse.

He turned it over and scanned the name. *Kingsville Family Planning Center.* Anxiety snaked up his spine as a hundred thoughts flew through his head.

He read the date on the card. Gloria had an appointment there in two weeks. Maybe it was just a regular pre-natal checkup. But a nagging sense of unease rippled through him. He searched his memory for something Gloria had told him and snapped upright in his seat. She'd said her obstetrician, Dr. Shepherd, worked out of the Kingsville Hospital. So what was she doing going to a Family Planning Center?

Doubts and suspicions swirled through the mist of his mind as he stared at the slip of paper. He had to get to the bottom of this — *now.* Tamping back his anger and confusion, Jason cut the engine and jumped out of the cab.

At that moment, Gloria appeared on the front porch, a confused smile on her face. "You're still here. Did you forget something?"

His feet became rooted to the spot like the ancient willow in the front yard. He swallowed and then slowly held out the appointment card. "You dropped this in my truck."

She came down the stairs, approaching him with wary hesitation, as though nearing a mad dog on a leash. Maybe his expression gave his thoughts away.

She reached out to take the card from his hand and her fingers brushed his.

"What kind of procedure are you having done at the Kingsville Family Planning Center?" The question erupted from him in a harsh accusatory tone. He hoped his blunt question would be enough to get her to tell the truth.

Horror filled her blue eyes. The cell phone in her hand clattered to the walkway and broke apart, the case flying into the grass.

He clenched his teeth together so hard his jaw ached. Her reaction told him it was nothing as innocent as he'd hoped.

"What are you talking about?" Clearly flustered, she bent to retrieve the fragmented phone.

"The appointment you have booked. What sort of procedure are you having done?"

She straightened, eyes wide. "You called them?"

"I did." He prayed forgiveness for this tiny lie to further his bluff.

A swatch of red bled across her cheeks. "How dare you —"

"I dare because it involves our child. Now answer the question."

Her whole body shook like a leaf in a windstorm. She bit her bottom lip and shrugged one shoulder. "Just one of those amnio things. A routine test."

Jason grabbed her arm, trying to control the urge to shake her until her teeth rattled. "Don't lie to me, Gloria. I know those tests aren't done until much later in the pregnancy, and they aren't routine. You're having an abortion, aren't you?"

Her mouth opened and closed. A film of tears formed in her eyes. She seemed incapable of answering him.

"If you don't tell me the truth, I'll go down to the clinic myself and get them to tell me."

She gasped. "You have no right —"

"No right?" A red haze obscured his vision. "I have every right. It's my child we're talking about here."

She wrenched away from him, causing red welts to rise on her skin. Tears now leaked down her cheeks. "It's my body. I can do whatever I want."

Outrage filled him until he thought he'd explode. "So you were going to marry me and then get rid of our child? And what? Pretend you had a miscarriage?"

She wrapped her arms around her torso and took one step backward, then another.

"I won't let you do this, Gloria. I won't let you get rid of our child like a piece of unwanted trash. I'll get a lawyer and a court injunction to legally prevent you from doing this."

Real fear and a spark of something else flashed across Gloria's pale face. "You can't do that. You have no legal rights because you're not the father." Her hand flew to her mouth as though she could recapture the words that had escaped.

His breath whooshed out like he'd been sucker punched. "What did you say?"

She stood, shaking her head.

He took a step toward her, adrenaline pumping through his veins. "I want the truth, Gloria. And I want it now."

She sank onto one of the porch steps, her shoulders hunched over her knees. Huge sobs shook her body, but he refused to feel

317

sympathy for her. Blonde hair fell like a pale curtain around her as she rocked back and forth.

Jason stood right in front of her, and despite the rage warring for release, softened his voice a notch. "Is this baby mine?"

After several beats of silence, she raised her wet face to look at him. "No," she whispered and buried her face into her hands, weeping inconsolably.

Jason stood rooted to the spot like one of the statues in their garden and let the words sink in. His mind could not comprehend the depth of her deception. "Whose baby is it?"

Her muffled reply was barely audible. "Marco's."

Another shaft of pain shot through him. She'd lied to him about Marco. His former best friend had finally succeeded in getting one of Jason's girlfriends to sleep with him. And now Gloria wanted him to raise Marco's child? How could she do this to him? "Why me? Why not Marco?"

She lifted her head again. "Because I love you, not him. I always have, Jason."

He gave a harsh laugh. "You have a funny way of showing it. Sleeping with my best friend."

"It wasn't like that. I turned Marco down

every time. Until after you dumped me. I felt so betrayed. So used. I wanted to get back at you for hurting me that way."

Remembering back, guilt and regret rose in his chest. Shame over his own failings had colored his thinking after that one night of indiscretion. He'd been convinced Gloria had seduced him on purpose and anger had him believing she deserved no explanation for his actions. He'd been mistaken.

"I'm sorry," he said, his voice gruff. "I never knew you had feelings for me. I thought it was all a big game to you."

More tears trickled down her cheeks. "I could never get your attention, Jason. When you finally asked me out, I was thrilled. But it wasn't long before I could feel you pulling away. I had to do something to keep you around. I thought if we slept together, you'd feel something for me, too." She gulped back a sob. "I wanted this baby to be yours."

He felt a tug of sympathy for her despite everything she'd done. The one thing he did understand was caring about someone so much you'd do almost anything.

"I'm sorry, Gloria. But you need to talk to Marco before you do something drastic. He has a right to know." He paused to gentle his voice. "And your baby has a right to live."

She bit down on her lip, staring at her hands twisted together in her lap.

He reached into his pant pocket, took out the marriage license, and ripped it in half. "Do what's best for your child, Gloria. Pray about it, and I know you'll find the answer." He should have taken this same advice — given to him by Nick.

Shoulders slumped, he turned back toward the truck.

"Jason, wait."

He looked over his shoulder to see her behind him on the walkway, eyes swollen in a pale face. "I do love you. Isn't there any way . . . ?"

He shook his head. "No, there isn't. I'm sorry, Gloria."

The misery on her face mirrored his own. For a few brief moments, Jason allowed himself to grieve the loss of a child he hadn't wanted in the first place.

28

Maxi fastened the cape around Madam Rothman's thin neck, thankful that at least one of her former clients had remained loyal.

She'd been back at work in New York for less than forty-eight hours and was still waiting for the thrill to return. She put it down to the lingering depression over losing Jason. Once her heart healed, her interest in her work would return. *It had to.*

"So what are we doing today? Highlights? Lowlights?" Maxi did her best to hide the dull ache in her chest behind a cheerful manner, however, she really didn't have to worry that her customers would notice anything amiss. Most of them were too self-absorbed to even consider she had a life outside the salon.

The aristocratic woman met Maxi's gaze

in the mirror. "No time for that, darling. Mr. Rothman and I have a soirée to attend. I need a fabulous upswing to match my new Vera Wang gown."

"No problem." Maxi tried to muster some enthusiasm. When had making rich, aging women look good become boring to her? An unbidden image of Dora Lee's enthusiastic face sprang to mind. With a sigh, she pushed the thought away and picked up a comb.

While Maxi worked her magic on Madam Rothman's silver tresses, Philippe entered the main salon. He stopped to speak with Sierra at her station. Maxi's gaze moved across the room and caught Cherise's curious look. Her eyebrows rose in a question as if to say 'What's up?' Maxi shrugged and continued her work before she earned another tongue lashing from Madame Rothman.

A few seconds later, Philippe crossed the room on a path toward her. Maxi's palms dampened as he approached. Had he come to let her know he'd made his decision?

"Bonjour, Madam Rothman. You look stunning as usual." Philippe flashed a wide smile at the woman in the chair, who actually blushed like a schoolgirl, despite the fact that she was at least fifteen years his senior.

"Why, thank you, Philippe."

He turned his attention then to Maxi. "When you're finished with your lovely client, I'd like a word with you in my office."

His expression gave nothing away.

"Of course."

"Bon." He bowed slightly and turned to march across the room.

"Is it me or is this something out of the ordinary?" Madam Rothman's shrewd eyes pierced Maxi's in the mirror.

She shrugged and picked up the hair spray. "Guess I'll find out soon enough."

"I hope you're not in trouble. Heaven knows Philippe has had enough complaints from customers about your long absence. But don't worry. I doubt he'd fire you."

Maxi ignored the woman's steely stare in the glass. Her attempt to pry some nugget of gossip from her wasn't going to work.

Ten minutes later, Maxi said good-bye to Lillian Rothman, pocketed her tip and mentally prepared for her meeting with Philippe.

"What's going on?" Cherise's conspiratorial whisper over her shoulder made Maxi smile.

"I'll find out in a few minutes. I have a

summons from the boss." She hoped joking would ease her building tension.

Cherise's wild perfume surrounded her as she gave Maxi a quick hug. "Good luck, sweetie. You deserve this promotion."

"Thanks. But don't celebrate yet."

Five minutes later, Maxi sat alone in Philippe's luxurious office awaiting his return after his personal assistant had shown her in. Instinct told her Philippe had made his decision and was about to reveal the new partner. She should be filled with anticipation, her nerves dancing with delicious delight. Instead, she sat in complete silence, feeling as wooden as the piece of artwork on Philippe's desk.

Today, the usually bright room was bathed in somber grayness. Rain dripped down the big picture window, obscuring the usual magnificent view, disguising it as one dark canvas. The weather matched her mood. Over the last few days, she'd done a lot of thinking about her conversation with Nick. She had to admit, she wasn't proud of her recent behavior. Striking out at Sierra and Gloria in anger had not been the right way to handle things. There was a difference between standing up for herself and wreaking retribution. Lashing out in anger made her no better than those who had hurt her.

She took a calming breath and vowed no matter how this scenario played out, she would accept her fate as part of God's plan. The events of the past several weeks made her realize she needed to turn control of her life over to a wiser force than she. To a God who knew what was best for her and loved her despite all her mistakes.

"Bonjour, Maxi. *Comment ça va?*" Philippe flew in like a proverbial tornado.

"Hello, Philippe." She mustered a brief smile. "Where's Sierra?"

"I will see her later. I want to speak to each of you alone." His sly grin told her he suspected a cat fight to erupt at the news he was about to impart.

Maxi didn't care. She'd rather hear the verdict without the smug Sierra present.

Philippe took his chair behind the chrome desk and opened a folder. He cleared his throat and looked over at Maxi.

Why wasn't her heart pounding? Her palms sweating? This partnership symbolized the realization of her childhood dreams. Everything she'd hoped for since those turbulent teen years. Yet she felt completely detached as she waited for Philippe to reveal his choice, almost as if she were watching someone else's life unfold.

"As you might have surmised, we have

made our choice for the partnership." He took a quick sip from a glass of water. "This has been a difficult decision. You both are strong, creative stylists with unique talents. You both bring many assets to our company." He paused and steepled his fingers together. He studied her for a moment as if wishing to draw out the drama. Then a huge smile broke out over his face. "I will not keep you in suspense. After much debate, I am pleased to tell you we've decided to offer the partnership to you, Maxi."

Her heart jolted in her chest. Her mouth fell open. Then she clamped it shut. She'd won the partnership despite all Sierra's tricks.

"Congratulations, Maxi. I have every confidence you will be a valuable asset to the *Baronne* team." Philippe stood and held out his hand across the desk.

She rose, still hardly believing what she'd heard, and shook his hand. Her knees quaked as a myriad of emotions washed over her. She'd actually done it. She'd shown her father she was worth something after all.

Except he wasn't here to see it.

She pulled her hand back and realized Philippe was waiting for her to say something.

"Thank you so much, Philippe. Your confidence means a great deal to me."

"It is well-deserved, *chérie.* Please sit. We have paperwork to fill out."

She sank onto her chair, willing herself to feel the joy she should feel at this most pivotal point in her life. Philippe opened a folder and shuffled some papers inside. As he did, the photo of Dora Lee peeked out at her. The beaming face of her new friend created a spasm of homesickness in Maxi's stomach. She pressed a hand to her midsection as if to settle the inner churning.

Why did she suddenly feel like she'd sold out on everyone who cared about her?

She thought about the years ahead, pandering to the likes of Madam Rothman, and a wave of nausea hit her. Perspiration streaked down her spine. This did not feel right at all. Almost without realizing it, she reached out and picked up the headshot of Dora Lee and then the one of Lily. She thought about the women she could help at the shelter, women who would really appreciate her input. Hot tears welled behind her eyes as a moment of clarity struck.

She'd achieved the goal she'd pursued with relentless zeal for the past two years, and now, she knew it wasn't what she needed anymore. She'd changed over the past few weeks, and her goals had changed as well. Her stomach roiled at the magnitude of the words she was about to utter.

She laid the photos down and looked up. "I want to thank you, Philippe. It has been such an honor to work here and mentor under your expertise." A slight frown appeared between his dark brows, and she released a slow breath. "Unfortunately, I must decline the offer."

She expected disappointment, hurt even. However, the anger that distorted his handsome features caught her by surprise.

"You dare turn down this opportunity after I have put so much faith in you? After you bring a lawyer here to fight your case?" Red blotches stained his cheeks.

She swallowed and gripped the arms of her chair. "Over the past few weeks, I've come to see that I belong in Rainbow Falls. It has nothing to do with your salon or how kind you've been to me."

"Kind? I have taken you from nothing and created the stylist you are today. Without me, you would be lucky to work at the Quick Clip on the corner."

Maxi absorbed his scorn, understanding its cause. She'd wounded his pride, and to a man like Philippe, his pride was everything.

"I'm truly sorry for disappointing you. I will always value my time at *Baronne's*. I hope, in return, you can respect my decision."

He pressed his mouth into a thin line. After several long seconds of silence, he blew out a breath. "There is nothing I can do to change your mind?"

"I'm afraid not."

She rose from her chair and held out her hand to him. It hung suspended in mid-air over his desk for a moment before he rose and shook it. The anger had lessened, but a certain coldness had set in. "I suppose I have no choice then. Good-bye, Maxi. I hope you will be happy back in your little town."

Happy? She doubted she'd be happy for a very long time to come — time she needed to get over Jason and heal from the disappointments of her past. "Thank you, Philippe. Give Sierra my congratulations."

Surprisingly, she meant it. One good thing had come out of all this — she'd somehow managed to let go of the anger that had simmered under her skin all these years. With Nick's help, she could now welcome God's hand in guiding her future. "I wish all of you nothing but the best."

She released his hand and walked with

calm certainty out of his office.

The closer Jason came to home, the bigger his grin became as realization finally dawned.

He didn't have to marry Gloria Johnson. The relief spilled over him like a tidal wave crashing to shore. The large boulder of guilt rolled off his shoulders, replaced by a bubble of joy rising through his chest.

He had to tell Maxi.

Jason hadn't been around much in a couple of days, afraid he'd run into her. Now he longed for the sight of her. The screen door banged shut behind him as he rushed into the house.

"Try not to rattle the windows." His mother looked up from her recipe book on the kitchen table with a scowl.

Jason only grinned harder and bent to kiss her cheek. "Hey, Ma. Any idea where Maxi is?"

Her mouth tightened. "She's gone back to New York. What do you expect with you marrying that Johnson girl?"

Maxi had gone back. He paused for a moment, letting the thought settle. Hadn't expected her to leave again so soon. No matter. A slight setback but nothing he couldn't handle. He opened the fridge door and pulled out a soda. "How long does it take to drive to New York from here?"

His mother slammed the recipe book shut and pulled her bifocals off her nose. "Why are you so happy? What's going on here?"

Jason popped the lid and took a quick swig of his drink, relishing the rush of carbonation in his mouth. Then he set the can on the table. His smile felt like it would crack his face in half. "I'm not marrying Gloria. The baby's not mine after all."

His mother let out one long whoop and jumped up, knocking over her chair. She threw herself into Jason's arms. He laughed out loud as he hugged her back.

"Alleluia. Praise the Lord. Praise the Lord." Her eyes glistened with unshed tears.

"I didn't know you were so religious, Ma." He winked at her.

"I am now." She hugged him again. "You have no idea how relieved I am."

"Oh, I think I have some idea."

She gave him a playful swat, and he laughed again. It felt so good to be able to do that.

"What's all the celebrating about?" Neither one of them had noticed Bernice wheel quietly into the open kitchen doorway. "Lord knows we could use something to celebrate right now." She looked from one to the other, an expectant expression on her face.

Jason knelt down in front of her chair and took her hands in his. "Mrs. North, I'm going to marry your daughter."

"Oh, my." She blinked as she tried to take his words in, and then a brilliant smile broke forth, creating a wreath of wrinkles around her eyes. "Can it be true?"

Jason grinned back. "Oh, yeah. Now the only thing I have to do is convince Maxi."

29

Maxi placed the treasured graduation photo of Jason inside the last box, closed the flaps and sealed it shut. It was a symbolic gesture, she knew, for packing away the past and preparing for the future, but it felt good nonetheless. She laid the roll of tape aside, and straightened to look around her New York apartment. All the furniture was staying, so other than the tiny mountain of boxes in the corner, the place would remain unchanged. She would miss this apartment, with its high ceilings and impossibly large windows overlooking the bustling street below.

She wiped perspiration off her damp forehead and peered down at her old gray sweats. A shower would be the next order of business. She'd been packing since she'd gotten up, and it was well past two o'clock. The image in the hallway mirror as she passed made her wince. Not a spec of makeup and her hair reminded her of a disheveled peacock. If Philippe could see her now, he'd most certainly rescind his offer.

She laughed aloud at the thought and headed through to the galley kitchen to get a drink. Despite the residual ache in her heart over losing Jason, she felt an unusual sense of freedom. It had taken achieving her life-long dream to make her realize it wasn't what she wanted after all. That and coming to terms with Drew's death after all these years. She finally understood she'd been running away from her father's disapproval as well as her own guilt.

Turning down the partnership had lifted a huge weight off her shoulders. She now looked forward to going home for good. Working with Peg at the *Cut 'N Curl* if she'd have her, and helping more women like Dora Lee at the shelter. That was where she'd found her joy and her true purpose in life. If she were honest, she never really belonged in New York. It would always be a place she loved to visit, but she couldn't live here. Not anymore.

She opened the fridge, grabbed a bottle of water, and then frowned at the loud knock on her door. She checked her watch. The landlord wasn't supposed to pick up the key and inspect the apartment until four o'clock. Oh well, he'd have to take her as is, sweat pants and all.

She peered through the little peephole just to make sure. Couldn't be too careful in the city. She blinked to clear her vision, and her muscles seized up like a victim of paralysis.

Jason?

Her unopened bottle of water slipped through her fingers and bounced off the hardwood floor. All the air seemed to evaporate from her lungs. She jumped away from the door as though Jack the Ripper stood on the other side.

Another knock, louder this time, echoed through the space.

What on earth was he doing here? And why did he have to come when she looked her worst? In a panic, she finger combed her hair and tucked her baggy T-shirt into her pants.

"Maxi. It's Jason. I need to talk to you."

The refrigerator motor knocked and sputtered in the kitchen, matching the knocking of her heart in her chest. She wet her dry lips, took a deep breath, and opened the door a crack. "Jason? What are you doing in New York?"

He stood smiling at her in the dim hallway light, his hair windblown over his forehead.

The familiar scent of his aftershave, his old battered leather jacket, and worn blue jeans all combined to overwhelm her with longing. He looked so good she wanted to cry.

"I've just driven fourteen hours to get here. Can I come in at least?"

Unable to speak, she stood aside to let him in.

He paused for a moment, then strode on through to the living room. His presence filled the space as he stood taking it in. Never did she dream Jason would show up here and be standing larger than life in her apartment.

He let out a low whistle. "Not bad." Then he noticed the boxes stacked in the corner and turned with a frown. "You moving?"

Shock made her mute. She couldn't bear to tell him the truth — that she'd given up her job and was coming home to Rainbow Falls with her tail between her legs, her big dreams nothing but an illusion. She ran her tongue over her lips and tried to pull herself together. "Why are you here, Jason? Shouldn't you be getting ready for your wedding?"

His expression turned serious. "Can we sit down? There are a few things I need to tell you."

He reached for her hand, but she snatched

it away. Instead she crossed the room and perched on the end of the stuffed armchair. Bracing herself for whatever Jason had to say, she folded her arms over her chest like a shield. Most likely he'd come to ease his guilt, to ask for forgiveness or some such thing. She wished he'd just say his piece and leave her alone.

He settled on the edge of the couch nearest her and leaned forward, his elbows on his knees. If she didn't know better, she'd say he was nervous. The way he clasped and unclasped his hands. The way he kept licking his lips.

Before he could say a word, the question that had been nagging at her burst out. "Why did you buy my parents' farm?"

He dropped his gaze to the floor for a minute as if contemplating his words. Then he looked into her eyes. "I figured it was the least I owed you."

Disbelief swirled through her system. "You bought my house because you broke up with me?" As well as she knew him, she didn't understand his logic there.

He shrugged. "You needed money for your partnership. I needed a home. It occurred to me that all those acres would come in handy and I could offer a portion to the city for a fire station one day. Seemed like a good idea all around."

The shard of pain in her heart dug deeper. "What about Gloria? I can't see her wanting to live in my old house." She still couldn't bear to imagine Jason living there with that woman and forced the terrible image from her brain.

Jason scrubbed his hand over his face. "Listen, a lot has changed in the past couple of days. That's what I came to tell you."

She tried to look away from his earnest eyes, but they drew her in like a magnet. What expression did she see there? Regret, guilt. Could it be hope?

She jumped to her feet and paced to the far side of the room. "Whatever it is, Hanley, just spit it out and go." She didn't care if she sounded rude. There was only so much nearness to Jason she could take right now. He needed to leave before she lost every shred of dignity and begged him to stay.

Jason rose from the sofa and let his pride and dignity fall away. He would take Maxi's rudeness, her disdain. He deserved all that and more. Maxi's slim back shuddered with pent up emotion, and fear crawled up his spine. How could he make her understand how much she meant to him? How his world wouldn't be complete without her in it? What if she couldn't forgive him and wanted no part of him? His hands shook so much he shoved them into his pockets as he closed the gap between them.

"Maxi, look at me, please."

She finally turned to face him with barely disguised anguish. "What do you want, Jason?"

He waited a beat until she met his gaze. "The baby isn't mine. It's Marco's. So I won't be marrying Gloria after all."

Her eyes grew huge and color seeped from her face. She raised one hand to cover her mouth but said nothing.

"I know this doesn't erase what happened, doesn't make up for the way I handled things, or my inappropriate relationship that led to this problem. I want you to know how sorry I am — about everything."

She stood stock-still, shaking her head. What did that mean? Was she refusing his apology? His chest tightened to the point that his breathing became labored.

"If you're willing to give me another chance, I'd like us to try again. I know how important your career is, and you shouldn't have to give it up for me. Once I get my firefighter certification, I'll move to New York. Try to get a job here." He paused for a breath, pushing back the fear that grew larger by the moment.

Her eyes darted around the room. "I — I don't know what to say."

He moved to stand right in front of her and pried one of her hands loose. Her stiff, cold fingers remained unresponsive in his. What was she thinking? For once, he couldn't read her. Panic fluttered in his stomach. He pulled out his trump card and prayed it would be enough to win her over.

"Maxi, the one thing I'm sure of after this whole fiasco is that I love you, and I don't want to lose you. No matter what it takes." Moisture impaired his vision. He didn't care; nothing mattered but what she would say. "I know it's a lot to ask, but I hope it's not too late for a second chance."

The vulnerability on her pale face made him want to wrap her in his arms and protect her. Make sure nothing ever hurt her again. A huge ball of emotion lodged in his throat, making speech impossible. Instead he reached out and caressed her cheek with his knuckles. Against the roughness of his fingers, her skin felt like velvet.

She closed her eyes and her whole body started to shake. When she covered her face with her hands and began to weep, he didn't hesitate for a second. He pulled her to his chest and enfolded her slim form against him. "Please don't cry. You know I can't take it when you cry."

His hands moved up and down her back. At last, the warmth of his body seemed to penetrate her stiffness. Her tears subsided. He pulled a tissue out of his pocket and gently wiped her face.

And waited.

Maxi took a cleansing breath deep into her lungs and blew it out. The fog seemed to clear from her brain. Had he really said he loved her?

"You — you're not marrying her?"

"No, I'm not. Can you ever forgive me for causing you so much pain?"

Hope began as a tiny bud in the pit of her stomach. She wanted to believe him, but she was too scared her lovely dream would burst like an overfilled balloon. As it had so often in the past. "I think so."

"Are you willing to give us another chance? This time with nothing blocking our way. Not my father, not Drew's death, not Gloria."

She took a step away from his intoxicating presence. It sounded like heaven. Her, Jason, and no baggage. She rubbed her hands up and down her arms. "You'd really move here?"

"If you want me to, I will. Whatever will make you happy, I'll do." The sincerity in his voice matched his eyes. He was laying himself bare for her. Laying his heart and his life on the line for her.

"I turned down the partnership." The words erupted out of her.

His mouth fell open as his eyes widened. "But why? That's all you've talked about for years."

The shock on his face softened her heart. He'd thought of her happiness first.

"It's not what I wanted after all."

He took a step closer. "What do you want, Max?" His voice was unbearably gentle. "Whatever it is, I'll get it for you."

She moved to the boxes in the corner and straightened the flap on the top carton. "I want a life in Rainbow Falls. Funny, isn't it? The thing I thought I hated the most is what I really wanted all along."

A tender expression softened his face. "And what about me?"

She watched the hope bloom in his blue eyes, overshadowed only by fear. With her answer, she held the power to make or break his heart. It was time for the truth at last.

"I love you, too, Jason," she whispered.

"I'd like to start over."

"Thank You, God." He sighed and stepped toward her. His hands framed her face as he lowered his lips to hers. She drank him in like a drowning woman. The familiar taste she never thought she'd savor again, the feel of his strong arms holding her, the smell of his leather jacket. Heat swirled up through her system, like steam rising off a lake.

Suddenly he pulled away from her. Dazed, she wondered what was wrong. He bent down, fumbling in his pocket to pull out a tiny blue box.

"I love you and want to share my life with you, Maxi. Will you marry me?"

She couldn't think, staring at the gleaming diamond encased in velvet. Everything was happening too fast for her to process. "It's a little soon for this, don't you think?"

The devastation that spread across his features shamed her. "I mean, we've only been on one official date. And you just narrowly escaped another marriage." A random thought crossed her mind. She pointed at the ring. "This isn't . . ."

"Of course not." He rose stiffly to stand before her. "I couldn't buy her a ring. Because I want to marry *you* — in front of God and everyone. It isn't too fast, Maxi.

343

I've known you since the first grade. I've loved you almost as long, only it took me a while to realize it."

She saw how much it had cost him to do this, to lay his heart open before her. Trust her with his soul. Marrying Jason was all she'd ever really wanted as far back as she could remember. Why was she hesitating now?

He pocketed the box. "You're afraid." His words came out as a flat statement. "I understand that. I haven't given you much to go on all these years." Strong hands reached out to settle warmly on her shoulders. "Whatever way you want to do this, I'm fine with. As long as we're together."

She met his warm gaze with her own and lifted her chin. If he could risk everything for her, she could take a step with him. "Don't put that ring away yet, Hanley. I'll accept it on one condition."

A slow grin spread across his face. "Name it."

"We go on at least ten dates before we get married. To make sure we're compatible."

He threw back his head and gave a loud laugh. "That's the Maxi I know and love. Ten dates it is."

"And I mean classy dates. Not Ruby's Diner or —"

He silenced her with a lingering kiss. She melted into his arms, her bones feeling as malleable as clay as all the weeks of tension drained out of her body. She grasped his shoulder to keep from falling while his lips traced a path down her cheek to the soft skin below her ear. She shivered, overcome by delicious sensations rippling through her system.

"We better make those fast dates," he whispered into her hair, "because I don't think I want a long engagement."

She laughed the first real laugh she'd had in weeks. A long beam of sunshine danced across the area rug, illuminating the room. She felt her own smile beam just as bright as she looked up into the eyes she knew so well.

"How about you load those boxes in your truck while I pack the rest of my things? Maybe we can even squeeze in one date tonight."

EPILOGUE

Eighteen months later

The sun shone down on the large crowd gathered in front of the new Rainbow Falls fire hall. Maxi set a large pitcher of lemonade on the table under the giant oak tree and took mental inventory. Iced tea, water, lemonade, her mother's homemade brownies, sugar cookies, and pumpkin loaf. That should keep the guests from getting restless after the ceremony.

She scanned the crowd for Jason's familiar face. A smile broke out when she spotted him standing with fire chief, Steve Hamilton, ready for the ribbon cutting. This was Jason's big day, the culmination of his dream. Her heart filled to the bursting point at the joy on his face. Jason had sold off some acreage on the outskirts of their property and used the profit to pay off his bank loan. The whole community had come on board with the project and funding had poured in faster than anticipated to build the station. And now, just down the road from their farmhouse, the sparkling new fire station was ready for the volunteer fire brigade to serve and protect.

Lily came up beside her, Annabelle glued to her hip. "I think they're about ready to start. Let's go get a better spot."

"OK. Everything's ready here." Maxi pulled the tie off her stubby ponytail and finger combed her now chin length hair into submission.

"Don't forget the apron." Lily pointed to her full-length flowered garb, which Maxi hastily whipped off and then smoothed down her simple green dress. Her hand lingered for a moment over her stomach and she smiled to herself. Today was Jason's day, but she had a surprise of her own for later. A slow roll of nerves hit her. She hoped his reaction would be as positive as hers.

The ceremony was quick and to the point. When Chief Hamilton cut the ribbon and declared the Andrew North Fire Station officially open, a huge cheer erupted from the excited townspeople. Jason's grin stretched wide enough to create two dimples. He peered through the crowd, and when his eyes met hers, he winked.

"I love you," he mouthed.

Tears of gratitude welled. "I must be the luckiest person in the world," she whispered.

Lily nudged her. "Well, maybe the second luckiest." Little Annabelle twirled one of her dark curls around the finger of one hand and sucked the thumb of the other. Lily smacked a huge kiss on the girl's plump cheek.

Maxi reached over and kissed the other cheek of her honorary niece. Her lovely little secret made her appreciate the toddler all the more.

"Here come the crowds. We'd better man the table." Lily handed Annabelle off to Nick standing on the sidelines and hooked her arm through Maxi's.

Once again, Maxi thanked God for bringing her back where she belonged, surrounded by family and friends. Her thoughts turned to Gloria Johnson who'd had her baby and had moved away to raise him. In her newfound state of serenity, Maxi could even forgive Gloria for everything she'd done to her and Jason.

Peg pushed Mama in her chair over to help serve the refreshments. Maxi had never seen her mother look so relaxed and happy. As much as Mama missed Charlie, the constant worry over his drinking had taken a toll, and now that the problem had been removed, she'd settled into her new life rather happily. Peg also benefited from having a roommate, and Jason slept easier knowing his mother wasn't alone.

Clint Hanley stood among the crowd. Maxi smiled at the pleased look on his face as he watched Jason accepting congratulations from the community. Maxi had never been more proud of Jason and the way he'd put the past behind him, helping Clint obtain janitorial work at Nick's church and doing his best to forge a relationship with his father. Now Clint would become one of the volunteer firemen at the new station named after her brother.

Life seemed to have come full circle.

Several hours later, after the festivities were over and everyone had gone home, Maxi finished putting away the last dish. She wiped her hands on the dishtowel, noting the slight tremor as she hung it on the rack. She licked her dry lips and took a deep breath before joining Jason in the living room.

Despite the warm fall temperatures, Jason had a cheerful fire crackling in the fireplace. He looked up from prodding the logs with a poker when she came in.

"Hey, honey. How's the fire?"

"Perfect." She took a seat on the well-worn plaid couch.

Jason put the poker down and came to sit beside her, his arm draped over her shoulder in casual familiarity. His warmth enveloped her, bringing a sense of calm to her nervous stomach.

"Jason, can we talk for a minute?"

Her voice must have given her away. He turned to look at her, a concerned frown wrinkling his forehead. "Sure. Is something wrong?"

"Not exactly."

This was coming out all wrong. She'd envisioned the perfect moment, like something out of a romantic movie, but this wasn't turning out as she imagined.

Concern became silent alarm. Jason pulled her hands into his. "What is it? Whatever it is, we'll figure it out together."

She tried to swallow, but her throat refused to cooperate.

"You're scaring me, Max. Just tell me."

All her fluffy words flew out the window. "I think I'm pregnant." Unwanted tears sprang to her eyes. Before her vision blurred, she saw the surprise register on his face. She prayed not to see anything negative, like horror or disappointment. "I know we said we'd wait a few years," she hurried on, "and I don't know for sure —"

He framed her face with his hands and silenced her ramblings with a kiss. She reached up and clamped her hands around his arms as if to anchor herself to him. When he pulled back, a huge grin split his face.

"A baby?" As quickly as it appeared, the grin faded and fear settled over his features. Jason jumped up and began to pace.

Her stomach roiled with a wave of nausea. What if he still didn't want children? What if he couldn't get past his fear of being a bad father?

She rose on unsteady feet. "You're not happy about this."

Jason whirled. He crossed the room in two strides. "No. Yes. I don't know, Maxi. I'm happy. I'm just terrified."

Her breathing calmed. Fear she could deal with. "You'll be a wonderful father, Jason. I've seen you with Annabelle. You're terrific with her."

He tugged her hand and led her to the couch. "That's not it. I can't bear the thought of you going through labor . . ." He paused. ". . . like Lily did."

It all came rushing back to her then. The way Jason had practically shot off Nick and Lily's porch the moment she'd mentioned having a baby. He'd been picturing her in labor.

Her insides relaxed their death grip. "Let's not worry about that now. It's a long way off. In the meantime, you get to deal with my nausea and hormonal mood swings."

With gentle fingers, he wiped away the moisture off her cheeks. "Not to mention the tears."

She gave a light laugh. "Yeah, that part's very annoying." She sobered. "You sure you're OK with this?"

His smile returned. "I'm more than OK. But you'll have to put up with my paranoia when it gets close to the time."

"Deal." She reached up to caress his cheek. "I love you very much."

"I love you more." He kissed her and then pulled her tight against his chest.

She rested her cheek against his flannel shirt and let out a quiet sigh. For the first time since Drew died, she felt whole again. God had taken the fragments of her heart and healed them with the power of His love and acceptance. Maxi knew that somewhere Drew and her father were smiling down on them, giving them their blessing.

With God onboard for the journey, she was sure the life she shared with Jason

would be just that — one continual blessing.

ABOUT THE AUTHOR

Susan is a member of the American Christian Fiction Writers (ACFW)® and the Romance Writers of America (RWA)®. She writes both contemporary and historical inspirational romance, and enjoys creating stories that explore themes of forgiveness, redemption, and healing.

In 2008, she became a Golden Heart Finalist with a Contemporary Inspirational romance entitled *Wyndermere House.* She has been a Genesis Semi-Finalist three years in a row, and recently, Susan's historical *Irish Meadows* won the 2013 Fiction from the Heartland contest.

Susan lives with her husband, two teenagers, and two cats in a busy suburb west of Toronto, Ontario, Canada. In addition to writing, she works part-time as a church secretary. You can visit her website at www .susanannemason.com and her blog at sue masonsblog.blogspot.com.